/-

D0193591

LOOSE
LIPS

LOOSE LIPS

A ROMAN À CLAIRE

Claire Berlinski

BALLANTINE BOOKS

NEW YORK

A Ballantine Book
Published by The Random House Publishing Group

Copyright © 2003 by Claire Berlinski

www.ballantinebooks.com

Library of Congress Control Number: 2004091998

ISBN 0-8129-6709-7

Manufactured in the United States of America

First Hardcover Edition: June 2003
First Trade Paperback Edition: June 2004

2 4 6 8 9 7 5 3 1

For the memory of my beloved grandfather

Espionage, for the most part, involves finding a person who knows something or has something that you can induce them secretly to give to you. That almost always involves a betrayal of trust: Whether it's a Japanese businessman giving you some technical information that his company has entrusted him with; whether it's an official of another government who obviously has a position of trust within that government; whether it's the wife of a military officer whom you've induced to betray the trust placed in her by her husband, in order to get information that might enable you to recruit him. There's a betrayal of trust. Espionage revolves around the many different forms of betrayals of trust . . .

—Aldrich Ames, convicted traitor

That's no righteousness where there is no truth. That's not the truth which leads one to deceit.

—*Mahabharata*

LOOSE
LIPS

I will never know the truth.

My friends thought I was a budget analyst who worked for the Department of Agriculture. It wasn't my choice for a cover. In fact, it would have been just about my last choice, but it was what the Agency told me to tell them. I had business cards that said SELENA KELLER, PLANNING AND ACCOUNTABILITY DIVISION, USDA, and if someone called the number on the card, he would reach a bank of sterile phones at the Central Intelligence Agency. In principle, a CIA flack would deftly look up who I was and who I was supposed to be on an electronic Rolodex. In practice, callers were likely to receive a "Selena? Selena who? You said Keller? Does she work here? Are you sure you have the right number? Selena . . . hold on . . . Department of Agriculture, right? Um . . . oh, okay . . . yeah, she's still in a meeting. Yeah, still there. No, no idea when she'll be done. Can I take a message?"

I wonder if any of my friends ever thought it odd, my abrupt change of careers. I'd spent most of my adult life in India, studying Sanskrit literature. When I joined the Agency, I'd just received my doctorate from Columbia University, and what I knew about budget analysis, or agriculture, for that matter, could have been inscribed inside a matchbook. After I'd been in Washington for six months, the head of my thesis committee called to invite me to the annual Ramayana Conference in DeKalb. I declined, telling him that I was up to my elbows writing a report on the industrial pet feed sector. If he suspected anything, he never let on.

I got the job at the CIA the way you get a job anywhere: I answered an ad on the Internet. That spring I was living in Manhattan, and nine major university presses had recently declined to publish my dissertation, *The Dialectic of Manjusri: Monasteries and Social Welfare in Northeastern India, A.D. 600–800.* To support myself, I was teaching an undergraduate section in multicultural studies at NYU as I sent out applications for postdoctoral fellowships and tenure-track positions. It was beginning to dawn on me that I might spend the rest of my life teaching at some godforsaken Midwestern university—a place with a name like Mongeheela State—writing articles that would be perused by no more than six geriatric scholars.

I found the ad while surfing the Drudge Report. Bernard Lewinsky was denouncing the treatment of his daughter, issuing an appeal for assistance with her legal bills. An article beneath this linked to the CIA's website, which in turn connected me to a section called "Employment." The text read:

> For the **extraordinary individual** who wants more than just a job, we offer a unique career—a way of life that will challenge the deepest resources of your intelligence, self-reliance, and responsibility. It demands an adventurous spirit, a forceful personality, superior intellectual ability, toughness of mind, and a high degree of personal integrity, courage, and love of country. You will need to deal with fast-moving, ambiguous, and unstructured situations that will test your resourcefulness to the utmost.

The accompanying photo displayed a black man, a black woman, and an Asian woman, all in their late twenties. The women conveyed rangy athleticism underneath their sensible professional clothes; the man wore no tie, and his collar was open beneath his blazer. Their expressions were alert and serious. All three were staring intently at a piece of paper I imagined as the order of battle for the Russian Mechanized Infantry Brigade.

I had a stack of copies of my résumé in front of me on my desk. On an impulse, I folded one into thirds and sent it to the CIA's Department of Human Resources. I never really expected that I would hear from them.

A few months later I was still only barely employed. I had all but forgotten the CIA when a woman who identified herself as "Martha from the federal government" began leaving messages for me on my machine. I had deducted *all* of my income on my last tax return on the grounds that I had been living in India for most of the fiscal year. I feared that I was about to be audited. Finally, Martha caught me at home. When she announced that she was from the CIA and not the IRS, I was relieved.

"Your résumé is a bit unusual for us," she said on the phone, "but you have overseas experience and a great education, and that's something we like to see. And we're always looking for people with foreign languages. I see you speak Sanskrit and Pali?"

"Well . . ." I coughed. "Well . . . yes."

She described the position she had in mind for me: "You would work overseas, probably under diplomatic cover. Your job would be to spot, assess, develop, and recruit human sources of intelligence for the United States. It's a job that requires good judgment and a lot of people skills. Is this something that would interest you?"

"Yes, I think it is . . ." I thought about Mongeheela State University. *Go, Heela Monsters!* "Yes, it *definitely* is."

She scheduled me for an interview in the Jacob Javits Federal Building in Manhattan. She told me I would be asked some tough questions about current events, and if the interview went well, I would be invited to Washington for further evaluation. Before placing the phone in the cradle, I stared at the receiver for a few moments in astonishment. It seemed to me that her call was nothing less than an act of divine intervention.

I prepared for the interview as if it were a set of grueling graduate boards. I read the major texts on the theory of espionage, memorized the names of all the Directors of Central Intelligence since the passage of the 1947 National Security Act, and pored over decades of testimony before the House and Senate intelligence-oversight committees. I studied the language of tradecraft: Only amateurs referred to CIA operatives as secret agents, evidently. They weren't agents; they were case officers; the foreigners they *handled* were the agents. An agent was also called an *asset,* like a country house or a fiduciary instrument. Promising targets for recruitment—assets in cultivation—were called *developmentals*. I committed the terms to memory and practiced using them, speaking aloud into the air.

I read about the Intelligence Cycle and about the Church and Pike committees. I found a tattered copy of Philip Agee's *Inside the Company* at a bookstore in the Village called La Lutte Finale. The passages on Guatemala were underlined in indignant red ink; someone had written *state-sponsored terrorism!* in the margins. When the day for the interview came, I could have delivered a nuanced discourse on the history of espionage from the Babylonians to the present.

I arrived at the federal building early, smoked a cigarette outdoors, scrubbed my hands in the ladies' room, shpritzed breath spray in my mouth, and took the elevator to the unmarked conference room to which I'd been directed. I knocked firmly. A man who introduced himself as Carl opened the door and shook my hand. He was about my age, and he wore a dark, baggy suit and sunglasses. I had brought my sunglasses, just in case, and when I saw that he was wearing his although we were indoors, I put mine on too. We sat down at the conference table, straining to see each other.

Carl warned me again that he was about to ask me some tough questions. "Ready?" he asked.

"I'm ready."

He began by asking me if I knew the name of the prime minister of Canada. By luck, I had read an article about Canada just that morning on the subway.

"Jean Chrétien," I replied, relieved that I knew.

"Good. Amazing how few people know that."

"Really? That's too bad. You know, Canada is the United States' number one trade partner, too."

He peered at me curiously, and I worried that I might have sounded overly eager to impress, too academic. I tried to look serious and alert, like the case officers in the photo on the website.

He asked me a few more questions about world leaders and geography. Who were the permanent members of the U.N. Security Council? Which former Soviet republics had nuclear weapons? I knew the answers and felt pleased with myself for knowing. He made notes that he shielded from my view, but when he set the pad down, I could see that he was filling out a form. He had placed all his check marks on one side of a ledger.

"Okay," he said. "I'm going to tell you about a hypothetical situation. There are no right or wrong answers—I'm just trying to get a sense of how you think. Okay?"

"Fine."

"Let's imagine you're working for us in Nigeria. You've just arrived, it's your first assignment, and you're undercover as the agriculture guy from the USDA. That's someone really low on the diplomatic totem pole, by the way. And the first thing the

Chief of Station tells you is that he's really glad you're there, because they have no one in the station who's deep enough below the local radar to meet a really sensitive asset—the Nigerian foreign secretary. So you're going to be the one who meets him. Okay?"

"I get it."

"So you drive out to pick up this guy, out on the edge of town, right?"

"Right."

"And everything goes fine—he gives you the intel and you give him the money, and you're driving him back, right?"

"Right."

"And then, you're out on the edge of town, and all of a sudden a dog runs in front of your car. And—*splat!*—you hit the dog." He smacked his right fist into his left palm.

"Splat." I nodded.

"Yeah, you hit the dog—*splat!* And an angry mob of villagers runs up and starts pounding on the window of your car. Kids, teenagers. And they're screaming and pounding and the foreign secretary is terrified. He's all pale."

"He's Nigerian?" I was suddenly worried I'd misunderstood something.

"Well, it's all relative. He's not looking so good."

"Okay."

"So what do you do?"

"What do I do?"

"Yes. What do you do?"

I thought for a few seconds. What the hell *would* I do? Cry? I asked: "Is there any plausible reason for me to be out with this guy?"

"Not at all. The Nigerian foreign secretary, some junior American agriculture officer—there *couldn't* be any plausible reason."

If there were no right answers, why was he asking this question? Of course there was a right answer. I tried to think through all the angles. "Well," I said finally, "I lived in India for a long time. And a few times, I got into a little trouble. I always found that the best thing to do was stay cool and try to grease my way out of it."

"Meaning?"

"Well . . . we're talking about Nigeria," I said.

Carl nodded.

"Life expectancy in the rural areas . . . probably not much higher than forty-five? Infant mortality is what—one in six? one in five?—and I've just hit a *dog*. That's just not such a big deal. A dog's life doesn't count for quite as much in these parts of the world as it does here." I decided from his encouraging expression that I was on the right track.

"I guess here's what I'd do. I don't think hitting a dog in Nigeria is such a big deal, and I think if I'm okay with this, well, maybe *they'll* be okay. I guess I stop the car, get out calmly— no, wait, I just roll down the window—and explain that I'm *so sorry*, I love dogs, have a dog at home, actually, so I understand why they're upset, and I want to compensate them for their loss by passing around all these *twenty-dollar bills*. Twenty-dollar bills and American cigarettes—no, wait, they're just kids—American *candies*." He nodded approvingly.

"I think if I pass around enough money, they'll forget they ever had a dog."

It must have been the right answer. The wrong answer, I later found out—and a surprisingly common one—was *shoot them all*.

We went through a few more of these problems. What would I do if I were out with a developmental who knew me as Angela, and I ran into an asset who knew me as Mary? His question put me in mind of that unfortunate time in college when Richard, my boyfriend, and I ran into Chris, my, um, *other* boyfriend.

"Chris," I said warmly. "Have you met Richard? Rich, honey, we're going to be really late." When Richard said, "Who was he?" I said he was some guy from my Comp Lit class, which was perfectly true. When Chris asked me why I called Richard honey, I said that I called everyone honey, honey.

I said to Carl: "You know, from my experience, the only thing that would give you away there is if you got flustered. I mean, really, people get confused about names all the time. You just get the two of them away from each other as quickly as possible, and if they ask any questions, you say, 'Gosh, I don't know. Did he really call me Mary?' "

Carl nodded sagely.

He asked me how would I convince an American businessman in Rio to let the CIA use his apartment as a safe house. I told him it would depend what I made of the businessman; perhaps I would appeal to the man's patriotism, if he seemed the patriotic sort, or play to his vanity, if he seemed eager to think of himself as the kind of man the CIA would trust. I answered Carl's questions as sensibly as I could, trying to look serious and responsible, but when I heard myself talking about assets and safe houses I felt a delicious frisson.

Then Carl placed his hands on his knees and leaned forward, fixing me with a serious gaze. "Selena, would you feel comfortable convincing another human being to commit treason?"

I knew this was the moment to convey my character: He was looking for depth, maturity, moral compass. "Well," I said slowly, "that would depend which government and it would depend why it was necessary." I hoped I sounded authoritative but thoughtful. But perhaps that response was too brief, too passionless? "*Of course* I could convince someone to commit espionage," I added, "if the information would be used to avert a war, or to prevent a hostile regime from acquiring weapons of mass destruction, or to prevent a terrorist attack. I would have no hesitation at all."

Of course I didn't have the first fucking clue what I was talking about.

Carl and I kept talking, using up far more than our allotted time. When I said that he must be hungry and suggested we go out for a slice of pizza, he accepted. Over lunch he told me what to expect from the rest of the application process. "When you talk to the shrink," he said, "be sure to wrap everything up in the American flag. Don't say you're in it for the thrills or the James Bond thing. I mean, of course that's why you're in it, that's why everyone is, but when you talk to the shrink, it's all about how you love the red, white, and blue." He also told me that he woke up every morning eager to go to work. I hadn't heard many Sanskritists say the same thing.

On the subway ride home, amid the chatter and babble of the city at rush hour, I fantasized about clandestine assignations, imagining myself spiriting away the secrets of the Iranian missile program, alone on a train to Marrakech, a desert sirocco whipping up the scent of jasmine in the hot night air. I was so involved in my fantasy that I missed my stop. I thought I might walk back, but when I exited the subway, the glares of the crack dealers suggested that this might not be a good idea. "Lady, you're lost," a pleasant Rastafarian observed politely. "You gotta get back on that train right away before something bad happens to you."

"Thanks," I said. "I guess I should pay more attention."

∽

Three weeks later, I received a letter from the Agency inviting me to an office in the suburbs near Langley, Virginia, for a medical and psychiatric examination. I took the Metroliner to Washington and then a taxi to a motel the letter recommended. I spent the evening walking around Tyson's Corner, an ugly cluster of strip malls about half an hour from the Capitol. It was an overcast evening in late summer, and even when the sun went down, the air was close. I tried to go to sleep early because my appointment was at six forty-five in the morning, but stayed awake with nerves, smacking the motel wall repeatedly in an unsuccessful attempt to kill a mosquito.

At dawn, I took a taxi to the address I'd been given. Nothing at the building's entrance indicated that it belonged to the CIA. It might have been the regional headquarters of Fidelity, say, or Costco. It was about the size of the other office buildings on the block, six stories or so; its smoked-glass windows reflected the broad, tree-lined suburban street. It was separated from the road by an unremarkable parking lot and a neatly groomed lawn. But an armed guard at the gate stopped my taxi and asked to see my identification. He examined my credentials carefully, then told me to step out and walk the rest of the way to the building's entrance. More armed guards manned a reception desk behind the sliding-glass front doors, surveying the premises via closed-circuit television. They too asked for my identification, and compared it to a typewritten list. Finally finding my name, a guard picked up one of several phones. "Miss Keller is here," he said.

A woman with hair teased and sprayed into a kind of curly blond plumage came to meet me at the entrance. "I'm Tammy," she said with the musical vitality of a game show hostess, offering me her hand. She was in her late forties, I guessed; she was made up in heavy foundation and false lashes. A laminated badge hung around her neck, knocking against a big, glittering brooch in the shape of a giraffe on her lapel. She escorted me through the turnstiles by the reception desk, swiping her badge against an electronic sensor and punching in a code. "Darn it!" she said when the machine rejected her code three times in a row. "I *swear* that thing hates me!"

She asked me if I was nervous and, without waiting for a reply, told me to "just relax and do your best. We're not looking for geniuses, so don't worry about that. The problem with geniuses, you know, is that they don't have any common sense." She kept chattering as we walked down the hall, her high heels clicking like castanets. She said that the Central Intelligence Agency was like a family and that she had been with the Agency since the age of nineteen. "Nineteen?" I asked. "How did you end up working for the CIA when you were so young?"

"Oh, they found *me,*" Tammy answered, and before I could ask what she meant, we arrived at a small medical laboratory, where she deposited me with a flourish. "See you in a few!" She waved and bustled off.

The walls had the usual doctor's-office decorations: a poster featuring the food pyramid and another about Lyme disease. I filled out a form about my medical history, proffered blood and urine on command, and suffered myself to be inspected by a physician with an old-fashioned lantern on his head. He tested my vision, whacked my knees with a mallet, listened to my chest, and then sent me back to the waiting room.

Tammy returned and took me to the psychological-evaluation clinic. At exactly ten o'clock, the door opened and a man with a neatly trimmed beard peered into the reception area. He introduced himself as Dr. Mason and invited me to follow him.

His small office was tidy and unornamented, as was he. He held my résumé in his hands as if he were looking at it for the first time. I sat down and waited for him to speak. "Well," he said after scanning the paper for a few more seconds. "You've had an interesting life, haven't you?"

"I've been very lucky," I answered, wondering when I should mention my *outstanding* patriotism.

"So . . . let's talk a little about you," he said.

"Sure, I'd like that." I met his eyes and tried to project stability, self-awareness, a positive outlook on life.

"Have you ever had any emotional problems?" he asked.

"Well," I replied, trying to sound as if I experienced appropriate emotion, neither too much nor too little. "Of course I've had difficult times in my life. But I've never suffered any mental illness."

"Mmmmm. Ever hear voices?" he asked. I admired the way he cut right to the chase.

"Voices? You mean ones that don't really exist? No, never."

"Mmmmm. Ever feel agitated?"

"Well, sure—sometimes, I guess."

"When have you felt agitated?"

"Well, you know—when I get stuck in traffic or when I get put on hold trying to reach a customer-service representative, you know, the usual."

"Mmmmm. Ever feel suicidal?"

"No, no. Never."

"Ever feel worried that everyone is watching you?"

"No, not really."

"Would you say you're in good emotional health?"

"Well, sure, yes."

"Mmmmm. What makes you want to join the CIA?"

"Patriotism, Dr. Mason. I want to give something back."

He nodded; his face gave nothing away.

He asked a few questions about my parents and my education. I looked for opportunities to mention my patriotism again, but I couldn't find any. Did I have a history of sexual deviancy? "I think my tastes are pretty normal for an upper-middle-class white woman," I said.

"Mmmmm . . . well," he answered. "Well. I guess that's good." He sounded disappointed.

He walked me to a nearby conference room and handed me a series of multiple-choice psychological batteries. He told me he would be back in two hours. *True/False: I will go to hell because of my thoughts about my mother.* I carefully avoided the answers that would peg me as a schizoid or a borderline.

And then I was done. Tammy took me to the accounting office, where a white mouse of a man reimbursed me in cash for my hotel and travel expenses. I shook hands with Tammy, who wished me luck, and took the Metroliner back to Manhattan that same evening.

One month later, a letter arrived offering me the job on the condition that I pass an extensive background investigation and a polygraph. The offer came on plain white stationery without letterhead, and nowhere did it mention the CIA. It referred instead to "our organization." "You will be joining our organization at a very exciting time," it read. I stared at the letter in astonishment, then called my mother.

"Mom, you will not believe this," I began. "You simply will not believe this."

⊘

I'll never know how I got through that background investigation. Mind you, I didn't really have any skeletons in my closet. I'd never killed anyone, if that's what they wanted to know. I'd always lived a more or less lawful life. But I'd smoked a *lot* of dope. For God's sake, I was a Sanskritist.

According to the CIA website, "recent" or "frequent" drug use could prove disqualifying. The terms weren't elaborated. I admitted on the form they sent me that I'd had some acquaintance with the cannabinoid family, as they called it, but I left ambiguous the issue of quantity, hoping they wouldn't ask. When the background investigator, a gray man in a gray suit, came to my apartment to interview me in person, he asked me *exactly* how many times I'd ever gotten stoned, as if I would have the faintest idea. I fished around for a number that sounded plausible but not excessive.

"About ten?" *Actually, it would probably be easier just to tell you about the times I wasn't stoned.*

"Are you sure of that number?

"Um . . . it's a little hard to remember. It was a while ago. Maybe less?" *Well, sir, I was pretty much stoned all through college. Yeah, I was pretty much stoned the whole time. Once or twice, I stopped smoking to take finals or something, you know? So I'd just say I was stoned, well, technically, four or five times, but for a very, very long time each time, okay?*

"And would you consider this to have been experimental usage?"

"Yes, exactly." *The experiment indicated a strong relationship between smoking dope and getting high as a kite.*

He looked suspicious. "You sure about that?"

"Yes." *How could I be sure about anything? I was stoned out of my mind.*

His team was going to interview as many of my friends and neighbors as they could find, he told me. That didn't concern me; I expected that most of them would describe me as friendly and studious. But I did have a small, nagging anxiety.

Directly after coming back from India to write up my research, I'd shared an apartment in Manhattan with a librarian named Mildred and a failing jazz pianist, Antonio-the-Untalented. I'd moved in with them following a desperate search for an inexpensive place to live. Mildred had met me at the door when I came to look at the room for rent. She was a stooped, weird sister with black teeth and a shock of white hair. But she was pleasant enough and the room was only $500 a month. The apartment was clean—dazzlingly so, in fact—and the neighborhood safe. I think she was taken with the fact that I was a Sanskritist; she wanted to talk about the Eightfold Path to Enlightenment. When she asked if I'd like to move in, I accepted gratefully.

On the night I arrived with my bags and books, I found a handwritten note under my door. The letters were crabbed and close:

I should mention my long-term, murderous struggle. People with very good intentions seem to have great difficulty in ascertaining the truth and discerning who is a credible source. So I usually say to roommates that you are free to believe what you choose (though it can be hazardous to hold false beliefs). But I expect you to behave with perfect integrity.

I am sure that is your intent.

Mildred.

I read the message several times, trying to make sense of it. Then I moved the heavy dresser in my bedroom against the door.

The next day, I asked Antonio what the hell was going on. "Don't worry about her." He waved his hand. "She's a fruitcake."

I soon ascertained that Mildred was, indeed, a full-blooded schizophrenic. She believed that a cabal of doctors had stolen her left breast and was conspiring to steal the right one. She held that the government was sneaking into the apartment at night to poison her food and spray toxic chemicals in her face as she slept. She regularly boiled and bleached everything in the house, trying to get the poison off. She believed that my predecessor, whoever he was, had been working as an informant for the government. Sometimes, I would find her sleeping on the living room floor, wrapped in a black plastic bag. "They can't find me in here," she'd mutter. I became used to the sound of coins tinkling: She cast the I Ching constantly, allowing the ancients to

determine her every decision. "Dark birds," she crooned, looking at the coins. "*Very* dark birds." She wrapped her food in
brown paper to keep the government from spraying it with poison.

One day, Antonio came home to find that Mildred had
thrown away his entire week's groceries. "What the hell did you
do that for?" he asked her, his eyes popping with exasperation.

"They got poison over your food too. You would have been
sick if you'd eaten it."

"Mildred," Antonio said slowly. "How precisely do you think
'they' got into a locked apartment on the fourteenth floor?"

"You should know!" she hissed. "You're the one who's been
helping them!"

Antonio stared at her, at a loss, then backed out of the room,
shaking his head.

I lived there until I could afford my own studio—it would
have taken more than Mildred to make me abandon a $500
room in midtown Manhattan—and I never had a problem with
her. She cast the I Ching for me whenever I needed to make a
tough decision, and she kept the apartment spotless. Sometimes
she sanitized the toilet eight times in a day.

But the questionnaire I'd been sent by the CIA required me to
list everyone I'd lived with for the past seven years, and when I
put down Mildred's name, I felt a dark foreboding. What on
earth would she do if a strange man in a dark suit showed up on
her doorstep, claiming to be from the federal government and
demanding to know whether she'd ever seen me engage in any
suspicious activity? Would she scream? Would she try to whack
him? I imagined Mildred raising a shovel into the air and tri-
umphantly smashing it down on the investigator's head.

I tried not to think about it. It was in God's hands.

∽

The Columbia Law library housed an extensive collection on the legal admissibility of polygraph results in court, which I studied closely. The luminaries of American jurisprudence were unanimous: The polygraph was a sham. The CIA might as well have invited Mildred to Langley to cast the I Ching—and perhaps they should have, since Mildred was often eerily accurate, having predicted to the month both the collapse of the Berlin Wall and the Asian stock market crash.

The fallibility of the polygraph was an axiom of forensic science, yet members of the national security community reposed in it an almost reverential confidence. Evidently, the polygraph functioned as an aid to interrogation; people believed it worked, so they told the truth. I was anxious about it. While I had nothing much to lie about, I had many things I didn't care to discuss. More important, the polygraph returned a disturbing number of false positives, and I didn't want to become a victim of bad luck.

I read on the Internet that passing was a matter of evidencing stress when asked the control questions. The trick to showing stress, according to an article I found posted to a chat group, was the cloacal clench. The author of the article claimed to be a former police interrogator. He promised that one well-timed squeeze of the sphincter would cause the subject's heart rate and galvanic skin response to rise exactly as if he were telling a shameful porky.

I arrived for my polygraph, in another unmarked building in the suburbs of Washington, with apprehension. The polygrapher came to the waiting room to fetch me. He and I walked together to the polygraph chamber down the hall and exchanged pleasantries about the weather. He then spent a great deal of time emphasizing how scientific the polygraph was, making it sound like electron microscopy. I listened politely. He discussed the questions he was planning to ask: Had I ever committed a crime? Had I ever attempted to gain unauthorized access to classified information? Was I working for a foreign intelligence service? I nodded to signify that I understood.

I was confused. All of these questions seemed perfectly reasonable. There should have been, according to my research, a relatively trivial question among the others, one designed to evoke a lie—*Have you ever told an untruth to a supervisor? Have you ever stolen office supplies?* That was where to manifest the strongest response if you wanted to pass. But all of his questions concerned issues with which the government would legitimately be concerned. Oh, what the hell, I thought. I'll just hope for the best.

The polygrapher strapped me to the chair and hooked me up to the electrodes and the breathing monitor. The chair was ample and squishy, actually quite pleasant. He switched on the device, intoning the questions in a hypnotic voice. When he asked me the question about my criminal history a second time, I suddenly wondered whether *that* might be the control question. After all, everyone breaks a few laws now and again. Afraid that I would fail if I didn't have a strong reaction to something, I made a sudden decision to energize my *mula banda,* as the yogis would say.

When it was over, he left the room, saying he needed to review my results. I knew from my research that he was doing no such thing; he was leaving me alone to increase my anxiety prior to the interrogation, the interrogation being the real point of the polygraph. The tactic worked; I was anxious. I sat there by myself, uncomfortable and apprehensive, nervously picking my nose until I realized that I was doing so in view of the tiny camera on the wall before me. I put my hands to my side and straightened myself.

The polygrapher returned to the room. He sat down across from me and stared at me, his thin lips peevish and cold.

"Selena, we seem to have a problem here," he said.

That was exactly what I'd read he would say. This was where, had I been lying, I was supposed to realize that the polygraph had trapped me and spill my guts. If I hadn't been lying, I would simply be puzzled.

"Problem?" I asked.

"You showed a very strong reaction one of the questions. Do you know which one it was?"

"Er, no, I'm afraid I don't," I said. *You lamentable witch doctor.*

He leaned in and glared at me, eyes inches from mine. "The question was whether you've ever committed a crime."

Oops. Yep, that's where I squeezed, all right. I guess that wasn't a control question. "I don't understand that. I've never committed a crime," I answered.

"Well, the charts don't lie. The charts are *scientific*. There's got to be some reason they're telling me that you haven't been a hundred percent with us today."

Yes, sir, there is. I was squeezing my sphincter when I answered that question. "Well, perhaps I was a little nervous? Could we try that again?"

"This isn't something you just try until you get it right, Selena. This is *science*. The machine is a carefully calibrated *scientific tool,* and it is telling me that you have something you need to get off your chest."

Wrong part of the body, Columbo. I was angry with him and furious with myself. This would have gone fine if I hadn't been, literally, a smart-ass. I explained again that I hadn't lied, the irony of it being that I really hadn't; and he explained to me that the charts never lie, and back and forth we went until he agreed to hook me up again. This time, I abandoned all scientific experimentation. When I left, he was still muttering over the charts.

In all, I calculated that my chances of getting a security clearance were no better than half.

. . .

It took them another three months to adjudicate my case, three months in which I ran to the phone every time it rang, like an impatient lover. When the call finally came, I had almost given up hope. But when the call did come at last, they told me I had been cleared to the Top Secret level. To this day I have no idea how I slipped through.

They told me to report for duty in Washington in January, with the rest of my class of trainee spies.

∽

Training would take place over eighteen months and would be divided between the CIA's headquarters in Langley and the mysterious facility they called the Farm. During that time, they warned me, I would be scrutinized carefully. At some point, I would be asked to jump from a plane. At the end of training, if I met their expectations, I would be taught a foreign language and then sent overseas. My destination would be determined by the needs of the service.

I packed up my studio and moved to Virginia, renting an airy, modern apartment with a balcony in the completely uninteresting suburb of McLean—condos, cul-de-sacs, lawns with little swing sets—about ten minutes from CIA Headquarters. It was easily four times the size of my place in Manhattan and half the price.

The move was uneventful save that it was the first time I'd driven a car on my own. Like many New Yorkers, I'd never really learned to drive. The deficit marked me as an alien elsewhere in the country, quite likely mentally infirm or dangerously unpatriotic. I hadn't needed to drive when I lived in India; I'd spent most of my time in a village with exactly one car, a 1978 Lada that was more rust than engine. Judging from the garlands strewn lovingly around its antenna, that car had functioned primarily as a religious icon.

I bought myself a used Ford Taurus, the safest car in its class, and captained it through the suburbs of Virginia like a Sherman tank. I hesitated at every intersection. I braked when the wind blew. I signaled when I shouldn't have and I didn't when I should have. I couldn't read a road map. My sense of direction was terrible and I kept getting lost: I tried to go to the grocery store and found myself well on my way to the Appalachians before I realized my error and corrected my course. The mirrors confused me; I couldn't figure out the relationship between the reflected image and reality. If objects in the mirror were closer than they appeared, did that mean I should merge faster or not at all? Why did people keep honking at me even when I was driving exactly the speed limit? On my third day in Virginia, I stopped at a tollbooth and tossed my change successfully into the basket. Then I threw the car into reverse rather than drive and promptly rolled into the car behind me.

On the morning of my first day at the CIA, I dressed in a fresh cream-colored winter suit with gold buttons and brocade trim. I wore silk panties, sheer nylons, pearls that looked real, and earrings to match. My Ferragamo pumps came from a thrift store, but they didn't look it. I put expensive serum in my hair to make it shiny, and I wore three very thin gold bracelets on the same wrist as my watch. I checked myself in the mirror one last time before I left: I decided I would look right at home in the photograph on the CIA website.

I had been told to return to the same anonymous office building where I had been polygraphed. I left an hour early in case I got lost, then waited in the parking lot, fussing with my lip gloss and adjusting the seams of my nylons. I was still the first of my classmates to walk through the sliding glass doors. Then more appeared—three women and a man. We introduced ourselves with pleasantries and affable, firm handshakes. Presently we were met by a silver-haired man, well into middle age with a careworn face; he introduced himself as Ned. Ned told us that he would drive us to Headquarters in a minivan, where we would meet the rest of the class. We bundled ourselves into the van, and Ned pointed out the local landmarks as we drove. "I remember my first day," he said. "You've got an adventure ahead of you, that's for sure." He blinked quickly a few times. "I wish I could start all over again."

We eased into the left-turn lane on Route 123 at the sign that said CENTRAL INTELLIGENCE AGENCY, pulling up beside a small makeshift memorial to the two Agency employees killed at that traffic light by a deranged Pakistani gunman. They had been ambushed while waiting for the light to change. The site was marked by two small wooden crosses and a straggle of limp pansies. I looked at the memorial with dismay; the light seemed to stay red for a long time.

At last we turned into the long driveway, cruising past ominous signs that said WARNING: OFFICIAL GOVERNMENT FACILITY and a barrage of other prohibitions: no photography, no firearms, no recording devices, no cellular phones, no unauthorized entry, no alcohol, no tourists. We drove past twelve-foot-high gates topped by razor wire and over a mechanized road barrier designed to rear from the ground and flip unwelcome vehicles like pancakes. Once, Ned told us, a flustered security guard, new to the job, had accidentally upended a visitor from the Senate Select Committee on Intelligence, who had hung inverted in the air until the rescue crews arrived. The damage to his car had been considerable. But on the day we arrived, the armed guards seemed on top of their game. The motion they made to wave us in was something between a beckon and a salute, a welcoming but respectful gesture, full of gravitas.

Our minivan continued down a road that circled the vast parking lots. Ned explained that titles to the reserved spaces, close to the building, were bitterly contested. "It's not worth it," he advised, describing the viciousness of the battles for parking supremacy. "Don't get caught up in that game. So you walk a few minutes every morning. It's good for your heart." The lots were full of dark economy sedans, mostly Dodges and Fords. There were a few SUVs; some had bumper stickers. MY SON IS AN HONOR ROLL STUDENT AT MCLEAN MIDDLE SCHOOL, read one. Ned showed us where we should park our cars. The lots open to trainees were practically in Montana.

The Headquarters compound was something like a small college campus. The two main buildings were adjoined; the older building, heavyset and somber, was made of precast concrete; the newer one, of steel and glass. A walkway linked the old building to a freestanding, domed auditorium. This nucleus was surrounded by woods, lawns, and endless parking lots from which soared satellite dishes and radio towers of surreal gigantism. The scene conveyed business and motion: Rolls of chicken wire and PVC piping sprouted from a large construction site near the main buildings; helmeted workers rattled pneumatic drills. From somewhere in the middle of the compound a generator pumped steam into the air.

We took a footpath from the lot through a small wooded park, which led to a lawn with picnic tables and a triptych made from a fragment of the Berlin Wall. A cluster of smokers, shivering in the cold, stood outside the entrance to the main building. Ned ushered us past the guards and the security turnstiles. The CIA seal, carved in granite, spread magnificently over the floor of the foyer. Ned pointed to our right, showing us the stars on the marble walls that commemorated the Agency's fallen. There were seventy-seven stars, he told us. A glass-encased book below the stars listed forty-two names: The names of those remaining were, even in death, too sensitive to be revealed. Etched into the wall ahead of me was the famous legend *And ye shall know the truth, and the truth shall make you free.*

We proceeded down the hall and assembled in a dark-paneled, carpeted auditorium. A heavy, matronly woman rose to take the podium, standing between the Stars and Stripes and a flag with the CIA seal. She moved only with effort, but her deliberate stride and sturdy carriage conveyed enormous confidence. An assistant rushed up to her with a glass of water; she acknowledged him with a nod. She waited until we were all seated.

"Welcome to the Central Intelligence Agency," she began, then allowed those words to sink in. "Some of you may know me as Maxime Shroeder." Her matron's lips creased into a knowing, sly smile. I recognized the name: She had signed the letter offering me a job. "In fact," she said, "my name is Brenda Argus, and for the next eighteen months, I am your boss."

There it was, my first secret—the real name of the head of the Clandestine Service Trainee Program.

She gave a rousing speech. We were embarking not only on a challenging career but an honorable one. We would serve the people of the United States with little recognition but with much satisfaction. She expected the very highest standards of integrity and accountability, and we in turn would have the pride of knowing that we worked for the finest intelligence service in the world, an organization that was more than just a service; it was a family. We had been chosen because we were outstanding, talented young people. We would work hard, and we would have extraordinary lives.

When she finished, we took our oaths. We swore to uphold and protect the Constitution of the United States. I held up my hand with everyone else, and when I repeated the words, I felt profound conviction, a deep, thrilling pride.

The trainees spent the rest of the day in a large conference room, where long tables were arranged in the shape of a horseshoe. There was a Central Intelligence Agency seal on the wall. I met the rest of my classmates. As instructed, we introduced ourselves by our first names only and said a few words about our backgrounds and our hobbies. There were twice as many men as women. Many of the men looked as if they had arrived straight from military service. They had very short hair and excellent posture; they addressed the authorities as sir and ma'am. My new colleagues were athletic and trim, with healthy, pink complexions; the men had large and well-developed upper bodies, from what I could discern beneath their sober suits and neatly pressed shirts. There were a handful of attorneys, a few former investment bankers, and a man who had worked for Microsoft. One woman had worked for a multinational energy corporation headquartered in Singapore; another had been a regulator for the Federal Emergency Management Agency.

To my right sat a woman from Vermont named Allison. Crisp and professional in a slim gray suit and an eggshell silk blouse, she was a champion triathlete and a prizewinning show-jumper. To my left was Kevin, from Florida, a licensed scuba instructor who had learned to speak Farsi at the Defense Language Institute in Monterey. Most of my new colleagues had graduated from mid-rank universities—Dartmouth, Penn—where they'd majored in political science or government. There were two graduates of West Point. Some had master's degrees. One woman had an MBA.

My classmates were largely from midsize cities such as Philadelphia and Atlanta; they enjoyed vigorous outdoor sports such as rock climbing and white-water rafting. Several of the men had served in the Gulf war. The men were mostly married and the women mostly single. There were no nerds or geeks; even the man from Microsoft seemed hearty and sociable. No one but me seemed eager to go outside to smoke during the breaks. When it came my turn to introduce myself, I thought I noticed a look of polite bewilderment in everyone's eyes as I described my former life.

At the end of the day, we were taken to an office to be photographed for the laminated identification badges we were to wear around our necks at all times while in the compound. In the photograph, I appear eager, flushed, excited. A great adventure, my expression seems to say, lies ahead of me.

The woman in the photograph is gone now, of course. Gone to wherever people go when things don't work out the way they planned.

CHAPTER 2

The first three weeks of my intelligence career were spent in an introductory course called CIA 101. On my second day, I was assigned a pseudonym to use on all Agency paperwork. It would be impossible to tell from CIA records that someone named Selena Keller had ever set foot in the Headquarters compound: I was to be Caesaria A. HESTER for the rest of my career—the capital letters and middle initial signifying that the name was an invention. All the pseudonyms used internally were by long tradition bizarre, although aliases used in the field were commonplace and unremarkable. Someone told me that the pseudonyms came from a 1926 London phone directory, which accounted for such rare treasures as Lundquist X. FENSTERWASSER.

I read and signed hundreds of documents during those first days. I promised never to reveal any classified information, to be drug-free and low-profile and wary of strangers who asked probing questions, to report the names of all of my foreign friends. I catalogued everyone I could recall meeting in India; the list went on for pages. I'd made friends with my entire neighborhood in Gujarat. There hadn't been much else to do. The form requested addresses as well as names. "Vishnu," I wrote, thinking of the one-legged man whom I'd often found sleeping on the steps outside my flat. "Last Name Unknown." Address? Finally I wrote: "Second landing outside the largest concrete-block house directly northeast of the train station, opposite the paanwalla."

I asked the security officer directing the proceedings for clarification about the regulations: Was Vishnu really the kind of foreigner they had in mind? She asked if I felt bound to Vishnu by ties of affection. I thought of the times I had brought Vishnu my leftover chapatis or crouched with him on the landing, smoking bidis and chewing paan, exchanging trivia about our favorite Hindu movie stars as the red sun set and the day cooled. What was that if not affection? I suppose I did, I answered. "Report him," she said briskly. So I did, although I am not sure that had he known or understood, he would have seen being reported to the Central Intelligence Agency as a token of affection.

What about romantic liaisons? someone asked. Must we report them? "First time is free," she said. "Second time, you have to report it." I wondered whether Agency officers ever spurned advances overseas because it wouldn't be worth the paperwork. *It was a beautiful night we shared, Boris, but I am afraid it is never to be repeated, because I cannot face filling out any more forms.*

We were given a lecture about protecting our covers. Only discreet members of our immediate families were ever to know where we really worked. We could tell them nothing about what we did. We practiced answering awkward questions about our daily commutes and why we didn't know cousin Lenny's wife, who'd worked at USDA for fifteen years and knew *everyone* there. I wondered how serious they could be about never discussing our work with our families. It seemed unreasonable to expect that we could really keep our lives a secret from people who knew us that well. My mother had already called three times asking how the first week had gone. If they thought I could say, "Sorry, Mom, you changed my diapers and paid for my college education, but I'm afraid from now on I will be a complete cipher to you," they obviously didn't know my mother—the woman who had figured out that I'd been smoking at summer camp even though the offense took place a full week before I returned home. (I had gone swimming, showered, and scrubbed at least a dozen times in between.)

The majority of the briefings involved the Agency's leviathan bureaucracy and its security regulations, and after the sixth or seventh lecture, I felt the first stirrings of impatience. For someone who had planned to spend her life in a university, I'd never much liked lectures. The instructors spent a day explaining the details of the retirement program and the thrift savings plan, showing us an animated feature-length film about a talking nest egg. An attorney from the Office of General Counsel explained the Agency's policy on frequent flier miles: We couldn't keep them, but we could use them to upgrade—but only to business class, not first. The American taxpayer did not want his public servants flying first class, period. We learned to use the internal computer system and how to file our time sheets; we learned the regulations for taking sick leave and collecting disability insurance. We were warned to be particularly cautious about using the telephone, even with one another. There was always a chance—even in the United States—that someone was listening. There was a lecture on computer security, but when they began to explain how far from the window we should keep our computer screens, measured in millimeters, I tuned out. I figured I'd pick up what I'd missed later.

Then came the presentation from Officer Molly, the bomb-sniffing Labrador retriever. She took her job every bit as seriously as any other officer in the Agency. She was very proud and very responsible. I could tell. Officer Molly could detect more than thirty kinds of explosives. What did she do, someone asked,

if she smelled a bomb? Did she bark? "Er, no," her handler explained, shifting back and forth on his feet. "No, Officer Molly
wouldn't bark. With some of the things she might be finding,
that could be, er, *counterproductive*. She'd just sit down real quiet,
like she's been trained. She doesn't make any sudden noises *at
all*." Officer Molly looked at him with working-dog dignity, her
silky ears cocked, and swished her tail from side to side.

I noticed Paul for the first time during CIA 101. I hadn't spotted him at first, but during some of the dull moments I caught
him eyeing me, hands behind his head, fingers interlocked, leaning back in his chair. I decided I didn't mind. He was an Army
captain from Mississippi, still serving in the Reserves, and a long-
distance runner. He had a very lean athlete's body and a preda-
tory, vulpine face, with hollows under his high cheekbones. He
spoke with a slow Mississippi drawl. He flirted with me during
the breaks, but he flirted with the other women, too.

During the lectures on CIA accounting principles, I imagined
Paul pulling my head back with my hair and exposing my neck,
then pinning my arms against the wall.

∞

February brought a heavy snowstorm that shut down the federal
government for two days, putting CIA 101 behind schedule and
forcing the lecturers to rush through the material. By the time
we completed the class, we were tired of learning how to fill out
paperwork and eager to get on with spying. At the end, we were
assigned to rotations in various operational divisions. Brenda
Argus told us she had tried to match our assignments to our interests and experiences. I was sent to work in the Indian Subcontinent Operations Group.

I was pleased by her choice. It was logical: It could fairly be
said that I was an India specialist, at least in some respects. I was
an authority on the iconography of the ancient Indian monastic

tradition, at least. Whatever my qualifications, I certainly believed the CIA's mission in India was worthwhile.

Few things in the world frightened me more than the Indian nuclear program. I realized how outrageous it sounded to the Indian ear when someone like me proposed that America was mature enough to have the Bomb but India wasn't. I realized it, but it didn't change the fact that it was true. I had lived in India long enough to see that most Indians had a wondrous inability to calculate risk; it was an aspect of the national character as evident as Italian sensuality or Prussian militarism. Indifference to danger can be a fey and thrilling trait, but not when it's mixed with nuclear technology.

Once, a young boy I met on the streets of Bubaneshwar, a kid of fourteen or so, invited me to see the temple at the top of a hill. "Please," he begged me. "You must come to see my dynamic God." I agreed. As we climbed to the hilltop together, he nervously inquired whether I was a vegetarian and whether in America we had heard of Govindar's munificence.

As we approached the idol, the crowds thickened and surged, calling out the god's name, pressing toward the temple in a wave of hot delirium. Presumably to prevent the crowds from climbing over one another, the path to Govindar was enclosed in thick wire mesh, like a chicken coop. I was swept up and crushed in the mad press, scarcely able to breathe, surging forward with the others because I had no choice. *Govindar! Govindar!* The women were weeping and stretching their hands to the deity, imploring, overwhelmed with passion. Before I caught even a glimpse of the idol, the crowd pushed me ahead, and it was over. Two days later, I picked up the paper: Seventy-two pilgrims had been trampled and suffocated at another temple some several hundred miles to the north. The conditions were identical.

Everywhere I went in India, I saw unspeakable accidents waiting to happen. Unstable kerosene lamps lurched atop wooden tables in houses built of straw and dung. Unsupervised children crawled determinedly, inexorably, toward those tables. Electrical wires frayed underneath leaking kitchen sinks. Men hawked and spat in the street amid an epidemic of tuberculosis. Buses sped over narrow bridges during monsoons, without benefit of windshield wipers.

I had been in Bombay when they detonated the Bomb at the Pokhran test site, and had watched as the old, the young, the rich, the poor, the lame, the halt—every Indian alive, it seemed—danced madly in the streets, stringing garlands around mock missiles and burning effigies of the Pakistani prime minister. They whirled and danced all night.

The CIA failed to predict the test. Outraged congressmen justifiably asked what the hell the Agency was *doing* with its classified budget if it couldn't even provide warning that the whole subcontinent was about to go nuclear. A representative from Ohio had proposed turning over the Agency's funding to CNN, which had reported the test first. Jay Leno sneered that CIA must stand for Can't Identify Anything.

I could have told them the test was coming: Everyone in India knew it. Even Vishnu had been talking about it.

Now, I wished India only good things—let me make that clear. I just believed that if the United States were to do a better job of keeping tabs on the Indian nuclear program, it would be a *particularly* good thing—for India as much as for the rest of us.

Tom, my amiable new supervisor, showed me to my cubicle and my computer. There was a plastic fish on my wall that sang "Don't Worry, Be Happy," apparently a hand-me-down from the cubicle's prior tenant. For some reason, everyone in the federal government seemed to own one of those fish. I explored the drawers of my new desk. The last occupant had left behind a jumbo-size bag of butterscotch candies, a copy of *Culture Shock:*

India, and a stack of legal documents relating to her divorce proceedings. My supervisor told me to make myself at home, and suggested that I occupy myself with the office's backlogged filing.

Within a week, I realized that because of the enormous cost involved in getting security clearances for clerical workers, almost all of the Agency's paperwork was done by case-officer trainees like me. The amount of paper moved daily was considerable. Virtually every document created by the Agency was classified, largely because the most elementary facts about the Agency—its budget, the number of employees who worked there, the names of the employees who worked there—were classified, and even the most routine correspondence contained clues about secret information. I often thought of this later when from time to time I would read in the papers that some schmuck had been arrested for passing secrets to the Chinese or the Russians. "The accused spy is charged with passing over six thousand classified documents to his Russian handlers," the journalists would exclaim breathlessly. Six thousand classified documents? That was hardly enough to process a health insurance claim.

I filed requests for Kevlar vests, and surveillance logs, and expense reports. I filed the daily cable traffic. Cable traffic was always written in the uppercase, a vestige of the days when cables were literally cables, written in Teletype. Now they were transmitted over a dedicated CIA satellite, but the correspondence retained its urgent, frantic appearance.

I soon found myself caught up in the story of the unfolding courtship of a diplomat we called PINEAPPLE, who worked for India's Directorate General of Foreign Trade in Colombo. He and the case officer developing him, Armand R. HIGGEN-BOTTOM, had met at a diplomatic reception. PINEAPPLE had accepted C/O HIGGENBOTTOM's invitation to lunch, and the two men had been dining for several months at progressively more lavish restaurants. C/O and MRS. HIGGENBOT-TOM played tennis with PINEAPPLE and MRS. PINEAPPLE, and once they had traveled together, the four of them, to visit a distant golf course.

C/O HIGGENBOTTOM regularly reported encouraging signs: PINEAPPLE claimed to admire the United States; he had a cousin and two nieces in Los Angeles, where he hoped one day to visit. He was especially keen to see Sunset Boulevard and Malibu Beach. He liked American cinema very much, our prospective traitor did, especially movies with Sharon Stone. He had a big family, with too many mouths to feed, and a son whom he wished to send to America to educate—"I have heard there are many Indians at Texas A&M University, yes? It would be possible to be finding vegetarian food in Texas, they are not only eating cows there?" He had four daughters: How could he afford to marry them, he asked, on the salary he made? He complained of aches and pains in his back and his knees—"I am having much lumbago today," he babbled sadly. He wished he could fly to America to see a real American doctor—real American doctors, he thought, being possessed of almost preternatural healing abilities with their special machines and devices. He confided sadly that his wife was maddening him with her complaints; their apartment was too small and their kitchen smelled, but how could he afford a bigger apartment or a new kitchen with four daughters to marry? I could imagine the man vividly, waggling his head and lamenting his woes.

Once, at tea, PINEAPPLE's wife had served C/O and MRS. HIGGENBOTTOM a plate of Kraft mini-marshmallows. She explained that she had received them through the mail from that distant cousin of theirs in Los Angeles. She served the revolting things with mango chutney, much to our amusement back on the desk. "I am thinking you will be liking this American dish," she said with shy pride. "We are very much liking foodstuffs from America." From then on, C/O HIGGENBOTTOM arrived at each meeting with PINEAPPLE bearing Oreos, Doritos, boxes of Cap'n Crunch, all pouched from Headquarters and secured with tamper-proof sealing wax. Pouched by me, in fact: I was responsible for driving to the supermarket and choosing the comestibles that best represented the American Dream. Into the tamper-resistant bag they went, accompanied by the myriad detailed bill-of-lading forms. PINEAPPLE always accepted these offerings with chortles of delight, examining them minutely and remarking at the cleverness of the American packaging.

C/O HIGGENBOTTOM was convinced that PINEAPPLE was a highly promising candidate, and so were we back at Headquarters. He planned to pop the question—*Would you like to earn money for your family by doing a vital service for the American government?*—within the month.

Privately, I wasn't sure PINEAPPLE's litany of complaints indicated that he was disposed to commit espionage. If PINEAPPLE had a brain in his head, he would have dined at our expense indefinitely, all the while enjoying the chance to complain to this wonderfully sympathetic American, and he would never do a thing for us in return. Who knows how long he could have kept the gravy train running that way? I kept these thoughts strictly to myself, though; I didn't want to appear as if I might not be a team player.

After a few weeks, my supervisor let me start drafting responses to these cables. I always wrote that Headquarters was greatly encouraged by HIGGENBOTTOM's progress: "HQS OFFERS ITS HEARTFELT SUPPORT TO THE DEVELOPMENTAL EFFORT AND COMMENDS C/O HIGGENBOTTOM FOR HIS ENERGETIC PURSUIT OF THE INDIAN COMMERCE AND INDUSTRY TARGET." I wrote this because this is what Headquarters always writes; by long tradition, I learned, Headquarters cables were—each and every one—small, cheery sunbursts of praise, inevitably congratulatory even in the face of monumental failure. The rationale was that case officers needed encouragement to counteract the isolation and frustration of working undercover in the field. Rarely did a cable escape Headquarters without the word kudos in it. I never used the word myself, but someone usually added it before it went out.

After reading the daily PINEAPPLE news and pouching the Lucky Charms or the Pop-Tarts, I spent my time exploring the compound. I made excuses to take files to the other side of the building so I could take a good look around. The corridors at Headquarters were long and dingy, with visible piping and wiring overhead. Around every corner stood vending machines with cheerless adjacent snack areas, reminding me of the huge public high school I'd attended on the Lower East Side. Peeling gray-green paint covered the walls and ceilings, sullen under cheap fluorescent lighting. Some divisions made attempts at decoration: Africa, for example, hung tribal masks in the hallways, and Latin America tacked up jolly ethnic weavings from Colombia and Mexico. But nothing could temper the massive, gray-grim seriousness of the place. Case officers in the field called Headquarters the Death Star and did everything in their power to avoid returning.

The place was huge and the layout confusing, especially for me, with my poor sense of direction. It could take fifteen full minutes to walk from one end of the building to the other. The basement—where, the trainees nervously joked, the aliens must be kept—was a dark rat-warren of offices containing files and records in huge, mechanized stacks. It was easy to wander for ages only to realize that you had circumnavigated the basement without finding the office you were looking for. Many offices had closed doors and discreet nameplates that indicated nothing whatsoever: Special Office, or Wiring Closet. Someone told me that one of those anonymous offices was actually an ultrasecret emergency command-and-control center capable of withstanding an atomic attack, but I think that may have been one of those little jokes the old hires liked to perpetrate on the new arrivals. Another was to tell us that we were obliged, when we put bags of classified documents into the incinerator, to shout our badge numbers down the garbage chute until we heard "the guys down there" call the number back. In every class, there was someone who fell for it, hollering his number repeatedly into the silent flames until his new co-workers took pity on him and let him in on the joke.

Every day, when I drove through those front gates, I felt a sense of wonder and astonishment that they were actually letting me in, letting me in with a *wave and a smile,* no less, when I presented my laminated badge. The place was mythical, its iconic power lending it an almost magnetic resonance, like the Taj Mahal or the Great Pyramids. I was not the only one to feel it; not a day passed without some nut trying to get past the front gates, driving up to the vehicle barriers with a 12,367-point list of demands from his alien masters or a desperate plea that the Agency stop beaming those obscene broadcasts into his fillings. Once, I heard, a woman had driven to the gates, departed her battered camper van, and removed a carefully constructed helmet from her head. The helmet, as she showed the guard, was lined with tinfoil and an elaborate nest of tangled copper wires. "I am here to tell you," she told the guard, "that I am receiving radio transmissions from your organization, and I *will not obey* your orders anymore! *I will not obey!* "

The guard had apparently seen one too many wackos that day, and he eyed her appraisingly. "Ma'am," he said politely. "Let me ask you. Are the transmissions you've been receiving in VHF or UHF?"

The woman looked slightly taken aback but quickly decided: "They're VHF, young man, they're VHF!"

"I'm sorry, ma'am, but our transmissions are exclusively in UHF. What you'll be wanting is the Department of Defense, down the road."

The woman thanked him and, clutching that lunatic helmet, shuffled off, never to be seen again.

One day, I came to the office to read that HIGGENBOT-TOM had invited PINEAPPLE to lunch, only to be abruptly re-buffed. PINEAPPLE had been curt to him. "I am too busy to be going lunching now," he'd said. He had sounded frightened. We suspected this meant that someone on their side had warned him off. C/O HIGGENBOTTOM, ever the optimist, specu-lated in his cable that the PINEAPPLE case might yet be salvage-able with time and patience. He proposed giving PINEAPPLE a few weeks to compose himself, then inviting him out again, holding out the prospect of an evening watching previously un-released Sharon Stone videos with a bucket of Orville Reden-bacher's.

We doubted it would work—the game was, obviously, up—but we wrote something encouraging anyway. I felt disappointed. I'd been hoping that the recruitment would occur while I was still in the branch. Soon I would be transferred to another division, and I would never know the end of the story, because I wouldn't have the need to know.

A while later I mentioned that I needed to have a poster framed, and Paul, the Army captain, told me he dabbled in carpentry. I watched him in his wood shop as he measured the poster. He scored the foamboard with a utility knife and sanded the edges, then sawed the legs of the frame to fit. He grooved the inside of each piece to hold the glass, inserted the joint connectors, and dabbed wood glue on the corners. Then he tapped the pieces to-gether with a tack hammer. He surveyed his work to make sure the pieces were squared together properly.

He told me his pretty, blond wife had left him for a golf in-structor, and he'd left two women back in Mississippi. Kathy and Emma were unaware of each other. He felt ashamed of lying, but not so ashamed that he was willing to stop.

"Selena, don't you fall in love with me too," he said.

"Why would I want a lying womanizer like you?"

"Because I'm so goddamn handsome and charming," he said.

A few weeks after this conversation, Paul invited the whole class over for homemade pizza. The students had a lot of get-togethers back in those days, and we often went as a group to happy hours at local bars or for beers after work at one another's houses. These evenings were admittedly dull—when you bring together that many men and women who have never been ar-rested, never tried to subvert the U.S. government, never suf-fered major psychiatric illnesses, never done drugs, and never been in debt, you don't get the world's liveliest parties. But we felt the need for these social engagements with one another, tame though they were, for we could no longer enjoy natural and unforced contact with anyone else. Even the most banal en-gagement with outsiders was laden with traps. We quickly came to dread the question "Where do you work?" For inevitably, any response—"Oh, I'm a budget analyst"—invoked a counter-parry: "Oh, really? Where? Oh, sure, of course—hey, you couldn't put me in touch with the HR people there, could you? I've got a nephew, a great guy, who's thinking about USDA—what's the name of the gal who does the hiring?" The questions weren't unanswerable, if you were nimble, but the exercise wasn't relaxing, either.

I helped Paul take the pizzas out of the oven, and then I ended up in conversation with someone else. Later, after almost everyone had left, I saw Paul out on the porch talking to Rita, a dark-haired, perky trainee with a wide smile. She had a kind of 1950s sweater-girl appeal, but when the men in our class found out that she was a devout Catholic with a commitment to chastity, they figured that making time with her would be more effort than it was worth. But there was Paul, leaning in toward her and giving her that intense stare that said *I'm positively riveted by what you're saying, Rita,* and there she was, leaning back and matching him, stare for stare.

I went to get myself another drink.

When I came back, Paul and Rita were still deep in conversation. Now she was laughing at every word he said, tossing her fluffy hair and twirling her necklace, with its crucifix pendant, around her forefinger.

Finally, after what seemed like hours, she yawned, made her excuses, and left. I stayed. When Paul then suggested we open a bottle of whiskey since it was Friday night, I accepted, drinking with him until the last stragglers returned to their wives or their cats. Despite my promises to myself, when at last Paul reached across the table and traced the outline of my lips with his finger, I didn't even pretend to resist.

The next morning I tiptoed down the stairs, praying I'd woken before Paul's roommate, Nathan. Nathan was another trainee, but he wasn't on the same career path as Paul and me. He was slated to become a reports officer. Reports officers direct intelligence collection and disseminate reports; they don't work directly with human assets. On the few times I'd visited their house before, Nathan had been congealed to the living room couch, watching reruns of *South Park* with a half-defrosted Swanson's TV dinner in his lap. There was something about Nathan that made me worry that one day I would come over to find he'd hanged himself in the attic.

The Agency's bureaucracy was slow and inefficient, but its gossip network worked like a fine Swiss timepiece. If Nathan saw me, this particular report would be disseminated faster than word of a plot to blow up Air Force One. I had hoped to sneak out silently, but I tripped and crashed down the staircase. I composed myself gingerly and found myself staring right into Nathan's glittering eyes. He took in my smeared lipstick, the torn brassiere in my hand, my unbrushed hair, the bruises on my elbows. He backed wordlessly out of the room.

My affair with Paul lasted little more than a month. At first he dropped by my apartment whenever the spirit moved him, then he stopped calling. Then Emma, one of his girlfriends from Mississippi, came to town to spend the weekend with him, and I realized it was over.

I had been warned, but it didn't matter.

After another month, I saw him sitting alone in the cafeteria, and I sat down next to him. "I'm not so angry anymore," I said.

"I really didn't want things to get all fucked-up and weird," he answered gently. "I really did want to be friends."

"I know," I said. "It's okay."

A while later, the class was called to the conference room for a briefing on our training schedule. At a break, Paul stood up to get a cup of coffee from the vending machine in the hall. As he walked out of the room, I caught sight of Nathan. His eyes, for an instant unguarded, followed the muscles of Paul's back, flexed underneath his cotton shirt. A look of blurry yearning passed over Nathan's face, and suddenly I understood.

༒

As spring neared, everyone in the class began to prepare for the fitness test we had to pass to qualify for the summer's paramilitary training course. I started running and lifting weights. Some of the other women began to get together to work out every afternoon, trotting companionably together around the Agency's little loop trail on the Headquarters campus grounds. Deer appeared along that path from time to time, watching the runners with shy curiosity.

I would have liked to join them, but Jade, who had been a drill sergeant in the Army and had served in Somalia, had unofficially taken charge of the training. Jade's Vietnamese parents had perished in the war. She had been taken into an orphanage until she was adopted by an American couple. In general, the Vietnamese are rather small-boned. Not Jade. She was large and strong, with well-developed shoulders and quadriceps. Her face was broad; there was the hint of something Inuit or Eskimo in her features, and her voice was deep and husky, almost expectorating. She walked with a muscular, determined stride. She had been a tennis champion in college and still looked as if she were aching to smash things.

At first, I found Jade unobjectionable, if perhaps unnaturally affectionate. Although we didn't know each other well, she often hugged me and put her arm around my shoulders as if we'd known each other for years. I received a birthday card from her that read "You are such a *Sweetie,* you have a heart of gold and I'm so proud to know you!" Although we were officially forbidden from sending personal e-mail over the Agency network, everyone did anyway, and frequently I received messages from Jade with greetings such as, "Whazzup sister! Hope you're having a great day!"

But at the same time, Jade seemed always to be in high dudgeon with one or another member of the class, usually because of some perceived slight or snub. She wrote indignant letters to those who invoked her ire. "You are always cold and arrogant to me!" she wrote to Allison, the triathlete and show-jumper. "You do not even say good morning when I walk into the room! I feel that I have tried to behave with civility to you, but you continue to treat me with bad manners and disrespect!"

Allison printed out the letter and showed it to some of the other trainees: "She's obviously wacko," Allison said to me. "But still, what if someone takes her seriously? Has she been going around saying these things to everyone behind my back?"

She had been, of course. None of us had stood up for Allison, either; we were all vaguely afraid of Jade.

Paul shrugged when I related Allison's story to him: "I told you so. Jade's like the Department of Defense. She needs an enemy to justify her existence."

Shortly after this, a remarkably odd thing happened: Brenda Argus, the director of the Clandestine Service Trainee Program, received a missive comprised of letters and words cut out from newspapers and magazines, like an old-fashioned ransom note from the days of silent movies. It denounced Jade for sending slanderous personal letters via interoffice e-mail. "INVeSti-gAte thIs WomAn!" the note demanded.

Word of the weird letter spread quickly, with everyone wondering who could have written it. Jade might have a few screws loose, we agreed, discussing the matter in thrilled whispers among ourselves, but anyone who had the time or disposition to sit home alone clipping words out of the *Ladies' Home Journal* to denounce a colleague shouldn't be trusted with our nation's security. Brenda Argus launched an investigation but never found the author of the note; it was untraceable, even by the CIA's finest forensic experts.

Jade took the event as the occasion to launch a campaign of extermination against her enemies. She pulled each of us aside in turn to question the patriotism of the others and cast aspersions on their characters. Driving home one afternoon, I had a flash of insight: The author of the note was *Jade herself*. It was her personal Reichstag fire. Of course, I had no evidence for this; it was just an intuition. And the mystery was never solved, proving that while the author may have been mad, he or she had something of a talent for covert ops.

After the incident, Jade's disapproval came to focus on me. Perhaps she sensed my suspicions about her, or perhaps it was because of my relationship with Paul, whom she hated. The friendship cards and the sisterly hugs came to an abrupt end, and she began to snort and roll her eyes every time I entered the room. No matter what I said in her presence, she would shoot meaningful looks at the people around her, as if to say, "Do you see what I mean?" I ignored her as best I could, hoping she would lose interest. And when she began leading the other women in the afternoon fitness training, I decided to go running alone.

Sure enough, after a few weeks her animus turned to someone else. The next object of her vitriol was Iris, the only black woman in our class. I'd noticed Iris from the start, because she was strikingly pretty. She was tall and gazelle-slender, with aristocratic high cheekbones and long, sooty eyelashes that raised and lowered like Japanese fans, causing her to appear perpetually caught in a moment of childish wonder. She dressed in the Chanel suits and St. John's knits she had purchased in her former life—as an investment banker in New York—wearing them with dramatic jewelry and matching scarves, walking down the gray corridors at Headquarters with a model's prancing, swivel-hipped gait. With her delicate elegance, I expected Iris to be a tender flower, but I couldn't have been more mistaken.

Jade had a habit of honking her nose like a foghorn, then excavating its contents with pistonlike motions at very great lengths, then examining her handkerchief, then blasting the damned thing again. She could make a lecture unbearable. Iris was sitting next to her during a mandatory security briefing, and after Jade's fifth honk in so many minutes, Iris lost her patience:

"Jade, *sweetie,* you think you could wait until after class before launching any more steamships from that harbor?" Jade was mortified, and thereafter spared no opportunity to question Iris's devotion to country and fitness for service. "I knew women like that in the Army," Jade told everyone who would listen. "I can spot a team player and I can spot someone who isn't, and believe me, she is *not* the person you want covering you in a fire-fight."

One night during happy hour at Fajita Pete's, after a few margaritas, Iris overheard Jade making a catty comment about the shortness of Iris's skirt, which displayed her endless legs. Iris lost her temper. She stood up. "Jade, would you mind enlightening me? *Why do you feel obliged to be such a goddamned bitch?*"

Jade, squaring her broad shoulders, asked Iris how she dared to "get in my face like that" and launched into a lecture that began "Let me tell you what I think of your—"

And then, to everyone's astonishment, Iris hauled off and punched Jade in the nose.

The other students separated them as they grappled like fairground wrestlers on the floor, Iris's Persol sunglasses spinning across the room, never to be found again, Jade energetically attempting to force Iris's shapely head into a plate of refried beans.

Somehow, miraculously, word of the spat never made it back to Headquarters, and neither of them was ever disciplined. But among the students, the imbroglio became legendary almost before Iris's fist connected. *Did you hear about the catfight? They had to be pried apart with a crowbar.*

I admired Iris's nerve and told her so in the ladies' room the next day. "It's about time someone stood up to her. You're a brave woman. I'd sooner tangle with Mike Tyson." Iris looked pleased with herself. She invited me to lunch.

Iris came from a hardworking family in South Carolina. Her mother was a housekeeper and her father a mechanic. After putting herself through business school by waiting tables, Iris discovered that she loathed business, so she decided to join the CIA instead. I never understood exactly why. She spoke quickly and breathlessly and had a short attention span; talking to her was like having a hummingbird land on your arm: She fluttered for a few seconds and then flew off.

Soon, when it was warm enough, she and I began to take our lunch outside every day, at the picnic tables by the triptych constructed from a fragment of the Berlin Wall. I loved that monument, with FREEDOM spray-painted on its facade. It was a communication through time and space that made the Agency and its mission feel noble. We chattered and gossiped. I told her about Paul and swore her to secrecy. She clucked sympathetically. "He's not that great-looking," she said. "Skinny as a bag of bones." She made the word *skinny* sound like a moral defect.

Iris had been dating a security officer since the week we'd joined the Agency. Brad was a handsome, gentle man who had come to brief our class during CIA 101. He had taken one look at Iris and determined that he would consecrate his life to worshipping at her feet. "You're like some exotic bird who flew into my house," he told her after the first night they spent together, "and all I want to do is figure out how to make you happy so you'll stay." Iris's desk was covered in the cards he sent her. Iris seemed fond of Brad—she was clearly congratulating herself for at last having the maturity and self-respect to choose a man who treated her well—but I could tell that she was already bored out of her tree.

Spring arrived. The cherry trees on the Mall bloomed like giant tufts of cotton candy. I finished my rotation, never finding out what had happened to PINEAPPLE. I began another rotation, working on the Balkans. Jade and I stayed out of each other's way, but whenever Iris and Jade found themselves in the same room, they eyed each other like lions circling the body of a freshly killed antelope.

I was eager to get down to the Farm, where it was said the real training began. The novelty of driving into Headquarters every morning was still keen, but the desk work was not as dramatic as I'd imagined it would be. I carried files from one office to another, and I went to administrative meetings that no one else in the branch wanted to go to, taking the minutes.

I went out a few times with men I met on my rotations. Most of the men in our class were married. Gordon, who worked in the Directorate of Science and Technology, had dark Latin good looks, but he drank too much and his conversation was focused entirely on things he wanted to buy: a Bang & Olufsen stereo, a Miata, a big-screen television, a satellite dish. I went out once with Mark, another trainee, but over dinner I noticed that he made smacking noises when he ate. When he asked me out again, I declined politely.

Seeing men who didn't work for the Agency was problematic: How do you construct a relationship with someone when you begin by lying about where you work? What do you talk about over dinner if you're supposed to be a budget analyst but you don't know a thing about budgets? The standard wisdom was that you couldn't tell someone you were dating where you really worked unless you were engaged to be married. I'd heard that some men waited until after the wedding, just to be on the safe side. My aunt, who truly believed I worked for the USDA, set me up on a blind date with a Defense Intelligence Agency analyst. He spent our dinner carefully impressing it upon me that he had access to classified information. "It's an enormous responsibility," he assured me.

So at night, I went home alone. I told myself that was just fine, and on most evenings, it really was.

CHAPTER 3

I can't say much about my first impressions of Stan, because I don't remember meeting him. Some people form part of a nameless, faceless mass, and Stan was among them, anonymous and vague. He was a pale, fat man with small eyes and very spiky thick red hair that stood straight up from his head like the bristles of a shoe brush. He made no impression on me, none, one way or the other. I had probably been introduced to him, but I didn't remember his name; I once heard someone refer to him as "you know, that guy who looks like a cockatoo." I believe Paul once told me he was very clever and knew a lot about computers.

My first clear memory of Stan dates from the first time our class went down to the Farm, about six months after our induction into the Agency, for the fitness test. We traveled in a bus driven by bald-headed Eppie, a man who held Top Secret clearances in order to chauffeur CIA employees from one clandestine facility to another. When we escaped the Beltway traffic, I could see wildflowers from the window; it was my first spring in Virginia and the countryside was apple-green and lush. We stopped at a shopping mall for burgers and fries, and chattered enthusiastically with excitement, dribbling fries and Coke all over the bus.

It was still light when we arrived. The Farm did indeed look like a farm or a summer camp, with rolling green hills carpeted in violets and dandelions, shimmering in the pale gold light. The scent of pitch pine creosote mingled with the smell of laundry soap. A woodchuck stood on its hind legs; a deer ran across the road. Mother ducks and geese paddled in circles around a small pond, trailed in earnest defiles by fuzzy chicks. Signs pointed to dormitories with names like Daisy and Blossom. The instructors met our bus at the dormitories, just as years ago my counselors had met us at Chief Spotted Snake Camp in the Adirondacks. When they directed us to our bunk beds, I felt for a moment that I had tunneled back in time and that archery lessons and pony rides were about to begin.

We were taken to an enormous depot where the training supplies were kept, and fitted for camouflage gear. The instructors told us that the fitness test would begin at five the next morning. We all went to the campus bar that evening, a shabby little affair with cheap beer, an ancient billiards table and a dartboard. We drank too much, thrilled to be in the country and finally beginning what we imagined would be the real adventure. When the alarm went off the next morning, we were all hungover.

Spring that year lasted all of about a week: It had turned hot and humid overnight. The instructors warned us to drink a lot of water. We were divided into teams, and Stan was in mine. For the first exercise, we were handed the parts of an M-16 and told to assemble it. I might as well have extracted my own appendix with a pair of pruning shears and a bottle of disinfectant. Fortunately, someone else on the team knew what to do, and we managed to put the thing together in reasonable time. We then used ropes to ford a chasm and carried a dummy—he was supposed to be an injured man—across a swamp. I had no idea what the point of these exercises was, but we were all extremely keen to excel at them.

Next, we were put through an obstacle course that involved crawling through mud, swinging overhand across ravines, shimmying up ropes, and hopping from one tree stump to another. Midway through the course, which began with a half-mile run in our heavy boots, Stan, sweating horribly and panting, announced that he was suffering from heat exhaustion and had to stop for water. He said this as if it were somehow our fault. *He's faking it, the lazy fuck,* I thought, annoyed because until that point our team had been acquitting itself decently.

Later, he told me that he had been crushed with embarrassment—it was the first time he had been near me and he'd hoped to cut a manly figure. But I barely noticed him that morning; my attention was elsewhere. Paul was swinging and shimmying through the obstacle course as if it were an amusing little bagatelle. His skin seemed caramelized in the light, and he glowed with sweat and the exhilaration of assembling machine guns.

I passed the fitness test. Stan failed, and I didn't see him again for months. He was sent back to Headquarters to ride a desk. They didn't fire the people who failed the test: Paramilitary training was now optional. In the CIA's early days it had been mandatory, of course; recruits had spent a full year in battle fatigues, learning to shoot straight and blow up bridges. But in an age of satellites and high-tech gadgetry, these skills were obsolete, so the course had been shortened to a single summer. If you had other talents, you could skip the class entirely and still expect a rosy career. It was more a hazing ritual than anything else, a rite of passage that linked us in spirit to the Office of Strategic Services and Wild Bill Donovan. We felt that we were somehow carrying on an important tradition. Those who failed the fitness test were held in contempt by the rest of the class.

Those who passed were divided into teams of eight. Paul was on another team and so was Iris. Nathan was on my team, but at least Jade wasn't. She was on Iris's. I looked at Iris sympathetically when the team assignments were announced. Jade caught my glance and pursed her lips disapprovingly.

The instructors issued our gear—water bottles, army-issue uniforms, backpacks, heavy plastic rifles—and sent us to our communal dormitories to prepare for the weeks ahead. I spent that evening organizing my new equipment and trying to catch glimpses of myself in camouflage.

As ordered, the class assembled the next morning at dawn for a hike in our combat boots, carrying backpacks weighted down with sandbags. Calisthenics followed, then a sprint around the obstacle course. Jade sang out the cadence as we hiked. A small woman named Annette couldn't make it through the pushups; she gave up and rolled over on her side. "I grew up in an orphanage," Jade hissed, "and I just don't understand people who give up at the first sign of *hardship.*"

Paul rolled his eyes and said, loud enough for everyone to hear, "It's *paramilitary* training—not military, *para*military. If I wanted to be in the fucking military, I'd still be in the fucking military. And I don't give a fuck if she grew up in a tiger trap."

Annette looked at him gratefully.

After the morning workout, we traipsed off to the chow hall. The cafeteria was staffed by large, slow-moving black women with security clearances who served up flapjacks, waffles, eggs, gravy, and grits, all accompanied by thick slabs of bacon. Well-built men sauntered in wearing camouflage gear or black paramilitary trousers and T-shirts, and we could overhear an odd covert-action patois—"Where ya been, Jake?" "On a *mooge hunt,* man."

After turning that over in my head for a while, I finally understood that Jake had been out looking for mujahideen—although God knows which or where or why.

After that vigorous workout and heavy breakfast, I could have gone right back to bed, but instead we were marched off for lessons in land navigation. I found myself dressed in full camouflage ensemble and combat boots, shlepping a compass, a protractor, a flashlight, a topographical map, night-vision goggles, a radio, a two-day supply of water, a first-aid kit, a couple of dehydrated meals, a sixty-pound pack, and a plastic-replica M-16 through the humid Virginia woods, skulking under the bushes for cover and pretending to be staging a raid on an enemy arms depot.

At first I felt pretty slick, in my camouflage gear and mirrored sunglasses, until I realized that those gentle rolling hills I had admired on the bus ride concealed at least ten thousand acres of dense forest, seventy billion mosquitoes, chiggers, gnats, bats, poison ivy, poison oak, thicket, ticks that carried Lyme disease, and strange things that made spooky noises, especially at night. Every tree looked to me like every other tree—every hill looked exactly like every other hill—and I spent the first few days wandering from one clump of thorns to another, scratching my bites, picking off ticks, swatting at flies, bandaging and rebandaging my blisters, inadvertently hiking in circles, and finding nothing whatsoever.

Joe, the kindliest member of our team, tried to help me, but Nathan proposed to leave me in the bushes to let me shift for myself. "She needs to learn to do this on her own," he said, and since Nathan was team leader that week, in the bushes I stayed. Nathan kept yelling at me for smoking, because the flash of the cigarette lighter and the glow of the embers could draw attention from the enemy. I found that a bit rich, and murmured under my breath that if the enemy was already in Virginia, I hoped someone had had the presence of mind to alert the President. I think he may have overheard me; our relations didn't improve.

By the end of the week I was covered in bites, scratches, rashes, and bruises, and I had poison ivy of the ass from peeing in the underbrush. That weekend we returned to Headquarters by bus, and when I arrived home, I slept for twenty hours.

We went back to the Farm on Sunday night. We studied emergency medicine the next week. In the classroom, we learned to perform triage, stabilize the cervical spine, fashion bandages out of our underwear, and tape a sucking chest wound. Then we were sent back into the heat for a practical exercise, a simulated safe-house bombing. The instructors drove us to a house in the woods purpose-built for the lesson. When we broke down the door, we discovered that the interior of the house was pitch-dark. We heard screaming and moaning and smelled smoke. I immediately stepped on the first victim. I stepped on her twice, actually.

Students from other teams played the victims. When we dragged them outside, we saw that they had made themselves up to look injured, using props and cyanotic-blue makeup. Latex moulage allowed them to create lifelike effects: burns, blisters, amputations, even a convincing avulsed eye. Thick liquid-latex blood covered every surface, collecting in slippery pools on the floor. The casualties pretended to shriek and limp. They were hysterical; they fought the rescuers. Fighting rescuers, the instructors had told us, is a common response to stress, but I reckoned my classmates were enjoying the chance to give one another a few sharp raps to the kneecaps. One of them nearly crippled me. We had no idea how many victims were in the house. The members of the rescue team quickly lost track of one another, and I wondered whether Nan, our team leader that week, had succumbed to smoke inhalation.

I dragged a screaming two-hundred-pound man whose intestines were bursting from his abdomen down a staircase in the dark—while choking on smoke and tripping over bodies—and hauled him across the lawn to the triage area. Once hauled, he refused to stay still; he lurched up, intestines in hand, insisting that he had to return to the house to find his family, all the while bleeding spectacularly on my clothing and his makeshift bandages. I didn't know what to do about his wounds: They had told us that intestines should be placed on one side of the abdomen and taped with nonporous material to what remains of the stomach, but the intestines—made of rubber and some kind of slime—wouldn't hold together. I symbolically cleared his airways and monitored him for shock and scrunched his intestines together as best I could.

The instructors had said that once we touched the cervical spine, we must immobilize it until the victim reached the helicopter. But how? The guy was writhing and I had nothing with which to immobilize him. "Stay put!" I finally barked in frustration. "It's for your own good!"

He stopped moaning long enough to fix me with a look of contempt. "Yeah, that'll work," he said.

We were dripping with sweat in the heat and direct sun, and the sweat and blood together made it nearly impossible to see the wounds and distinguish the serious from the superficial. The bandages wouldn't stick to the slick of fluids. The victims kept pretending to die.

I'd never before had such a keen appreciation of what emergency medical technicians and firefighters do for a living. By the end of the exercise, I was exhausted. We were allowed to shower. As I was scrubbing the blood off myself—it was made of something viscous that stained—I remembered that after the Oklahoma City bombing, a warning of a second bomb was received immediately. The firemen rushed into the Murrah Building anyway, and had they not, many more would have perished. Whether I would have been brave enough to do that, I didn't know. Later, when we were preparing to jump out of a plane, the instructors often spoke of "conquering our fear." I could never accept that it was anything but plumb stupid and pointless to jump out of a plane. But rushing into a burning building to save a stranger—that's something else.

The following week saw lessons in hand-to-hand combat. The instructor was a former inner-city street cop. God forbid, I thought, looking at his brute face, you should ever find yourself on the business end of *his* nightstick. He called himself the Bull-dog, and his eyes lit up demonically every time he described the satisfying sound of a miscreant crumpling in agony to the ground. He told us to line up against the wall. "How many of y'all have studied martial arts?" he asked. "Ju-doo, Achy-doo, that sorta stuff?" About a third of my classmates raised their hands. "Well, you get into a real fight, that stuff ain't gonna be no use to you."

He explained: "Someone's comin' at you with a broken-off beer bottle, you better believe me, you'll forget everything you ever learned about acting like a crouching crane or a hidden lizard." He raised his arms like wings, wrists limp, in an absurd parody of a crane, and snorted. "Tunnel vision. They call it that for a reason. You see that mother comin' at you and you'll lose yer fine-motor skills and yer depth perception. Everything'll look like a tunnel. And the only thing you'll see in that tunnel's a broken-off beer bottle. Biggest damn beer bottle in history. I promise it."

The reptilian brain takes over and the panic reflex kicks in, he said. People with no experience of violence can no more remember how to administer a roundhouse kick or precision jab than invoke Jedi mind control. The advantage will always be to the opponent who is accustomed to violence. Looking at the Bulldog as he lazily masticated his gum and slapped his fist against his palm, I knew he spoke the truth.

That day, we learned one crude tactic and practiced it a thou-sand times—a single blow to the brachial plexus. The advantage of this move was precisely that it was crude; there was nothing to remember by way of proper form or technique. It was just a good, solid club to the complex of nerves at the base of the neck and, if you could remember it, a thumping kick to the nerve bundle between the foot and the shins. The Bulldog insisted on demonstrating the power of these blows to each of us—"just a little one so as y'all can understand how it works"—and then supervised as we practiced on one another. The men quickly overcame their scruples about hitting women. The best part of the day was giving Jade a good thump to the brachial plexus, then sneaking off to the bathroom before she could find me to return the favor.

By the fourth week, I had ripped off the blisters I'd developed on my palms, exposing the flesh underneath. I had shin splints and a persistent rash. My classmates were going down one by one to sprained ankles and torn ligaments. That was the week we received instruction in surviving interrogation. Since they couldn't really beat us, they settled for annoying us. We were blindfolded and chained to trees until we got hungry and were bored out of our wits. After some time—I'm not really sure how long—I was hauled into a small room. A guard took off my blindfold. Dazzling klieg lights poured into my blinking eyes; a rat-faced woman whom I didn't recognize called me an arrogant imperialist running dog. She told me to tell her the names of my classmates or I would be shot. I gamely assured her that I would be killed before giving up my comrades. It was easy enough to be heroic, since I knew no one was *really* going to be shot—if nothing else, that would violate about seventeen thousand OSHA regulations. But oddly enough, I later heard that when it came Nathan's turn, he gave us all up anyway. We were a little dismayed to hear that.

We were scheduled for rappelling and maritime exercises the next week, then firearms training, then something the schedule listed as the "fundamentals of drowning." Following that, we were to be trained in building explosives from household materials. I was tired. We all were, but we were too competitive to admit it to one another. The lack of privacy had the predictable effect, and we began sniping at each other. It was curious to see who retained a sunny disposition under those conditions and who turned into a whining pain in the ass or a minor-league tyrant. The results weren't what I would have predicted. Those who had been in the military thrived, and rarely lost their tempers. I admired that and I admired them. I wished I were more like them. Competent and cool.

Joe, a Green Beret who had fought in the gulf war and taken a bullet—in the ass, from friendly fire, alas—always had time to gently explain things to me, and then to encourage me, even when I was slow to catch on. During firearms training, I was unable to remember how to disassemble and clean my weapon. He showed me how again and again. "Don't feel bad," he said. "This can be pretty tricky if you've never handled a gun before." As I practiced, he entertained himself by shooting targets at the end of the firing range with a Browning nine millimeter, methodically plugging the flapping paper with bullets. When he was done, the neat holes he'd left formed a perfect smiling face.

On the day we practiced with automatic weapons, they brought the first-aid crew and an ambulance to stand by in case of an accident. I asked the paramedic what they would do if someone accidentally shot himself with one of those monstrous things. "Get the mop," he said economically, gesturing with his head in the direction of the utility closet.

"No reason to be afraid of it," Joe reassured me as I contemplated the M-16 I'd been handed, packed with live ammunition. "It's just a tool like any other. Follow the instructions and you're safe as houses." When I finally pulled the trigger, lying on my belly and bracing the rifle against my shoulder, the recoil slammed me back so hard that on the next day I had an angry bruise in the shape of the butt of an M-16.

Joe always beamed with a genuine boisterous gratitude to find himself still alive, no matter how little sleep we'd had, and he never once expressed irritation or shortness of temper. Despite having a jack-o'-lantern's face and a head shaped like a lightbulb (rather like the screamer in Munch's famous painting), he had recently convinced a ravishing, limpid-eyed blond schoolteacher to marry him. When I saw how kind he was, I decided that his bride had done well for herself.

Nan, on the other hand, who had always seemed perfectly pleasant to me before, if in no way especially interesting, became the hair shirt of my short paramilitary life. A thick-legged woman from Michigan with a moon face—formerly a commercial real estate saleswoman—Nan had a voice that registered a single note, an adenoidal whine elongated with the diphthongs of the Midwest. She had blisters. She had a *mye*-graine. She thought someone wasn't pulling his *wei*-ei-ght. The cigarette smoke *sickened* her. Whenever I lit up, she would start waving her hands in front of her face and making coughing sounds, as if she were discharging a hairball. *"Do you mind?"* she'd say, wrinkling her nose. "I'm *allergic* to cigarettes." I wondered if she would specify in her assignment request that she would work only in the *nonsmoking* section of Kazakhstan. I began to light up in front of her just to annoy her.

I made a vow to myself that I would be like Joe: I wouldn't complain or lose my temper. I stuck to it pretty well. But the tension built up to a point where we were all irrational. One evening we found a group of strangers in our bar, men who looked like our men—alert and clean—but whose faces were unfamiliar. They were drinking beer and swaggering as if they owned the place. We asked them who they were, and they told us they were Secret Service trainees, sent to the Farm for training in explosives detection. Our men puffed themselves up, and soon both groups of men were trading tales of masculine daring. They might fly on Air Force One and take bullets for POTUS, but we used aliases and fake I.D., and since when did John le Carré ever write novels about the Secret Service? The men from the Secret Service asked questions that slyly suggested that anyone who had to work undercover must not have the balls to go face-to-face with his opponents. They managed to imply that espionage was somehow effete. Our guys suggested in turn that anyone whose job description was to make his face look like a bull's-eye must be a little short on candlepower.

Later in the evening, one of the Secret Service men sidled up to fluffy-haired Rita, the perky trainee with the wide smile. Something inappropriate was said. Our boys and the Secret Service rumbled. We kicked them out of the bar and told them not to come back. Our boys were very pleased with themselves. Everyone felt better the next day.

At last, the summer came to an end. The mornings and evenings grew cool. We reached the final week of the course. I'd been dreading the final week. I loathe airplanes. I've always loathed airplanes. I need three shots of vodka just to board a 747. Once I went to a hypnotist to try to overcome my fear of flying. Her office was decorated in purple and potted ferns; there were macramé skirts around the planters. The mating cries of a whale, superimposed upon harp music, played in the background. *When you buckle your seat belt,* she intoned in an oleaginous voice, *you will feel safe and calm. Safe and calm. Safe and calm. When you buckle your seat belt, you will feel safe and calm.* It had cost a hundred bucks, and it didn't take. The whale music was an abomination, and I still hated flying. The idea of jumping out of a Twin Otter made me absolutely nauseated.

On the first day of jump week, Ed, the jumpmaster, lined us up. "This week is the heart and soul of your training!" he cried. "The one week where you *cannot make a mistake!*"

Ed had been a Navy SEAL. Judging from his face, he was past sixty, but below the neck he looked about nineteen, all sinew and brawn. When he met us at dawn for our morning hike and calisthenics, he was always in a sweat from having been up an hour *before* us, running and pumping iron with his two demented, drooling Rhodesian Ridgebacks. "Sanskrit," he had repeated slowly when I answered his question about what I had done before joining the CIA. "Not very practical, now, is that."

"Jumping from an airplane," he bellowed on the first day of jump school, "is *optional.* You do not have to be *airborne!*" He surveyed the class, arms folded across his chest. "Raise your hand if you're a *pussy who wants to stay on the ground!*"

The pussies in the class, of whom I was the prime example, looked at each other nervously. I tried to convince myself that the real act of courage would be to raise my hand in the face of this kind of pressure. Wouldn't that take courage? More courage than jumping out of a plane? I tried hard to persuade myself that it would. My hand stayed by my side, as did everyone else's. Ed smiled a narrow, mirthless little smile. "Good. No pussies here. *Airborne!*"

Recreational jumpers usually exit at some five thousand feet, allowing themselves a half minute or so to respond to a malfunction. But we were going to jump military style, Ed told us. "Military jumpers exit at the lowest altitude possible to minimize the time they're targets in the air! So you are going to jump from 1,250 feet! If there is a malfunction in the main canopy, you will deploy the reserve in four seconds or less! Otherwise, you will not survive! *Airborne!*"

We rehearsed on the ground for several days, wearing harnesses attached to pulleys that lowered us to the ground when we jumped from a thirty-foot tower. We practiced landings and did emergency drills. As each day passed, I knew with greater certainty that I did *not* want to jump out of that plane. Nan had gotten all gung-ho about it and kept telling everyone how excited she was. "Airborne!" she squeaked every time Ed addressed her.

I hoped her chute wouldn't open.

On the morning we were supposed to jump, it began to rain, and the flight was canceled. *Thank God*, I thought. But at lunchtime the sky cleared, and by the afternoon it was bright and cloudless. The aircraft sat on the tarmac, engines growling. Ed told us to suit up.

The day had turned positively radiant, with green fields and woods as far as the eye could see. The grass and milkweed swayed in the fine breeze, and a monarch butterfly settled on my packed parachute. I shooed it away furiously.

I put on my helmet and Joe helped me into my parachute rig, tightening the harness around my legs and chest. Jumpmaster Ed checked each of us personally before we left the shed where the equipment was stored, making sure the metal clasps were fastened securely. I begged him to check me twice. The annoyance I'd felt with his fanaticism for order and discipline had completely disappeared.

We boarded the Twin Otter by climbing up a metal ladder. The jumpmaster fastened our static lines to the heavy metal rings on the interior roof of the plane. The static lines connected to the parachute's deployment bag; when we jumped, we were told, the static line would pull the bag off the parachute. In principle, the parachute would then catch air and inflate.

We arranged ourselves on the hard, narrow benches against the walls of the plane, tight against each other and sandwiched on all sides by our rigs. Ed had divided us into lifts of three students. One lift would jump each time the plane passed over the field. We sat in the order we were to exit; I was in the middle. Ed checked our rigs once more and tugged our static lines.

The pilot, a wild-eyed lunatic with terrible teeth, began idling down the runway. He wasn't watching the road; in fact, he was looking over his shoulder, howling gleefully in the general direction of the passengers, driving with one hand and using the other to light a fresh cigarette from the smoldering butt of its predecessor. He tossed the spent embers behind his shoulder with a flick of his forefinger. I supposed that if he ignited the gas fumes in midair and turned the plane into a fireball, I would for once be prepared. We gained speed and took off with a great deal of groaning from the engines. The small aircraft was cramped and fetid. We were told it had a heroic history of covert missions: Propaganda leaflets and weapons caches had been kicked from its yawning door, just as we were about to be. The fumes were sickening, and the harness was heavy. The pilot turned to us, and over the roar of the engines I heard him shriek maniacally: *"Thank you for flying with us today. We realize you had your choice of covert airlines—"*

I looked to Joe at the stern of the plane for reassurance; he looked, as he always did, unperturbed, as if he were taking the crosstown bus to the zoo. He flashed me a brilliant smile of encouragement and gave me the thumbs-up. "You're gonna love it! It's beautiful out there!" he yelled.

We reached altitude, and Jumpmaster Ed, lying on his belly with his head out the door, began dropping ribbons from the plane to check the wind direction. Not satisfied with our position, he told the pilot to circle the airfield again; we tilted and rolled. Through the maw of door I could see the features of the earth. I could see the training camp from the air, and the flares that marked the drop zone. They looked like toys.

Finally satisfied that our position was favorable, Ed shouted for the first lift to line up. He hollered the commands as we had practiced them. *Stand up! Hook up! Check static lines! Check equipment!* The words were clear despite the noise of the engines. Joe hopped out first. He was at the door one second, then there was a hideous, unspeakable sucking sound, and he was gone.

The rest of the jumpers in the lift exited the cabin one by one, their bodies vanishing with a violent lurch at the command—Go! GO! GO!! My lift was next. We circled the field again. I felt a numb sense of disbelief as I stood in line for the door, and, when my turn arrived, sheer horror. I placed my feet on the step beneath the door and my hands on the wing struts. The wind screamed past at eighty miles an hour. Then the command: GO!!

I leapt.

Instantly, there was an obscene force and pressure and violence as the wind yanked me into the void, then a sickening, anarchic tumbling. Then the chute opened and suddenly I was caught, and I floated, held tightly by the harness. The canopy was above my head, as it should have been, and all was still and eerily silent as I hung 1,250 feet above the earth. I remembered what I was supposed to do—check the steering toggles, gain canopy control—and somehow made it to the drop zone, landing as I had been taught by curling my body into the shape of a banana. It was all over quickly, much faster than I had expected. Even with a parachute, it doesn't take long to fall 1,250 feet.

I was told I would find the experience beautiful and exhilarating. I was told I would be proud of myself for conquering my fear. I was told, in fact, that I would never fear flying again. But that's not the way it was.

The experience was hateful. If there was a spectacular view up there, I was too worried about breaking every bone in my body to notice, and when it was over, all I felt was relief. I was glad I wasn't a pussy, but that was about the only reward in it. And since then, I've been even more afraid of flying. It reminds me of jumping out of a plane.

The first thing I did upon reaching the ground and assuring myself that all my limbs were still correctly attached to my torso was look for my cigarettes, which had departed the plane along with me, strapped to my leg. I figured if the chute didn't open, I'd surely be wanting one on the way down. The instructors were shouting at me to get up and pack up the parachute, but I ignored them. When I lit up, Nan, who had hit the ground two jumps ahead of me, started waving her arms in front of her face and wrinkling her nose. "Do you have to smoke?" she whined.

"Nan, shut the fuck up," I said.

At the end of it, I was given my jump wings and a certificate proclaiming me to be a qualified parachutist. There is a photograph of me standing by the plane, in my fatigues, with my parachute and helmet, but it is classified and must be stored in a secure facility, so I don't have it anymore. I sustained only minor bruises from my landing, but others weren't so lucky; we had a broken nose, several sprained ankles, a serious knee injury, and a tree landing, the jumper winding up in an eighty-foot hardwood and dangling from a branch for several hours. Iris missed landing in live power lines by inches. How stupid, I thought, to risk everyone's life for a hazing ritual.

But I did it and I survived. I was a full-fledged member of the secret brotherhood. I had truly joined the CIA.

CHAPTER 4

I n the end, it wouldn't matter if we could shoot straight or if we had the *cojones* to jump out of a plane. They had specialists to do that. *We* had been hired to convince other human beings to commit treason, and the real education was still to come. In a few months, we would return to the Farm for the bone-crushing tradecraft course. But first we were to go back to Headquarters for the fall, where we would learn to determine whether we were under surveillance. The course was taught there rather than at the Farm because the urban environment was more like those we might encounter overseas. It was the first training exercise that *really* counted: Anytime a spy meets an agent, he must first assure himself that no one is watching, and if you could not do this successfully, each and every time, you could not succeed in the training.

I returned to my apartment in McLean on a Friday evening, wishing I had more time before the class started on Monday morning. My bills were on my kitchen counter, unpaid; my plants had died. I hadn't seen any member of my family in months.

But the class began immediately, and as soon as it did, blurry-faced strangers began tracking me. I was supposed to identify and describe them, but I kept missing them completely. I saw ghosts. I was certain that one man in a blue parka was tracking me with his eyes and speaking into a hidden microphone, but the instructors told me he was just a casual; his artful pretense of indifference was in fact the real thing. Meanwhile, I missed the real shadows, who slipped in and out of the twilight, merged into the crowd, then produced reports chronicling my every gesture.

I didn't seem to improve with practice. A few weeks into the class, I met Morris, my instructor, at our prearranged rendezvous point, a picnic table outside a Safeway. "So," he asked. "Were you under surveillance?"

"I don't think so," I said. "I didn't see anything out there." I had driven through most of northern Virginia, pretending to tour the plant nurseries. I'd traveled long, lonely country roads. I'd wandered in and out of stores alone. I'd seen nothing out of the ordinary.

"How sure are you?"

"Pretty sure."

"Sure enough that you'd have met your asset, gone ahead with the meeting?"

"I think so . . . yes, I think so."

He picked up the surveillance report and read from it. "Subject entered Gro-n'-Green nursery in Oakton at 1437 hours. Looked at hydrangeas and inquired about price. Did not seem genuinely interested in flowers. Made no purchases. Appeared nervous and distracted. Subject looked over shoulder twice at entranceway for no apparent reason. Subject exited store at 1446 hours. Upon pulling out of parking spot, Subject sideswiped surveillant's adjacent vehicle, damaging said vehicle's paint. Subject swore loudly. Subject did not inspect the damage to the other car and did not leave a note. Please remind Subject that hit-and-run is a felony offense."

Morris stared at me furiously. "Still think you weren't under surveillance?"

"Um . . . I guess not."

"Let me tell you something. If you hit a surveillant's car like that out in the field, they'll slash your tires and pour sugar in your engine. On top of it, you just led the whole surveillance team right to your asset. Congratulations. You got him arrested and shot by a firing squad."

I had never been so inept at anything before. Every time I got into my car, my inexperience behind the wheel led me to do something only a woman with something to hide would do: I drove too slowly or too quickly. I rode the brakes. I left my turn signals on for too long or not long enough. I took forever getting in and out of parking lots, often scraping my fenders. I was nervous and distracted. I kept looking over my shoulder.

I told Morris that I wasn't behaving erratically on purpose, but it didn't matter. "What are you going to do?" he asked. "Hang a sign on your bumper that says, Don't worry about little old me, I'm not with the CIA, I just grew up in Manhattan and I'm new to this whole driving business?" He spoke as if I were driving poorly on purpose, to humiliate him. He told me that if I didn't improve, I wouldn't pass the class.

Morris tended to speak in clichés and homilies, one after another. "Gotta keep your eye on the ball. Practice makes perfect. Look before you leap." He carried himself with shoulders hunched, his body compacted, in the manner of a man who had been injured by life and hoped to shield himself from further blows. He had served in Laos and Cambodia. "Can't make a silk purse out of a sow's ear," he said when I asked him how he remembered his time there. I was never quite sure what he meant, but his frustration with me came through—clear as a bell, as he might have said.

The other students seemed to be mastering the subject much

faster than I was. In the supermarket, I ran into Jason, a classmate who was rumored to be related to the Director of Central Intelligence. I asked how the course was going for him. "God, it's so good to be able to sleep as late as I want," he replied, running his hand through his pompadour. "I don't know about you, but I really needed this break."

Unlike jumping out of a plane, this class wasn't optional. I knew I'd never be able to bear it if an asset who had placed his trust in me was shot by a firing squad because I couldn't do my job properly. The thought of returning to academia, humiliated, because I was a bad driver—of all idiotic handicaps—was unbearable. I didn't even know if I *could* return to academia: I'd been off the job market now for too long. I'd published nothing since receiving my doctorate; my name had never been well known among Orientalists, and those who did know it thought I had left the world of scholarship to take a job as a budget analyst. The move didn't suggest my commitment to Oriental studies, and I doubted they would welcome me back.

It was a glorious fall; one sparkling day passed after another. The leaves were blazing ocher and crimson. Farmers by the side of the road sold autumn squash and great cheery pumpkins. All I thought about was becoming a better driver. The key to detecting surveillance was knowing whether you'd seen the same car twice, but I knew nothing about cars. The guys in the class could tell the year, make, and model of a car from the shape of its headlights, but I wasn't even aware of the relationship between a car's manufacturer and its hood ornament until one of my classmates mentioned it to me. I spent hours in the parking lot at Headquarters studying hood ornaments. I made flash cards and created mnemonic devices for myself: *Fords are All-American, like the Gipper. Ronald Reagan liked jelly beans. Fords wear jelly beans.* I took to the road day and night, studying *Car and Driver* at the red lights so I could bone up on the shapes of headlights. Sometimes

I didn't notice that the light had changed until the drivers behind me began honking furiously.

But as I grew more fatigued and anxious, my skills actually deteriorated; within a month my car had so many dings and nicks that body-work repairmen stopped me in parking lots. I kept getting lost in the dense Beltway traffic, wasting hours trying to find my way home every night. One evening, at twilight, I nearly struck a wandering toddler.

I recycled dirty clothes rather than doing laundry. I stopped reading, eating, doing yoga. My eyes were bloodshot; I felt haggard. I forgot my mother's birthday.

My sister left message after message; I never had time to return her calls. Once she managed to catch me just as I was walking out the door. She asked what was wrong. I told her I couldn't talk about it. She exhaled sharply and I could imagine her pursing her lips. "I'm your sister, Selena. It's not reasonable to ask me not to be concerned when I haven't heard from you in months. Can you at least give me some idea when you plan to return to this astral plane?"

I told her that perhaps we could discuss it in person one day. She didn't sound happy. Neither did I.

In the end, I still failed the class. Morris was terribly upset, he took my failure as his own, and I found myself in the odd position of comforting *him*. "You did all you could, Morris," I said. "You were a great instructor; you just can't make a silk purse out of a sow's ear."

Everyone else passed. My classmates got diplomas at a convivial little graduation ceremony with coffee and Krispy Kremes. I got a "Certificate of Attendance."

When I got home that evening, I burst into the tears of humiliation and frustration I'd been choking back all day. I would have eaten nails before letting any of my classmates see me cry. Every one of them had passed but me.

I checked my e-mail; I'd received more messages from my mother and sister, both complaining again that they hadn't heard from me in ages. Lilia politely inquired whether I had, perhaps, been brainwashed. I replied, telling them both to stop kvetching, because I'd probably be back in New York any day, unemployed and sleeping on Lilia's couch. I was on the verge of washing out, I wrote rather dramatically. I couldn't spot surveillance if it came up and bit me on the ass, and it would be for the best when they fired me because I'd just get my assets killed. I remonstrated with my mother. "Why did you waste my time with those piano lessons and ballet school?" I wrote. "Why didn't you make sure that I learned to *drive*?"

My mother wrote back as every mother would: She would love me no matter what happened. She also pointed out, rather tartly, that at the age at which I had taken those piano lessons, I couldn't have seen above the steering wheel. Lilia, somewhat to my surprise, wrote that she was delighted that I might abandon espionage, voluntarily or not. I suppose I was expecting a pep talk from her, the *you-can-do-anything-you-set-your-mind-to* speech, but I sure didn't get it. Since I'd joined the Agency, she wrote, she never saw or spoke to me. She resented the fact that when we did speak, I couldn't talk to her about what I did. "I accept that there's good reason for all of that," she wrote, "but from my point of view, my sister's been assimilated by the Borg." She asked me whether this was really how I wanted to live my life.

Lilia was pregnant with her second child. I meant to answer, but I didn't have time.

⚭

Morris sent me to see Brenda Argus, the head of the Clandestine Service Trainee program, to determine what this meant for my career. She looked at the memorandum announcing my failure and shook her head; her matron's lips turned down at the corners. "We can't keep you on if you can't spot surveillance," she said. "Maybe you should be working harder."

I sat on my swivel chair with my knees together and head bent, hating her with all my heart. I assured her that I was very committed and would work harder.

"Maybe you can make it up when you go back to the Farm," she said. She decided I would continue there with the rest of the class, but she would caution the instructors at the Farm to keep their eyes on me. From then on, she implied, I was on probation.

∞

Soon after my talk with Brenda Argus, I came down with a stomachache. It was early winter, a few days before we were to return to the Farm to begin our final marathon of training. I took an antacid and went to bed.

By the morning, the pain had moved to the lower right quadrant of my abdomen. I looked up my symptoms on the Internet. I checked my temperature: slightly above normal. Pain, swelling, fever, vomiting—I checked off the symptoms, one by one.

Two hours later, I called a cab and I told the driver to take me to the emergency room. A nurse drew my blood and the attending physician ordered an ultrasound. I watched the screen as the images of my organs flickered. When the results of all the tests came back, the attending physician called the surgeon and booked an operating theater.

I vaguely remember asking the surgeon if he had done this before, and telling him to be sure to wash his hands. I was wheeled into a cool room by a complement of chattering phantoms in green masks. Sometime later, I awoke in the recovery room. I was told that the surgery had gone well and that I was fine. I didn't feel fine. I was in pain—not "discomfort," as the nurse kept calling it. I had a self-administering morphine drip, and I kept poking at the button, but I think they'd rigged it so that I couldn't accidentally overdose. I couldn't sit up at all, and my stomach was swollen and purple. I drifted in and out of sleep and fog. My parents called; they wanted to come down from New York immediately, but I talked them out of it. My mother was saying something insane about appendicitis being caused by apple seeds; I thought about trying to explain that it was a kind of infection, but it seemed a terrible effort.

I called the office via the special number we were given for emergencies. Only Paul and Iris visited me in the hospital. Iris brought flowers and a shiny helium balloon printed with GET WELL SOON! and a picture of Garfield. She fussed over me. "Oh my *God*," she said, fluttering around the bed, arranging things. "Trust *you* to get appendicitis right before the toughest part of training."

I spent the week after returning home sleeping. The only consolation was that at least I could lie in bed until it was time to go back to the Farm.

∞

I was by no means back to normal by the day I drove back to the Farm, and I had none of the sense of ebullient expectation I'd had the last time we went down. The surgeons seemed to have removed not only my appendix but my bravado. Many of us were expected to flunk out in the coming months, and I suspected I was a prime candidate.

There were to be no more boisterous weekly bus rides. We would be driving ourselves to and from the Farm each week; the curriculum would require us to meet imaginary assets throughout the region, and we needed our cars to drive to the meetings. I drove to the Farm alone through a vile hailstorm, traffic heavy and ominous on the interstate, praying that I would remember the way. When at last I arrived, I saw that the once green hills were covered in frost and the trees were bare, their branches like spider legs.

I hauled my suitcase over the icy parking lot and up to the room I'd been assigned. We had shared communal barracks in paramilitary training, but now we each had a small room to ourselves, in a utilitarian dormitory. Mine was small, simple, and clean, almost antiseptic, with a concrete balcony that opened onto a view of another concrete building.

I set down my suitcase and stood in the doorway, contemplating the twin bed with starched white sheets and the powder blue blanket tucked around the mattress in neat hospital corners. Above the bed, a bland seascape stared from the wall, the kind of mass-manufactured pastel one finds in a motel. The carpet was thin and fuzzy, wall-to-wall drab, a color immune to staining. I looked in the bathroom, half expecting to see a ribbon around the toilet indicating that it had been sanitized for my protection. No ribbon, but the bathroom smelled of industrial-grade cleanser, so perhaps it had been sanitized nonetheless.

I sat on the bed. The sheets smelled of bleach, and the blanket was neither soft nor warm. There was no television, no radio. No plants. I was the only living thing in the room.

I wondered if there were cameras installed in the walls. I looked closely at the fire detector, which sat sullenly on the ceiling like an eye, but I found nothing—not that I would have known what to look for. I had brought a few books with me but didn't feel like reading. It was too cold to go for a walk.

I had sublet my apartment in McLean and put my things in storage to save on rent while I was away. I would be spending weekends here as well as weeks.

I realized that I was feeling sorry for myself. I told myself to suck it up. *After all,* I said to myself, *you joined the CIA, not the Girl Scouts.*

⚭

Hal Hertz, the course director, strode to the center of the stage to address us. He gripped the podium with both hands. "Listen up, gang," he said. "You're in for a tough time. If you think this is all bullshit, you're gonna be in for a rude surprise. The day after you graduate, you could be meeting assets. You could be on a plane for Bogotá or Moscow. People's lives and this country's security will depend on you. So take this seriously, because if you don't, you're out of here. Look around you: A lot of the people you see aren't going to be here at the end of this class. Because if we don't think you have the chops, we aren't going to let you graduate. Everyone understand?"

He was bald and angular; he wore a goatee and a narrow tie. The veins stood out along his temples and forehead. His dark eyebrows pointed to the tip of his long, thin nose; he had flared nostrils and bloodless lips; his face was lean and cold.

"We're going to test you. We're going to see how you handle surprises. We're going to see how you handle stress. How you perform when you've had no sleep. How you handle being watched. How you handle criticism. We're going to see if you make mistakes. We're going to see if you make them twice, and if you do, you won't be around for long. We're going to see how you work with other people. Yes, those are closed-circuit cameras in the conference rooms. No, there aren't any in your bathrooms. There are some things they don't pay us enough to watch. *But everywhere else, we're going to be watching you.* And what we want to know is: Do you make the grade?"

⚭

Stan smoked. He was the only other smoker in our class.

We had a full week of introductory briefings. At the end of the second day, I realized that I was out of cigarettes. I checked all my pockets but found nothing. The Farm's little commissary was already closed. I walked out of my room, prepared to drive all the way to the 7-Eleven, a good twenty miles away. It was raining and already dark.

Stan's room was down the corridor from mine, and I nearly walked into him as he opened his door. He was very large, with a pale, doughy face, and his thick, brushy hair stood straight up. "Hey, you!" he said, beaming cheerfully.

"Hey yourself," I answered, and then remembered that he smoked. "Stan! You wouldn't have any cigarettes on you, would you?"

"Of course I do," he replied. "Come on in." He held the door open for me and extended his arm as if flourishing a cape. I walked into his room. It was extremely tidy. I went out to his balcony, because it was against federal regulations to smoke indoors. He followed, and offered me a Balkan Sobranie from a sleek silver case.

"You know, I've never really talked to you before," he said, lighting my cigarette with a matching filigreed-silver lighter.

"Now's your chance."

"I've been curious about you. This kind of work doesn't usually attract Sanskritists. How did you end up here?"

"The alternative was the tenure track at Mongeheela State University. I just couldn't face it."

An intelligent understanding sparkled across his face and he chuckled. I liked that. I'd explained that to another classmate, the one who made noises when he chewed. He'd looked confused, then said, "Mongehecla's a pretty good school, isn't it? I think one of my sister's friends goes there."

We bantered a bit and finished our cigarettes, and I thanked him. "Anytime," he said. "It's always good to have a partner in vice."

The class began with lectures about the proper format for intelligence reports. The subject was dull, but like tax code, the details were critical and getting them wrong could land you in a heap of hurt. Reports had to be slugged so that they reached all and only those with a need to know, but determining who precisely comprised this set was as much art as science. If you sent the report to too many people, you increased the risk to your source; if you sent it to too few, it could be missed by the one person who fully understood its significance.

Wally, the lecturer that first week, was a nervous public speaker, and the class was cruel to her. On the fifth day, some of the students made bingo squares out of her pet phrases: *I cannot stress this enough,* or, *You really need to be detail-oriented, guys and gals.* They marked their cards covertly every time she used one of these locutions, and the student who filled his card first had to lift his hand and use the word *bingo* in a question. "Wally, excuse me for a moment, I'm not sure I understand. Let's say you have a report already in dissemination, but the next day your asset shows up and—*bingo*—he tells you that some part of the information he gave you was inaccurate. Do you have to issue the whole report again, or can you just issue a correction?" I think Wally figured out what was going on, and her feelings were hurt. I felt bad for her.

I started borrowing cigarettes from Stan at the breaks and smoking with him in his room after class. "Don't worry about it," he said when I wondered whether we'd get in trouble for smoking indoors. "It's cold out. The housekeeper won't rat on us—I've got things arranged with her."

"You do? How?"

"We've just got an understanding."

Stan's room was identical to mine, but his was more appealing: It was orderly and fresh. He lit scented candles to keep the air from smelling like smoke. He had arranged his crisply pleated clothes into neat stacks on his shelves and organized them by color. A burnished wooden box on his dresser contained two small, perfectly symmetrical pyramids of imported cigarettes. On his bedside table, water murmured over the smooth pebbles of a feng shui fountain. He had brought a portable CD player to the Farm, along with a few collections of piano sonatas. When I knocked on his door, his room was always calm, and he always seemed happy to see me.

As we smoked, we talked about the same thing everyone there talked about—everyone else. Stan was dismissive of Joe, the vigorous Green Beret I'd admired during paramilitary training. "Sure, he's good at jumping out of planes," he said. "That's great. Except that our job isn't to jump out of planes, it's to recruit assets. And if you want to get up close and personal with some Palestinian terrorist, jumping out of planes won't help you much, will it. I'd much rather use someone who, say, speaks Arabic. Or maybe someone who's read the Koran. Or *any* book your target might have read. Or, hell, any *book*. And I'd really like someone who knows something about the history and the culture of the Middle East. Frankly, I'd prefer a guy who doesn't have a jar haircut that screams 'Duck for cover! I'm CIA!' Nine-tenths of the people we'd want to recruit would be *terrified* if they met someone like that. Joe's a relic. He's CIA circa 1961. He's Bay of Pigs. He has *no* subtlety."

A few days later, I asked Stan if he regretted having missed the paramilitary training. "Not really," he said. "I mean, I'm sorry I failed the fitness test. That was embarrassing. I used to be in great shape, in college, when I fenced, but—" He shrugged and gestured vaguely at his paunch, as if it were just something he happened to carry around, like an umbrella. "I have other priorities now. I just don't have the time to spend hours in the gym. And not going to the Farm over the summer was a good thing for me. A very good thing."

"Why?"

"I was working on some pretty interesting stuff back at Head-quarters."

"What did you do?"

"Can't talk about it."

"Oh," I said, since there was nothing else I could say. I finished my cigarette, and we rose to go back to the auditorium.

∞

"Let's say you were kidnapped by terrorists," Stan said that evening when I came over again. "They've got you blindfolded and tied to a chair. They've got a gun to your head. One of the people in our class is going to negotiate your release. Which one would you want it to be?" Stan loved gaming out espionage scenarios, and he loved sizing up our classmates.

I thought through the group. Nathan would tell them they could keep me, I supposed. I imagined Iris and had a swift vision of her calling her interlocutor a camelfucker and punching him in the nose. What about Kirk, who had been assigned to the seat next to mine in the auditorium? Kirk had been a Marine before joining the Agency. Wiry and pockmarked, he still wore his hair shorn to his skull; he walked with the tense, erect posture of a professional soldier. He kept a wad of tobacco between his teeth and gums, and spoke out of one side of his mouth so the juice didn't run down his chin. When he sat down, he splayed his legs far apart. I once heard him talk about the safest way to meet an asset who might cause trouble: "You put the guy in the front seat. You sit in the back, so you can pop him if he gets squirrelly. Make sure you put plastic on the seat or it'll get ruined when his sphincter goes."

"Kirk," I answered.

"*What?* Why the hell would you put your life in the hands of that *psycho*?"

"Because he looks mean as hell, and I want them to believe

that we might just be crazy enough to drop the Big One on them."

Stan shook his head as if he were disappointed. "Why, who would you choose?" I asked.

"Marcia."

"Marcia?" Marcia seemed like a sweet girl. Youngish, a little younger than everyone else. I didn't know her well. She had slim legs and an ample bosom and an unassuming face. Paul had put the moves on her once; she'd turned him down.

"Marcia. I don't know if anyone here could do it right, but at least Marcia's charming. She wouldn't have the faintest idea what to do, and she'd admit it. So she might try asking politely. And that might have a hope of working."

I had no idea whether he was right. I'd have never thought of Marcia. I was chagrined that he'd thought so little of my answer. "Maybe," I said, and wondered whether Stan was more cunning than I, or Marcia more charming.

∞

We had been at the Farm for two weeks. Wally finished her lessons on reporting formats, and an instructor named Bill took over, lecturing on defectors. *Make sure you offer him a beverage,* Bill stressed. *See if he needs a hot meal. He's a human being. He's just made the biggest decision of his life, and he doesn't know if it was a good idea. He's frightened. People in trouble are like baby ducks. They imprint on the first thing they see. He'll be looking at you and wondering, "Are you my mommy?"*

In the afternoons and evenings, we had exercises in writing cables and reports, which came back from the instructors the next day covered in red ink. We began studying dead drops—places to leave money and messages for our agents, who in turn would leave the secrets we were purchasing. The instructors told us to drive out to the countryside to look for suitable sites, warning that we might be under surveillance and had better not look like spies casing the area.

After class one day, Stan offered to help me. "I heard you had a few problems back at Headquarters," he said tactfully. "I could go out with you, sit in the passenger side, see if maybe I can give you some pointers. I've taught a couple of people how to drive. I'm pretty good at it."

Everyone knew I had failed surveillance detection, but only Stan had ever offered to lend me a hand. I accepted his offer gratefully. He started giving me lessons late in the evenings. We drove the back roads of the Virginia countryside, bleak and forlorn in the dead of winter. Every road seemed to lead to a strip mall, each one a featureless checkerboard of giant Kmarts and Tastee-Freezes, Denny's and Fashion Bugs, International Houses of Pancakes. Clumps of dirty snow were piled up by the sides of the parking lots. Treading gingerly over the ice, Stan and I searched for places to leave our packages, sketching sites in our notebooks. We practiced spotting vehicles that might be surveillance. He told me what to look for, giving me tips. "See the way that car is parked there? The way its nose is pointed out? Why would it be parked that way when no one else is?"

"I guess to make it easier to pull out in a hurry?"

"Exactly. Excellent. See, you can do this. Keep an eye on that car." Sure enough, the evil thing slipped out behind us, holding steady in our wake. "Gotcha, Ratface," he said, glancing in the side mirror, moving his eyes but not his head.

Then he looked in mirror again and muttered, "Damn, it's YWP-7182."

"Pardon?"

"YWP-7182. Just saw him again. We saw him up on the freeway. And by the Taco Bell."

"You were memorizing license plate numbers on the freeway?"

"I wasn't memorizing them—I just remember them."

"You mean you were just looking at license plate numbers and you happened to recognize this one from the hundreds of license plates we saw before? I mean, thousands?"

"Don't you do that too?"

"Are you kidding me? Of course I don't."

"How do you know when you're being followed, then?"

"Let me get this straight: You just *remember* thousands of license plate numbers? You don't write them down or anything?"

"No."

"Don't look: What's the license plate of the car three cars behind us, in the right lane?"

"YYT-9688."

Oh my God. He's right. He has a memory like Deep Blue.

I was intimidated, and impressed.

❧

Stan had been a corporate lawyer before he joined the Agency. His specialty was class-action suits—not filing them, but beating them. "You wouldn't believe," he said, "how much time and money my clients had to spend to defend themselves from people so dumb they don't even check to see whether the burger is hot before they put it in their mouths." Even in casual conversation, he often spoke as if he were closing a case before a jury, stacking articles of evidence one upon the other, marshaling his arguments to a vigorous conclusion. "The map says we should take the next exit," he said to me once, "but that's only dispositive."

Oddly, though, as soon as he began to plead his case before that imaginary jury, his voice would become high and thin, a strange counterpoint to his fluency and an even stranger contrast to his stout physique. One expected a rich, stentorian bass to emerge from that barrel chest, but instead his voice was reedy and compressed, almost womanish. It was unattractive. I noticed this with guilt. I wanted to consider his appearance charitably, but I couldn't. He was tall and huge, but his limbs were disproportionately short; his forearms were stumpy like flippers. He had a double chin and a broad bottom. His eyes were close and beady; his nose and mouth were too small for his large, fleshy head; his skin was pale and freckled and his hair stood straight up in a brushy orange tuft. He had a determined, stout man's short-legged stride. He was often out of breath.

He dressed very seriously. At Headquarters, Stan had worn a dark suit and tie to work every day, even though the CIA had a casual-dress policy. "This is the CIA," he told me, "not some Silicon Valley start-up. It's not a casual job." When we had visitors at the Farm from Headquarters, Stan put on a suit. He matched his good silk ties with his muted argyle socks and a display handkerchief, securing his French cuffs with the heavy gold cuff links he'd acquired on his litigator's salary. His casual wear was strictly prep school: crisply ironed khaki trousers and polo shirts, Ray-Ban sunglasses tied around his neck by a cord. I asked if he might be more comfortable if he wore jeans and a sweater to class like everyone else; he looked at me doubtfully.

I liked the way he said things that I'd never thought of myself. I liked the way he'd read every book that I'd ever read, and many that I hadn't. He had read the *Arthashastra,* an obscure Gupta-dynasty treatise on espionage that advocates the use of poison girls, as Kautilya termed them. I'd skimmed it before my orals, but even I hadn't finished it—it was almost unreadable—and I had an excellent reason for reading sacred Hindu texts.

We discussed it in his room one day. The CIA was just about the only intelligence organization in the world that didn't use honey traps—beautiful women who seduce a target and coax secrets out of him in moments of passion. Swallows, the Soviets had called them. Stan wondered aloud whether we weren't crippling ourselves. Espionage was a dirty business, he argued; we needed to use every tool in our box. I agreed in principle, but I wasn't sure whether the tactic was really that effective. "Your average Iranian rocket engineer isn't really going to say, 'Praise Allah, my sweet little raisin,' and then tell her about that plutonium the North Koreans are sending them in a vat of kimchi. Seems to me that all we'd really be doing is getting the enemy laid, don't you think?"

"Women always underestimate the things men will do to get laid," he said.

⌒

"I've had the most extraordinary life," Stan told me. "I've never known hunger or war. I never had to worry there would be a knock on the door in the middle of the night. This is the greatest country on earth, and I want to give something back."

I was only half paying attention. I was looking for our exit.

"What about you?" he asked. "Why are you here?"

I never knew how to answer questions like that. Of course I loved America—who wouldn't? But I never felt right making speeches about My Great Patriotism; it always came out sounding vapid, as if I were trying to win the Miss Iowa Grainball Pageant. Still, when you work for the CIA, it's important to talk about your patriotism often and loudly; otherwise people get worried.

"Well," I said, searching for the right words, "let's start with the fact that I've never seen an American city reduced to rubble by an earthquake. And it's not because we don't have earthquakes in America—of course we do. It's because in America, we have *building-safety codes*. And we have local inspectors who ensure that everyone adheres to those codes. State codes, county codes. And those inspectors don't take bribes. And when you read the papers, you don't read that an American nuclear reactor melted down yesterday because someone sold the spare parts to pay for a dacha on the Black Sea. And American children don't die of diarrhea that you could fix with a glass of water mixed with salt and sugar."

I looked to see if he was satisfied with that answer, but his expression remained expectant.

"Stan, my grandparents were refugees from the Nazis. They were incredibly lucky to make it to America. If they hadn't come here, I wouldn't exist. In America, they *never* send Jews to the gas chambers. They *never* shoot their own intellectuals." I thought that answer should be more than enough, but he kept looking at me, waiting. What was he waiting for? "Look, I believe deep down that the world would be a safer place if the U.S. just ran it—I mean, fuck all this covert stuff. Just have keen young men and women from Seattle and Kansas City working eighty-hour weeks to administer Rwanda and Uzbekistan. They'd do it in accordance with federal environmental and safety regulations and everyone would be better off, and . . . oh, shit! Did I just miss the exit?"

"You can take the next one. I know a shortcut back. How long are you planning to stay in the business?"

"I don't know. As long as they'll let me, I guess. You?"

"I'm out of here in seven and a half years."

"Exactly seven and a half?"

"Six years on the streets, at least eight recruitments. Then I take an eighteen-month rotation to the NSC. I'm here to punch the intelligence ticket. You need that in Washington. Then I run for Congress. Denny Hastert's seat, if he vacates it by then. I don't think you'll be around much longer than that either. You're too intellectual for this job. You'll see. It seems glamorous to you now, but after a few years you'll find out the glamour's like the Wizard of Oz—just a little man pulling ropes and a smoke machine."

I wondered how he knew that, so early in his career. It had the ring of truth; sooner or later that's the way most things are. "You might be right," I answered. "We'll see."

The other students started gossiping about Stan and me. Kirk, the tobacco-chewing former Marine, was at pains to remind me that "out there in the field, your friend *Stan* won't be there to help you." There was some bad blood between Kirk and Stan. Word had it that Kirk had botched our dead-drop exercises; he had hollowed the underside of a tree stump with immaculate precision, his handiwork so meticulous that the thing was quite indistinguishable from the rest of the ambient pasturage. A team of instructors marched for days up and down the remote bridle path where the stump was said to be but never retrieved the drop. Kirk had left a substantial cash payment inside.

"Too bad about that stump, buddy," Stan said to Kirk. "Lot of money to leave lying around in the woods, isn't it?"

"At least I can see my dick when I shower, asshole," Kirk answered, and marched off to the gym to clobber a punching bag.

Iris warned me that the others were saying Stan was doing my work for me. Jade, especially, was ecstatically broadcasting the word that I was cheating. "She's not even doing her own work— she's got that lovesick whale doing it for her!" I tried not to worry about it too much. I figured that with Stan's help, I might pass. Without it, I wouldn't. I wanted to pass, whatever people said.

∞

Stan applied his formidable memory to many things, not just license plates. He knew volumes of poetry and prose by heart. One evening he recited Tennyson's "Ulysses" for me, his voice soaring when he reached the last lines: "Made weak by time and fate, but strong in will / To strive, to seek, to find, and not to yield."

"There," he said with relish. "That's how I want to live my life. How about you?"

"I've never really adopted a personal slogan, to tell the truth. Right now all I want to do is get through this and keep my job. *Don't get fired* are the words I live by these days, I guess."

"Easy to remember. Hey, I want to talk to you, and I don't want you to be distracted by the road. Let's stop for a cup of coffee." I didn't want coffee, but he insisted. We pulled into an International House of Pancakes and found a table. The waitress's apron was stained; she had a black eye and an angry cracked lip. Stan ordered blueberry pancakes with whipped cream.

"You're really worried, aren't you?" he said.

"About passing this class? Of course I am."

He looked at me gently, and his face was soft, caring. He said, "What I don't understand, exactly, is why failing one stupid class caused you to lose all faith in yourself. You're just an inexperienced driver, that's all. You're not dumb and you're not lazy and you're not a failure. It's not a big deal—anyone can learn to drive." The waitress came back with Stan's pancakes; I noticed him taking in her sad face.

"How did you feel when you failed the fitness test?"

"I realized that I'd kind of let myself get out of shape, but I didn't think for a *second* that I couldn't do this job—I mean, most of this is easy. It's common sense. So I can't run fast—what's the big deal? I know I'm good at the things that are really important. And what's the big deal if you can't drive well yet? What's important is that you're smart." He put his elbows on the table and leaned forward, placing his chin in the cup of his hands. He stared at me. His eyes became shiny and moist; his pupils widened, and he was silent for a moment. At last he said quietly, "And what's not important to this job, but is very important to me, is that you're also very, very beautiful."

I put my coffee down and toyed with a packet of sugar. I didn't want to look back.

"Stan," I said at last, "I can't tell you how much I appreciate your help, and your kindness. I think you're the most interesting person here. I can't talk to anyone else here the way I talk to you. But that spark . . . it just isn't there for me."

I felt awful. I was about to speak again, but he raised his hand. "Stop. You don't need to say it. I know." His voice was dull.

"God, now you're making me feel like a shit."

"It's okay," he said. "I like being friends. Sometimes friends can be more intimate than lovers, in a way."

I reached for my handbag and pulled out a cigarette. The one good thing about Virginia was that all the restaurants still had smoking sections. He lit it for me and I inhaled. I hesitated, then decided to ask. "Stan, maybe it's not my place to ask this, but have you ever thought of making an effort to lose some weight?"

"We'll discuss your great concern for the healthy life when you quit smoking. My girlfriends accept me the way I am. Fat, happy, and oversexed. You're just superficial."

The waitress came back with the check. Stan reached into his billfold and left a twenty-dollar bill on the table, then glanced at the waitress in her stained uniform and added a little more.

But the next day, at lunch in the cafeteria, he ordered a salad with sunflower seeds, and that evening, he went to the gym, the poor fat thing. I was there to do yoga, and I saw him come in. He hefted his bulk around the weight machines like a bear clumsily performing circus tricks, pausing to pant for air. I was sorry for him, and moved.

∞

"What kind of man *do* you like?" Stan asked a week later. We were sitting on his concrete balcony at twilight, watching a large winter bird, a hawk maybe, swoop and glide against a gunmetal sky. We had spent almost every evening together since our conversation in the pancake house, driving through the countryside and talking.

"I don't think I really have a type," I replied, vague. "I've dated lots of different kinds of men. Why, what about you? Do you have a type?"

"Yeah, I guess I've always been with a certain kind of woman. Submissive. Kinky."

"Submissive?"

"Yeah, there's something about my personality—I'm pretty domineering, so I attract women who need that. I get women who need father figures, someone to take care of them. I get women who like to be tied up and spanked."

Despite myself, I was curious. "And you like tying them up and spanking them?"

"That and much, much more. You'd be surprised to know, Selena, that every single one of them considered me the best lover she had ever had. But of course you can't consider that, because you're too obsessed with superficial appearances."

"Stan, let me let you in on a little secret about women—we tell every man he's the best lover we ever had." Stan raised an eyebrow. "So what happened to all those relationships?" I asked.

"They ended. My last girlfriend didn't want me to join the CIA."

"Why not?"

"A lot of reasons. She was jealous—she didn't want me to have a career that took me away from her so much, didn't want me to do things that I couldn't tell her about, didn't like the fact that she wouldn't know where I was. Or who I was with."

"I can understand that."

"I couldn't. I don't really understand jealousy. That used to bother her. She *wanted* me to be jealous—she even tried to *make* me jealous. But I just don't work that way. She thought that meant I didn't really love her."

"Well, she must have been right, since you joined the CIA anyway."

He looked puzzled, as if this logic had never occurred to him. "I've always felt that the right woman wouldn't stand between me and what I need to do. I need someone who can really be by my side, because I have big goals."

"What are your goals?"

"I'm going to be the president of the United States." His voice was perfectly even, and his expression didn't change. His eyes stayed on the hawk, which flapped and plunged and shrieked and then rose again.

I stared at him with my mouth open. "Well," I said finally. "I guess that *is* a big goal."

"Like I told you—seven and a half years here, then the NSC, then Congress."

"What makes you want to be president?" I didn't laugh at him. This was America.

"I'm not a religious man, but I believe in destiny . . . do you believe in destiny?" I had the feeling it was important to him that I believe in destiny. I thought of the phone call that had rescued me from Mongeheela State, and I nodded. He said, "It's my destiny to lead this nation. I want to make us proud to be Americans again."

"I'd never noticed we weren't proud to be Americans, actually."

He stopped watching the bird and looked at me intently. He straightened himself in his chair and drew a lungful of cold air into his chest. "Our generation . . ." he said, and paused. "Our generation is so goddamned lucky. My grandfather fought at Okinawa. He lost his leg below the knee. The pitcher, the catcher, and the left fielder on the varsity ball team didn't come home.

Grandpa doesn't talk about the war much, but every morning when he wakes up—he's almost ninety now—the first thing he does is raise the flag in front of the schoolhouse, even if it's a thousand degrees below zero outside. Once when I was little I asked him why, and he told me it was for the guys on his baseball team. They died so he could go hunting in the winter and fishing in the summer and call himself an American and a free man. That's all he ever said about it, but it was enough. That's the patriotism I want to bring back to the White House. That's the dignity."

This was his stump speech. I imagined him at a podium, in rolled-up shirtsleeves and a loosened tie, stirring up the crowds at 4-H clubs across America. I saw the sage, approving nods from the retirees in old-age homes, the public halls filled with uncertain voters waiting to be convinced of something. I could see the pulse throbbing in his temples. Then his eyes narrowed. "Now we've got some lying piece of shit in the White House. The guy gets blow jobs from a fat, spoiled bimbo young enough to be his daughter while he sends American boys into combat. Is that proud enough? Is that what my grandfather deserves?"

"I see. So if you were president, you wouldn't allow me to service you under the desk in the Oval Office?" I smiled, but he didn't.

"Absolutely not," he said. "That is the *people's* house."

∞

Stan had brought a television and a VCR down to the Farm; one slow night we watched *Basic Instinct* together. When Sharon Stone took off her shirt, Stan said, "Your breasts are much better than hers."

"How would you know?"

"Believe me, I can tell."

"Pig!" I said, and threw a pillow at his head, but he must have seen that I smiled.

After the movie, I told Stan I had to leave to prepare for the next day's classes. "Okay," he said. "Come back later, when you're done, and flirt with me some more."

"I'm not flirting with you, Stan."

"Of course you are. When are you going to admit that you're attracted to me?"

"I'm not. I never will be."

"For God's sake, Selena, cut the crap. You're attracted to a fat guy, and it's making you nuts. You can't stand the thought of what people will think of you if you date someone who looks like me. I'm an insult to your vanity."

"I am not attracted to you and I'm not thinking that!"

"Then why are you here all the time?

"Because you're my friend. Because I have nowhere else to go."

"Iris is your friend too. I don't see you in her room at eleven at night every night, do I?"

"Stan, back off. It isn't going to happen."

"Don't bet on it," he answered.

I walked out of his room, vexed but also impressed by his nerve. Was he right? Yes, perhaps, I admitted to myself. Maybe I was a little bit attracted to him. But did that mean anything? The place was a hothouse, the environment so intense that any kind of unlikely passion could ignite. There were persistent rumors of affairs between the married men and the single women. Illicit couples were often caught sneaking off to the laundry room or the utility closet for a quarrel or a quickie. I thought about it as I went to bed, and when I fell asleep, I dreamt that Stan was holding me. I woke up full of inchoate longing.

CHAPTER 5

I sat next to Iris at lunch the next day. She was wearing stiletto heels, a pencil-slim black skirt, and a very tight sheer-silk turtleneck. I told her she looked terrific and asked her if she was planning to seduce her instructor.

"No, I'm planning to seduce my *boyfriend,* remember?"

I had forgotten that Brad was coming down to the Farm to attend a two-day conference for security officers. I asked when he would be there. She told me he'd be there any minute and looked around the room. I asked her how things were going with him. "The man's a puppy dog," she said. When I asked her what that meant, she changed the subject and asked me what was up with Stan. "He's stuck to you like white on rice these days."

I hesitated. I didn't know that I wanted to discuss Stan with Iris; I wasn't sure what I felt and I didn't know if there was anything to discuss. Finally I said, "It's horribly shallow to write someone off because he's fat, isn't it?"

She shook her head vigorously. "That's bullshit. Ever notice how the people who say beauty is only skin deep are always the ugly ones? If he's so deep, why isn't *he* interested in an ugly girl?" She pulled a slender ivory compact from her handbag and sketched cocoa lip liner around the contours of her mouth, then filled the outline with a slightly lighter shade, using a tiny sable brush. She blotted her lips delicately with a paper napkin. "You're just lonely, so you're looking for the nearest thing around. And it's not the right thing. And why doesn't he lose weight, anyway? Why should he feel entitled to attract women even if he's a pig? You *know* I'd never get a date in a million years if I was that fat. I mean, for the love of God, I haven't eaten anything today but a cup of oatmeal with skimmed milk and two Sweet 'n Lows. I'm hungry enough to eat the south end off a northbound skunk, and—"

I held up a hand to silence her; I was afraid she would go on like that all day. "I get it, I get it. You're suffering for beauty. It's noble."

But Stan *was* losing weight—quickly. He was starving himself, and he was doing it for me. He had lost ten pounds already. Every day, he ate a little green salad with sunflower seeds for lunch, and every night I saw him lumber off to the gym. No one had ever done *that* for me before.

∞

Stan had never known his real father. The man had abandoned his mother when he discovered she was pregnant. Stan and his mother had only discussed his father twice in his life. She told Stan that his appearance was hauntingly similar to his father's. "You're the spitting image of him," she said. Stan believed that his natural father had been an Air America pilot. "When my mother told me what he did, I knew it had to be Air America— she didn't know what that was, and I didn't tell her—she just knew he'd flown planes over Laos." Stan's mother had worked as a secretary to support him, and when Stan was a toddler, she married an upright man, who adopted her illegitimate child. Stan said his mother married "because she wanted to give me a name."

"Her own name wasn't good enough?" I asked.

"I come from an old-fashioned town. It's so small that the only place to go out at night is the ice cream parlor, and even *that* closes at nine. When I was growing up, we got excited about the state fair. It was the most interesting thing that happened all year."

State fairs were as far from my childhood as the running of the bulls in Pamplona. My mother was a curator at the Metropolitan Museum of Art. To her parents' horror, she'd fallen in love with a shiftless cabdriver who played bass in a band called the Baloney Ponies. My father, unlike me, was an ace of a driver. A fare once dashed up to his cab and promised him a fifty-dollar tip if he could get to LaGuardia Airport in fifteen minutes. They were there in less than twelve, but the fare dropped dead of a heart attack. Another piece of family lore had it that a Japanese tourist had arrived at the taxi stand at LaGuardia asking for a ride to Kennedy. My father threw his luggage in the trunk, told him to get in, and circled the airport three times. He dropped him off exactly where he'd picked him up. "There, buddy, you're at Kennedy," he said. "That'll be two hundred bucks." The poor schmuck paid him and toddled off with his luggage. I didn't tell Stan the story about the Japanese tourist; I'd found out over the years that a lot of people didn't think it was so funny.

I'd been a love child; my mother hadn't married my father until Lilia was born, and when she did, she told me, it was because she was worried that my father had no health insurance. When they married, he became eligible for coverage under her program at the Met. One thing for which my long-suffering mother did *not* marry my father was his name, Shtetlinsky. She never liked it, never took it, and never gave it to us, thank God.

As a teenager, Stan milked cows and shot pop cans from the roof of his neighbor's barn. "When I was in high school you called a girl up to ask her for a date for Saturday night. Then you

both dressed up, and you went somewhere special," he explained. "And maybe to the ice cream parlor afterward." I concluded that Stan had come of age in a Hardy Boys novel. The
town sounded god-awful to me, but Stan seemed nostalgic
about it, so I kept that thought to myself.

I asked him whether he had ever wanted to find his real father.
"Not much," he answered. "Why would I want to get to know
someone who left a woman to raise a small child by herself?"

"Aren't you at all curious about the person who gave you half
of your genes?"

"Nope."

"But you obviously have something in common with him—
doesn't that intrigue you?"

"We don't have the most important thing in common: He fled
responsibility. He didn't know right from wrong."

His father probably was a creep—he did abandon his child, no
arguing with that—but I found it hard to understand Stan's unequivocal lack of curiosity. Wouldn't he want to *see* the man who
was his spitting image? I too had always been told I was the spitting image of my father; my genetic legacy was so markedly obvious that I grew up hearing the same weary joke—"Well, no
question about the paternity *there*"—from everyone who laid
eyes on us. When once my father found a brochure about rhino-
plasty among my school papers, he was indignant: "We have
Roman noses," he told me. "They're *very* aristocratic." In fact, he
and I had Roman everything—not just the long, aquiline noses,
but the lampblack hair that curled exuberantly when exposed to
even a micron of moisture; we shared the same charcoal eyes
with high, arching brows, the same deep groove above our lips,
the same tendency to speak with our hands. In the winter, people often asked us if we *were* Italian; in the summer, we were
taken for Hispanics. We preferred being taken for Italians. We
both liked to imagine that we might pass for extras on a Fellini

set, strolling past the Trevi fountain, at our ease among the decadent glitterati of the Eternal City. As far as I knew, there was no Italian blood in my family whatsoever. Some recessive Sephardic gene probably gave us both our Mediterranean coloring. Lilia looked nothing like either of us; she took after my mother—fair, subtle, and enviably long-limbed. She was a full four inches taller than me, which seemed most unjust.

On occasion I would look at my father's face, so much like my own, and catch a glimpse of something I didn't want to see—a self-indulgent vanity, a sneering arrogance. His voluptuous and fleshy features warned of his inability to deny himself whatever he wanted. But I would far rather see that than have no idea where it came from. That, I suppose, was why it so puzzled me that Stan didn't even want to know what his father looked like. Perhaps he felt that exhibiting curiosity would be disloyal to his stepfather, who had raised him as his own child. Stan's mother and her husband never had children of their own.

He had been his mother's pride and joy, a child with an IQ, he told me, "so high the psychologist said it was technically impossible to measure—my mother loved hearing that." A gifted, thoughtful boy who took tuba lessons, he collected butterflies, loved science fiction, and once, at the age of twelve, won the state's annual student citizenship contest for an essay he had submitted on the topic "Why I'm Proud to Be an American." He still remembered accepting the award on the lawn of the governor's mansion, the audience before him vast, the crowd cheering and applauding. It was then that he had conceived the desire to be president.

When he told me that, I tried to recall what I'd been doing at the same age. I remembered wondering whether Rodney Fisher liked me, and getting stoned for the first time in the girls' toilets with my friend Sally Duxbery. I certainly hadn't thought about keeping my political options open. But I suppose if you're as bright as Stan and you grow up in a small town, you learn early in life to consider yourself something exceptional.

∞

Our classmate Annette was small and shy. She wore girlish clothing—white tights, heart-patterned turtlenecks, penny loafers— and she had a matching grade-school face, with round cheeks and an unspoiled complexion. She was from Connecticut, and she had been an urban planner before joining the Clandestine Service. Like Nathan, Paul's roommate, she was on the Reports track—slotted to evaluate intelligence rather than recruit agents. She was by no means beautiful; she was a cute girl rather than a pretty one, and her appearance certainly didn't suggest sensuality. But she was petite and somehow vulnerable, with hangdog eyes that conveyed a private sadness. Women like Annette are compelling to a certain kind of man, the kind of man who wants to believe that he and he alone has uncovered a hidden treasure. Our class was full of those men.

Paul and Annette had been assigned to the same team during paramilitary training, and as they worked side by side, Paul had become hopelessly smitten. He courted her the way he had never courted me. I saw him escorting her from building to building with his protective arm around her small shoulders; I heard he woke up early to scrape the ice from her car windows.

A few weeks into the tradecraft course, Paul and I had lunch together. "She's the one," he said. "She's the one I've been waiting for. I didn't even feel this way about my wife." I told him with what I thought sterling graciousness that I was happy for him and had heard that Annette was very nice. After lunch, I went to the ladies' room. Annette and her friends were deep in an animated conversation. I thought I heard my name as I opened the door. As soon as they saw it was me, they fell silent. Toilets started flushing.

Stan and I were sitting in my car in the parking lot after one of our driving lessons when Annette walked past, unaware that we were watching. "You know," Stan said, "I don't get what they see in her."

"What do you mean?" I asked, feigning casual curiosity.

"It tells you what the men here really want. Someone totally unthreatening. Not that pretty, not that sexy, not that bright. Kind of sweet, that's all. I'd die of boredom with her. And you know what? Give Annette twenty years and she'll be Wally. She won't be cute at all after twenty years on the Uzbekistan Reports Desk. She'll give those same lectures on reporting formats, boring everyone here to tears, getting upset because people keep falling asleep in her class. I don't get it. Why would you want to play with a pussycat when you could hunt for a tiger?"

I replied, gracious to the end, that I had heard Annette was very nice. Had I been a cat, of any kind, I would have rubbed against Stan's ankles and purred.

∽

Later, when I realized that Stan had been setting the pace all along, I saw that I had been recruited. Everyone sniggered during the introductory lecture on recruitment, not because it was funny, but because the instructor might well have been reciting from some unwritten manual on high school courtship. First you watch your target. You get to know him before he even knows you exist. You find out what your target likes to do. If the target plays golf, what a coincidence, you *love* golf. If he shoots birds, you just became *nuts* about shooting birds. Stan had been watching me from afar for months and he had learned my habits. I smoked, so Stan started smoking. (*Lesson one: Building*

*rapport is a matter of diminishing the sense of difference between two peo-
ple.*) My driving was giving everyone fits; Stan remade himself
into the world's most patient driving instructor.

Developing an asset for recruitment is a game of guile and
forbearance, akin to coaxing an honorable woman into an illicit
affair. Think of the Viscomte de Valmont corrupting the innocent Cécile de Volanges, and you'll have it about right. The case
officer spends time with the target—as much time as the target
will allow—but discreetly, of course, avoiding the bars the man's
colleagues are likely to frequent. He invites the man to good
restaurants, or out for a halcyon day on the embassy boat. He
buys the target gifts—maybe something the man's wife has always wanted but could never afford. If the target says "You
know, I'm not sure it would be, well, *appropriate* for me to accept
this," the case officer replies, "Look, this will be just between
you and me. I know your wife could use a little pampering. They
don't pay you half as much as you're worth at your office, we
both know that. She's a hell of a lady, your wife; I'd like to see
her have something nice for a change." The case officer listens
patiently as the target laments the cost of sending kids to college
these days. He ignores the man's habit of cleaning his ears in
public.

He watches to see where the man is soft: Does he have loose
lips? Does he say things that perhaps he shouldn't? Does he
seem dissatisfied, resentful? Why? Does he approve of his government's policies? Does he admire the United States? Perhaps
he has a sick child who might profit from medical attention in
the West. Perhaps he's vengeful, perhaps he's vain. Perhaps he
needs to be told that he's too good for penny-ante office politics.
*You were passed over for promotion? They're nuts to ignore a man of your
talents. They gave the job to the president's nephew? That little wretch?
He's only twenty-three years old! He knows nothing about foreign*

policy—he's just a playboy, a lightweight! That's appalling. Perhaps the man just wants money, plain and simple, which makes everything straightforward. Our job, they taught us, was to figure out what he needs and to give it to him. Give it to him better than anyone ever has before.

They taught us to plan the pitch, not wing it. The offer has to be made so convincingly, so compellingly, so *smoothly,* that the target can't find a single good reason to object. You should know, even before you open your mouth, they told us, that he will agree: You take no chances that he will report you to his people, landing you on the next flight out of the country with your name on the front page of *The New York Times.* It should seem to him that treason is *his* excellent idea. The pitch must be organic; treason should seem logical, natural, the obvious way to solve all his problems in one simple step.

We practiced our pitches for hours, in front of closed-circuit television cameras, in front of the instructors and one another. We were told to say whatever it took to convince our victims to betray their countries—but avoid the word *treason,* they cautioned us, for the word leads to thoughts of *firing squad.* Talk about *fostering international understanding. Going beyond conventional diplomacy. Helping our two countries get beyond all the jaw-jaw.* Don't talk about going to jail or being hanged (God, no!). Talk about *putting away a little nest egg for your kids' education. Earning a bit of pocket money with this great gig I can get for you. Doing some private consulting for the U.S. government.* Use the friendship; use the trust you've developed. Use the prestige of the United States. *Use, schmooze, be profuse*—one instructor had this legend engraved into a copper plaque on his office door. Of course, we were no more *truly* interested in the deep yearnings and aspirations of our targets than the Phi Beta who courts a cherry-lipped Sigma Mu is *truly* interested in her journey of feminist empowerment: It was just a means to an end.

When a case officer made his first recruitment, he was said to have lost his virginity.

We were all skilled manipulators to begin with; that was the personality type the shrinks selected, or so we were told. "Case officers tend to be compensated introverts," said the psychologist who drove to the Farm from Headquarters one day to deliver a talk on the psychology of espionage. That is, the typical case officer was outgoing not so much by natural disposition as by long-cultivated ambition and discipline. The instructors honed our instincts, giving lessons on the systematic exploitation of a man's vulnerabilities—how to handle a vain man, what to do with a man who pities himself. They instructed us to list his vulnerabilities on paper at the end of every meeting so that we had them firmly in mind. Think clearly, they said, about what you'll say to make him do what you want him to do. Anticipate his objections. Practice out loud.

That ability—to bend a man to one's will, all the while convincing him that it was the other way around—was the hallmark of a good case officer. Rarely did anyone at the Agency remark that this was not necessarily the hallmark of a good human being; professional competence was admired—revered, even—as I suppose it is in all professions. The ability to tell falsehoods convincingly, to swiftly discern the lacunae in someone's character, to convince people to behave against their own best interests—those were the traits that separated the excellent case officers from the herd. That, and a kind of low, animal cunning.

Long after we left the Farm, they promised, the rubric they taught would remain with us: Meeting someone at a party, a former spy will begin mechanically to tabulate the ports of entry: *Child suffers from debilitating illness. Envious of elder brother's success. Loves luxury. Drinks heavily.* Everyone notices these things, of course. But spies consider them the way mountain climbers consider handholds, and they scheme directly to exploit them.

How can a child's leukemia be used to convince a father to reveal the things he ought not? Can a target's yearning for his father's approval somehow be leveraged? How best to persuade him to take actions that would, if discovered, lead to his arrest and execution, the impoverishment and disgrace, perhaps even the death, of his wife and children? We were taught to sketch charts on large white paperboard, representing the architecture of a man's weaknesses: major and minor fault lines, primary and ancillary character flaws.

Never once did I hear anyone ask what, in the long run, it would do to *us* to consider other human beings in this fashion.

Vanity was a superb lever, and when a case officer used another man's vanity to advantage, he always felt a fine sense of superiority and contempt, for here was a man who would betray his people and his country not for money or ideals but because he was a weak, self-important little creep. "I know your insights are worth more than your prime minister realizes," we said to our prey with a meaningful, unwavering gaze, all the while congratulating ourselves and regarding the man before us as vermin. Vanity was so powerful a motivation that it often took pride of place on those diagrams, sitting atop the branching schema that represented another human soul, like a crown of thorns.

There was no sympathy for members of our own side who fell victim to the same tactics. Once, at lunch, I heard my colleagues discussing Jonathan Pollard, a naval officer convicted of spying for Israel. A prominent group of American Jews had been lobbying for his release on the grounds that Israel was an allied country; Pollard's crimes, they held, didn't merit the life sentence he had received. "That fucking traitor should be sent to the gas chamber," someone at the table said, "and so should those scumbags who are trying to free him."

Everyone at the table nodded emphatically. I waited for someone to say something. No one did. Finally, I spoke up. "I believe you've just suggested gassing a large number of Jews. It's quite an original idea. Where did you come up with it?" He looked at me blankly. I realized that no one at the table had a clue what I meant. I put down my napkin, took my tray, stood up, and walked away.

∞

One evening, Stan and I went out looking for dead-drop sites. I was driving, as I always did, for practice, and at an intersection I became confused. "Shit, Stan," I said. "I'm lost again."

"Straight ahead," he said unthinkingly. I pressed on the accelerator. Suddenly an SUV rocketed past and nearly clipped the hood off our car. The driver leaned on his horn. With the Doppler effect, the noise was hysterical at first, then reproachful. "Whoa, Nellie," Stan said evenly, glancing up from the newspaper he was reading. "You have a stop sign. He doesn't."

I pulled over to the side of the road. I was trembling. I braced my arms on the steering wheel and put my head between them. "Stan, I just nearly got us killed. *I nearly got us killed.* Why am I so bad at this? Why do you know where we are when I don't? I've driven these roads as many times as you have. How come you never get lost and I always get lost? Why didn't I notice he was coming?"

Stan handed me a clean tissue from the glove compartment and waited until I stopped sniffling. He put his hand on my shoulder. "When I started driving," he said gently, "I made all sorts of mistakes. I rear-ended my high school band teacher. I got lost all the time too. But I've been driving for fifteen years. I can devote more mental energy to navigating now because I'm devoting less mental energy to the basic, mechanical driving skills. I drive on autopilot. You have to think about just driving safely, so you have less energy for noticing landmarks and the other things that help you get your bearings. It's normal. But I promise you: You can learn this skill, and you will. I'll help you every night. You'll be fine. You're going through a normal stage that everyone goes through."

"I don't know if I'm cut out for this job."

"*Of course you are!* That's not even a question. I know you are. You're far more intelligent than anyone else here. If for a second I didn't think you could do this job, I would tell you honestly. I love my country, remember? I wouldn't encourage you to do this if I didn't think you could do it. You can do it *well*. You're so bright and talented, Selena. If anything, you're too good for this job—you're going to get bored with it."

"You think?"

"I think. You know," he said quietly, "you undervalue yourself. You really do. Not just in this job but in your whole life. I mean, what were you doing with Paul? He's such a fucked-up loser. He's sleazy. He uses women. Why would you have given a man like him the time of day? You're worth so much more than that." There was pain in his voice. He had never mentioned Paul before and I hadn't known he knew about it, but I supposed everyone did. "You deserve a real man, a gentleman, someone who cherishes you."

"I'm sorry, Stan," I said, rubbing my red nose. "I didn't mean to go all blubbery on you. I'm overtired. I'll get a grip. Thanks for being so patient. I really don't know what I'd do if you weren't here."

I put the car into drive and eased back into traffic.

∽

When I came to class the next day, Iris pulled me aside to tell me the news before anyone else did. Paul had resigned. Just like that. Annette had broken up with him, and he had decided that he would rather leave than go through training watching her from afar. His seat in the auditorium was empty.

He came to my room after class to say good-bye to me. "Paul," I said, grasping his hands. "Are you sure?"

He let go of my hands and sat down on my bed. He was unshaven; he had lost weight and the hollows under his cheekbones were deeply recessed. "Honey, it's okay," he said. He had never called me honey before. "It's okay. Don't be so sad. I just can't go back to living the way I was before I met Annette. I don't want to be a seducer. I don't want to keep lying to everyone. I've had enough."

"But it's just a relationship! You know you'll get over it. How can you let this destroy your career?"

He didn't look at me; he seemed to be contemplating something far in the distance, as if he were looking out over a vast desert, although the only thing in front of him was the bare wall. Finally he said: "Didn't I just explain that?"

He stood up. He told me I was the only person in the CIA whom he wished well; he kissed me on the forehead and he gave me the limp red rose that he had tried to give to Annette before she made her rejection unequivocal. He slung his duffel bag over his shoulder and he was gone. I sat on my bed looking at that rejected rose for quite some time.

I never saw him again.

∽

A few days later, we were instructed to attend a mock trade fair, where we were to begin practicing our lessons in recruitment. The instructors would play members of the government of the People's Republic of Turkrapistan, a country that looked remarkably like rural Virginia, where every government official had financial problems and a sick child and every minister sooner or later found his way onto the United States' payroll.

Each student had been assigned his own target. I was supposed to look for Elvis P. Avidoff, deputy undersecretary of trade and labor.

Stan and I agreed to help each other find our targets; he was looking for Lieutenant-General Felix G. Lustifer. Stan and I drove to the trade fair together. We were supposed to recruit our targets within three weeks. "Everyone will succeed at this one," Stan said. "By the time this exercise is done, Turkrapistan will be the most penetrated country in the world. The first one is supposed to be a confidence builder. Or anyway, they make it easy enough so that if you can't do it, you flunk out, because you're obviously a total loser."

"How do you know?"

"I've heard about it." He shrugged. Stan always knew this kind of thing.

That year, the Turkrapistan Ministry of Commerce and Trade rented a local conference hall for the Turkrapistan: We're Open for Business! fair. The reception had already begun when we arrived; the instructors were pressing against one another to get at the little shrimp on toothpicks and the bite-size wieners wrapped in pastry dough. Stan ambled up to me after fifteen minutes and told me where to find Elvis: "He's over there," he said, pointing discreetly at a thin-faced man with silver hair and a pallid complexion. "He's stupefyingly boring. Enjoy."

I sidled up to my target and made an excuse to introduce myself. Stan wasn't lying. The man spoke in a quiet monotone and had no hint of a sense of humor; his eyes were dead. I struggled to make it past the pleasantries and to find this man's passion, dropping hints about golf, music, gardening, cooking, but I struck out each time. He barely registered my suggestions. He mentioned eating lunch, and I thought that might be my entry— *You eat? Why, what I coincidence, I eat too!*—but his inanimate expression told me this wasn't the key. I looked at Stan, who had

found his target without my help and was making him laugh up-
roariously. Finally, Elvis dropped the big hint: "I like to collect
stamps," he said.

"Really!" I answered. "What a coincidence! I'm a *passionate*
stamp collector. I'd love to compare our collections!"

Stan told me after the reception that *his* instructor wanted to
pound tequila and go to strip clubs.

From then on, I contrived to invite Elvis to lunch or tea every
other day, attempting to build his trust and develop that elusive
rapport they kept talking about in class. I talked philately for
hours. I allowed him to suggest the restaurants he liked, and I always picked up the check. It all went on a government expense
account. I encouraged him to tell me about himself, behaving as
if everything he said were richly fascinating.

In fact, Elvis P. Avidoff was so aggressively boring and self-
involved that I yearned to strike him. I wondered if he was boring me on purpose to test my patience or if this in fact was the
nature of the man who played him. I smiled and nodded as he
launched into interminable, almost lobotomized accounts of his
failure to advance at his office. He told me about his daughter's
struggle to overcome a speech impediment. We both knew where
this was supposed to go: At the end I would offer to help his
daughter get the medical attention she needed in exchange for
clandestine updates on Turkrapistani trade policy. *Your daughter
drools when she says the letter* r? *That's a terrible shame. I know a doctor
who can help, in America. He's very expensive, but I think we can find a
way to make it happen.* Later I found out that he really did have a
disabled daughter, and I felt ashamed for hating him so horribly.

At our third meeting, Elvis confided that he had been passed
over for promotion yet again. "How shameful and shortsighted
that your government fails to recognize your talent," I said. "I
find our conversations so rewarding, and your insights about
Turkrapistani politics so incisive. My government would love to

have a man on the ground here with your knowledge and abilities." Elvis of course added that he was having money troubles and couldn't pay his daughter's medical bills. Stan was right; this exercise was paint-by-the-numbers.

Every evening, after class and my assignations with Elvis, Stan sat by my side as I drove through the back roads, gently correcting my braking technique, teaching me to anticipate the actions of other drivers. One day, I overheard a group of instructors talking about me. They were drawing straws to decide who had to ride with me in the next exercise. But then one of them spoke up: "Hey, guys, she's gotten a lot better lately. I went out with her last time and it was no worse than being with any of the rest of those numbnuts. Give it a rest—she's trying hard." I could have kissed him for that; it was like the sun coming out after a Scandinavian winter.

The sad sack who played Elvis seemed to relish his captive audience. It must have been wonderful for him that I was forced to listen while he behaved like the self-absorbed old fuck he was instead of the obsequious case officer he was usually obliged to be. He wallowed in his role, confessing decades of marital problems, financial anxieties, and professional frustrations in that soporific monotone as I listened sympathetically, cocking my head to the side and from time to time making small feminine noises of compassion and encouragement. I became certain that everything he told me was true, his life story conveniently masked behind the fiction of pedagogy.

He told me that his teenage son had come home drunk the night before and had said unspeakably cruel things to him. His eyes moistened. "He called me a liar," he said. I patted his hand. He told me that his sister had died of bone cancer and that he hadn't once visited her in the hospital. He had been too busy at work.

"That doesn't make you a bad person, Elvis," I told him over dinner as I imagined his sister dying alone. "You did the best you could."

"Do you think so?"

"Of course I do. You know, you undervalue yourself. You really do. Not just in your job but in your whole life."

I pitched him that evening and he accepted, ahead of schedule.

∽

We received reviews of our performance after every exercise, and Elvis gave me warm praise. "An excellent listener," he wrote. "Outstanding people skills." That evening, Stan and I drank scotch together in my room to celebrate my success. I allowed myself to become a bit lightheaded. We talked as usual about the day and our instructors and our classmates, and as usual he looked at me with misty, longing tenderness, as if I were the pot of gold at the end of the rainbow. As it grew late, he got up to leave, and when he left, the room was perfectly silent. I lay on the bed in that disheveled, sullen little room and felt achingly alone, a little drunk in a melancholy way, and I was sorry he'd left. On an impulse I picked up the phone. It rang in his room, and when he picked it up—he knew it could only be me, and he knew why I was calling, and his voice was so happy and warm— I said, "Come back. I don't want you to go."

"I will," he said, neither hesitating nor questioning, as if it were the most natural thing in the world.

When I reached for his hand and pulled him toward me, he answered by climbing into my bed and folding me in his arms. He felt strong—despite his soft appearance he was surprisingly muscular, ursine—and I lay against his chest as he held me and stroked my hair. We lay like that for a while, surprised by ourselves and each other. When I looked up at him, his face was sweet and happy, and his small eyes glowed brightly, like a raccoon's. He was delighted with himself and with me. I had never seen anyone so happy just to look at me. He whispered to me all night long, telling me stories and babbling gentle nonsense. "You're so soft and small and you smell so good," he said in wonderment, as if it were the first time he had ever touched a woman.

I told him I thought we should keep this to ourselves, aware that privacy in our group was impossible, but hoping against hope for a few days before our romance became public property. "It will be our little secret," he answered. "No, it will be our *great, big, enormous secret,*" he murmured, and I laughed. We didn't sleep at all, although that night we didn't make love. We talked and cuddled and exchanged secrets. He kissed the back of my neck, very gently, very slowly, and I felt it all through my body, the warmth radiating in waves. I felt safe and protected.

The next day, we struggled terribly to get through our lectures. I was so tired I thought I would die, but I felt peaceful, too. Stan asked me that day if I regretted what had happened, and I told him, honestly, that I didn't at all.

It was late winter, we were eager for spring, and we were nearing the halfway mark of the course. I began to make rapid progress. Our next exercise was a walk-in, an instructor impersonating a man who came uninvited to the embassy to volunteer his services. A mid-ranking officer in the Turkrapistani Police Constabulary, the walk-in had evidently embezzled money from the precinct to feed his gambling habit. The tip he'd received on a pony proved to be a bum steer, and he now feared his malfeasance would be discovered and he would spend his life in prison. He offered to sell us the constabulary's surveillance log. He claimed they had been following one of our officers. He said we could have it for ten thousand U.S. dollars.

I told him we were definitely, absolutely interested; I understood completely how a betting man could find himself in a little pickle like that; I would do what I could to help him, but I needed to receive authorization from Headquarters first. I arranged to meet him the next day at a discreet location in the woods so that he wouldn't be seen entering the American embassy twice.

On the afternoon of our assignation, it was pouring. I looked balefully at the rain, coming down in great thick silver sheets, making mud out of the entranceway to the classroom. It occurred to me that a diplomat ambling through the woods on a day like this would look mighty peculiar—distinctly suspicious, in fact. What would I say I was doing? One of the other instructors owned a chubby little terrier named Casey. I knocked on his office door and asked him if I could borrow Casey for the afternoon. "Sure," he said. "He's all yours. Show him a good time." If anyone asked any embarrassing questions about what I was doing, I could say I was walking my dog.

I fetched Casey at his master's house. He hopped into my car, trusting fellow, looking tickled by the prospect of going for a ride. Perhaps he thought we were setting out to chase rabbits. He sniffed the seats. We drove off into the rain. Casey found a half-packet of Swedish Fish under the seat and wolfed them down before I could intervene, then put his paws on the window and watched the woods go by.

I drove past the armed guards at the gates and merged onto the interstate. Suddenly, as if someone had plugged him into a power outlet, Casey went berserk. He began yapping and ricocheting off the windows, scrabbling at the upholstery, acting as if he were being deprived of oxygen. I tried lowering a window so he could put his nose out; he tried to jump out. I levered the window back up; he got his head stuck. I murmured something soothing; he yapped. I yelled at him to shut the fuck up; he yapped some more. Two months before, I'm sure the distraction would have caused me to drive into an embankment, but under Stan's tutelage my skills had improved, and I proceeded steadily through my surveillance detection route despite the rain and chaos.

When I reached my destination, Casey rocketed out of the car door as if someone had lit a firecracker under his ass. I bolted after him, caught him at last, and snapped the choke chain around his neck. He performed a melodramatic pantomime of asphyxiation, then began yanking me through the woods, zigzagging right and left, sniffing every shrub, every stump, every mushroom, pausing only to urinate every ten seconds. The rain worsened; thunder and lightning commenced. I couldn't control the umbrella and the dog at once and became soaked.

I met my instructor at the designated place, exchanged the prearranged safety signals—*Is the local dry cleaner careful with silk? I don't know, I hand-wash my shirts*—and made the swap. He took the money; I took the surveillance log. The dog leaped at his leg and attempted briskly to copulate. When I returned to the car, the animal did his best to smear every surface in the vehicle with mud, rainwater, filth, and dog hair. He made sure to roll and shake on every seat. I believe he urinated again.

Casey regurgitated in the backseat when I rolled over a speed bump. He was still soaking when I handed him back to his master; he was only a third the size he'd been when we left. "I'm sorry about this," I said. "I know this isn't the condition he was in when I borrowed him."

His master examined him with an air of annoyance. "You didn't give him anything sugary to eat, did you?" he asked suspiciously. I remembered the Swedish Fish. I decided to deny everything.

"Um, no, why?"

"He can't handle sugar. Makes him totally hyperactive. Made him bite a kid once."

Well, gee, mate, I wish you'd told me that beforehand.

But the instructor who played the Gambling Schnook, a shrewd, foxy, rather attractive man of Irish descent, liked the touch of bringing a dog to our meeting. He posted my cable describing the encounter on the instructors' bulletin board as an example of "a student who doesn't have her head up her ass." When I saw that, I ran to Stan to tell him. He smiled knowingly. "See? I knew you would be good at this," he said.

The next morning, Stan invited me to spend the weekend at his apartment, and I accepted. We drove toward Washington together, chattering all the way about American history and our favorite presidents. He told me how to make a soufflé that never collapsed. For about fifty miles, we sang Elvis songs together—he was surprisingly musical, and of course he remembered the lyrics to every song he'd ever heard. Finally we pulled up to a high-rise building in a working-class suburb. Stan showed me to the elevator, which we took to the seventh floor; it opened onto a dingy hall with shoe-scuffed green carpeting. He unlocked his door, picking up the advertising brochures for pizza delivery that had accumulated over the week, and I crossed the threshold.

I set down my bags and looked at Stan's apartment, a small, boxy studio with low ceilings that overlooked the Beltway. The room was furnished in heavy oak. I complimented him on the tall, patrician dresser. It had graceful curves, with rolled top drawers and precisely carved trim; it was polished to a high luster and smelled of Lemon Pledge. "It was a gift from my parents," he said. "Actually, all the furniture here, they gave it all to me—they usually give me furniture on my birthday, or when I tell them I've been promoted. My mother likes to give me things I'll be able to use for a lifetime. The dresser was a promotion gift."

Stan told his mother and stepfather that he had been promoted at what he thought were plausible intervals. His parents didn't know about the real promotions; they thought he was still a lawyer. He felt he had no choice but to lie. "My mother wouldn't sleep at night if she knew. My father wouldn't remember not to talk about it on the phone." I asked him how his parents would feel if they found out, especially if they discovered in the most terrible way possible, with a knock on the door from a dark-suited Agency envoy, a visit from the grief counselors. "They would forgive me. They're patriots too," he said, a rare note of hesitancy in his voice.

I sat down on the dark brown leather sofa, crowned with four identical square pillows, exactly equidistant, made of light brown silk. In front of the sofa, a crystal ashtray and an illustrated book about the flora and fauna of New England lay on a glass-and-chrome coffee table. There was a framed poster from a Broadway show on the wall, along with pictures of Stan posed among various Republican luminaries. The words *To Stan, with thanks for all your help* were handwritten on one portrait-size photograph that displayed Stan on the steps of the Capitol, his arm around the shoulders of his state's senior senator. Both men wore dark suits. The senator was some thirty years older and thirty pounds heavier than Stan. Both appeared immense, important.

A dark Oriental tapestry hung on the opposite wall above a collection of antique books arranged neatly in a small mahogany bookcase. Crossed fencing swords were mounted above a masculine affair of a bed with navy sheets and a solid bedspread. Another bookcase held debating trophies. A solitary rubber-tree plant gasped for light in the corner. I went to open the curtains, but Stan stopped me: "It's nicer when they're drawn," he said. "More private."

I opened the walk-in closet to hang up my coat. There was a collection of videos on the shelf—half action movies and science fiction, half pornography: *Lesbian Dildo Sluts, All-Orifice Action*. He had made no attempt to hide them. He hadn't been expecting my visit, obviously. I pretended I hadn't seen them; so did he.

That night, Stan caressed every feature of my body, touching me in that gentle way, talking to me softly, then thrillingly, telling me what he planned to do to me next. He seemed to know what I wanted without being told. I told him not to stop, and he didn't. When I told him he was the best lover I had ever had, I meant it—as I always do.

Afterward, he soaped my back in the tub, and an innocence stole over him; he jiggled my breasts delightedly, he watched them bounce, squished them into funny shapes, drew mouse whiskers on them with a bar of soap. He was as joyful as a six-year-old with a new skateboard. "I can't *believe* you're finally letting me do this," he said. "God, I've wanted to do this for the longest time. Look, they float!" He called me his little lizard, his little otter, his kitten. When I stood up, he took a towel and patted me dry, and when he reached my belly, he drew his finger carefully along the raw red scar.

"You're the only man who's ever seen that," I said. "It's kind of ugly."

"No," he said, looking at me with an odd intensity. "If I'm the only man who's ever seen it, it's the most beautiful thing about you."

He stroked my hair as I fell asleep. Every time I woke up, his arms were still around me. He watched me as I dried my hair the next morning, his eyes bright and shiny: "You're so beautiful. So beautiful. You're the most beautiful woman I know. Everywhere you go, the men stare and the women get jealous. How did a fat guy like me get so lucky?"

He went out to get the paper and came back with pink roses, tipped with silver and beaded with dew. He cooked breakfast for me and brought it to me in bed—cream of wheat, butter and honey in clay pots, green figs, yogurt. We didn't want to go back to the Farm. We didn't have the whole weekend off; we never did; we'd finished late on Friday and were expected back by Sunday afternoon. We wished we could take a vacation.

On the drive back, I took his hand and asked, "Stan, why are you so kind to me?"

"Because I'm in love with you."

He had been bursting to say that. In a way, I'd hoped he wouldn't, because I didn't know what I would say. But when he said it, I was touched. And proud. Stan's love felt like an imprimatur. Stan was not a mercurial or an impulsive man. He was *serious,* the kind of man who planned to lead the free world. When he made a decision, he made it for excellent reasons. His love was the judgment of a man who took good judgment seriously. I didn't say anything, but I smiled at him and stroked his cheek, and that seemed to be good enough.

From then on, he had surprises waiting for me in his room at the end of those long days—rum-filled chocolate truffles wrapped in golden ribbon (he didn't touch them; he was still dieting), crimson tulips, an exotic sticky liqueur served in a crystal shot glass. Our lives became completely intertwined. Every evening he asked if I would stay the night, and when I said yes, he looked as happy as he had the first time he touched me. He held me in the mornings before class, and watched me as I showered. "It thrills me to see you naked," he whispered as I soaped up. "I know that sounds silly, but it just thrills me. Your body is so beautiful. Wait . . . wait, don't get dressed just yet. You know, right now your nipples look like number-two-pencil erasers when they're fresh out of the box . . . let me touch . . . do you think I'm silly to get so much pleasure just from touching you?" He passed notes to me in class. Once he passed me a sketch of my face he had drawn during the lecture. In his portrait I had no flaws: I had no scar above my eyebrow; my hair cascaded in Pre-Raphaelite ringlets down my back—an effect it achieved in reality only twice a year, in weather conditions more specific than those required to launch the space shuttle. My eyes were innocent, enormous, sable-fringed; my bone structure perfected to the proportions of a Roman statue. It was the way I *liked* to think I looked, but deep down I knew better.

We ate lunch and dinner together every day, ignoring everyone else in the class, and talked about our exercises. He helped me plan my recruitment pitches and my surveillance detection routes. With his help, my driving improved, and I became capable. Every weekend, I drove us back to his apartment in Alexandria, and we would spend our only free day in each other's arms.

My birthday arrived in March. A year before, I'd dropped hints about the date to Paul, but he forgot it, or ignored it, and I spent the evening alone in my apartment surfing the Internet. When I woke up this time, though, Stan was already awake; he brought me coffee and a tiny cake with candles in bed and placed something small in my hand. I unwrapped the silver paper and found a velvet box. I lifted the lid. Inside was a diamond necklace, the glittering stone set amid tiny sapphires on a golden teardrop, the setting filigreed like lace, the pendant hanging from a slender chain, the whole thing shimmering like dew. "It's an exact copy of a piece that belonged to Empress Maria Theresa," he said.

He fastened the clasp around my neck. I felt the stones smolder in the hollow of my collarbones, and for a moment, I don't know why, I felt unbearably sad.

∞

One weekend we arrived at his apartment compound to find that the management had pasted a bright yellow sticker across the windshield of his rusted Chevy convertible, warning that his tags had expired and the building management would have his car towed if the situation was not rectified within forty-eight hours.

"What fucking business is it of theirs?" Stan swore, and kicked the tires. "This is between me and the state of Virginia, not the goddamned building manager!" After scraping off the sticker with a razor blade, which took nearly an hour, Stan called the property manager at home, interrupting his dinner, explaining that the building management was not only in violation of city, county, and state laws against vandalism—and that Stan would report this to the police—but that Stan was prepared to organize a class-action lawsuit on behalf of all the tenants similarly inconvenienced and to sue the building not only for damage to the vehicles but for the time he would spend preparing the lawsuit, which, he informed the stunned property manager, he would be billing at his standard rate, six hundred dollars an hour. "Your company will spend more than thirty thousand dollars paying for the costs of the discovery motions *alone,*" he said.

After slamming down the phone, he switched on the news. The headline story was a World Health Organization initiative to fund HIV treatment in Africa. Stan glared at the screen. "Why should a penny of my tax money go to that? You know, they've known how HIV is spread for years and yet they keep fucking around without taking precautions. They just keep screwing like rabbits. Why is it *my* responsibility to bail them out now?"

I'd never seen him lose his temper. He looked at my face and saw my dismay. He softened. "I'm sorry. I'm overreacting. I wait all week to get these few hours alone with you, and the weeks are

so long, and I come back and find the building management
committing extortion and I waste a precious hour scraping crap
off my car—I'm just frustrated."

I took him in my arms, cautiously. "We could both use a vacation," I said.

We ordered a pizza that evening and sat in front of the television, watching reruns of *L.A. Law* and *Hill Street Blues*. The next
day, he received a letter of apology from the management, a bottle of wine, and a promise to change the building's policy on the
use of the yellow stickers.

∽

Stan had lost twenty pounds. People were beginning to notice,
and his pants were loose. I told him he looked great, and I complimented him on his willpower. He looked at the cigarette I was
smoking. "Have you ever thought about quitting?"

"*Et tu,* Stan? I thought you were the only one here who
wouldn't give me grief about it."

"I wasn't a smoker before I met you. I'd have a cigarette with
a drink every now and again, but I only really started smoking
when I met you. You smoked, and it was the obvious way to
spend time with you."

"You've got to be kidding." I looked at him closely. He hadn't
been smoking much lately, it was true. He'd been saying he
didn't feel like it.

"I had such a crush on you. I'd had such a crush on you since
the first time I saw you. You smoked, so I smoked. But I'm worried about your health. You should cut back."

I had no idea how to react. "Well, maybe when we're finished
with training I'll think about it," I said at last.

"Think about it," he said. "If I can lose weight, you can quit
smoking."

When I thought about it, I realized that smoking had never

seemed natural on him. He had strong views on substance abuse. Once, I'd mentioned that I used to smoke dope. He became rigid. "I sure hope you're over that phase, because I can't be with a woman who does that."

He had his political career to think of, I supposed.

⌒

We expected that when training was over we would be sent back to Headquarters for a year of language study, although we didn't know for sure; we wouldn't receive our assignments until it was all done. "Have you thought about where you're going to live after we finish?" he asked me. I was sitting on his bed with his head in my lap; he was looking up at me. His tone was casual, but his face wasn't.

"I haven't been looking much beyond getting through this, really."

"You know, kiddo, we spend every night together now—and it's been wonderful. I don't want that to stop. Would you consider moving in with me?" He paused and said, "I know we're not married—"

"That's not the issue—"

"We'll get a bigger apartment. Someplace just for us. Someplace with a terrace—we can plant a garden. We can get parakeets. Think about it—it makes sense. What's the point of us both spending money on rent for two apartments that wouldn't be as nice as one we could afford together?" Stan and I had seen a pair of cheerful parakeets in a pet store once; I had admired them. We imagined naming them after our pseudonyms: Caesaria and Lou.

He saw my hesitation. "I don't want to pressure you," he said. "I don't want to rush you into something you aren't comfortable with. But think of the money we'd save. And, God, it would make me happy if you said yes."

I looked at his longing, loving eyes. I remembered Paul saying, "Selena, don't fall in love with me." I remembered going to the hospital alone. And, God help me, I said yes.

He took me into his arms. "Selena," he said. "I want you to know how much I love you. I would take a bullet for you, I love you that much."

I told him that I loved him too.

Stan had recruited me.

CHAPTER 6

A s spring neared, the most serious problem we faced was the People's Front for the Liberation of Turkrapistan. We suspected that the terrorist cell was producing sarin gas. Using overhead imagery, we'd identified the PFLT training camp in the inhospitable foothills of the Greater Turkrap mountain range. We were running a penetration of the camp, and one of our assets, GONZO, claimed to have seen Libyan chemical engineers in the compound's laboratory.

About a month before, the PFLT had bombed the hotel where the Turkrapistani government was holding its annual leadership conference, killing the deputy prime minister and more than thirty civilians, some of them children. The defense minister threatened to impose martial law. The Turkrap Broadcast Company brought us the news in a special bulletin, and when the TBC showed footage of the hysterical mothers, keening in agony by the bodies of their mutilated children, Iris sucked in her breath sharply and said, "What *animals* would do something like that?"

Iris wasn't the only one who was losing her grip on the distinction between Turkrapistan and reality. Instructors who had been there long enough behaved as if Turkrapistan were as real as any member of the United Nations. In the bar, they could be overheard arguing late into the night about local politics. *Look, Jim, even China's got MFN these days! Well, Bob, I say Turkrapistan gets MFN when they play by the rules. Not before. That's why they say "most favored nation," not "any old rat-ass piece of shit excuse for a country." Yeah, Jim, but you're biting off your nose to spite your face. Without Turkrapistani oil we'll be at three dollars a gallon by summer.*

At lunch one day, our classmate Kevin asked the assembled table whether we would blow GONZO if it was the only way to save lives. "Let's say he tells you that the PFLT is planning to put a bomb on a plane."

"How many people know?" asked Mark, who had been a stockbroker before joining the CIA.

"Only four—and the other people who know are all inner circle."

"How does GONZO know?" asked Mark.

"They're making him build the bomb," said Kevin. GONZO was an explosives technician.

"So if you do anything to prevent it, they know he sang."

"Right. GONZO ends up in an unmarked grave with his balls stuffed in his mouth."

Mark said: "Well, he's the only source we have reporting on the PFLT. We can't take the chance he'll be whacked."

Joe looked up from his plate abruptly: "Are you out of your *mind*? You'd let the people on the plane be killed? What if there were Americans on board?"

"Not if there were Americans," said Mark. "Of course not. Then GONZO's dead meat."

Sitting at the end of the table, Iris listened to this exchange in silence. The cafeteria smelled of long-forgotten grade-school specialties—Salisbury steak with gravy and sloppy joes with Tater Tots. We finished our lunches and took our trays to the revolving carousel that whisked the plates off for scrubbing and scalding. Iris asked me if I wanted to take a cup of coffee with her on the lawn, since we still had ten minutes before class began. We took our Styrofoam cups outside, under a shady elm tree. The lawn smelled newly mown. Iris fussed a bit, arranging herself, her handbag, her coffee, and her Chanel sunglasses. "I'm beginning to really hate those people," she said, nodding toward the cafeteria.

"Why more than usual?"

"Did it just occur to you in there that if you'd had the misfortune to be born without an American passport, those guys would have let the PFLT blow up your fucking plane?"

I thought about that for a moment and then turned my palms up in the air. "Let's not pretend you joined the CIA because you were expecting to meet Nelson Mandela. I mean, be reasonable."

℘

We had passed the halfway point of the class. I was melancholy because Lilia had just given birth and I didn't have time to go to New York to see her new daughter. When my nephew was born, I'd flown back from India. Lilia and I had pushed his carriage through Central Park together every day that winter. I woke up at night to keep her company; I warmed a saucepan of hot cocoa, the Mexican kind, with cinnamon and vanilla bean, and as he nursed and gurgled and then fell back to sleep, we talked, drinking our cocoa with afghan blankets over our shoulders. We spent long, lazy afternoons playing with the baby's fingers and toes. We had no secrets from each other.

The pace of this job wouldn't let up when training was over, they said; case officers worked equally long hours in the field. They rarely spent time with their own children, much less their sister's. I was beginning to wonder if I'd ever have children. I'd never seen the point of bringing a child into the world only to leave the poor creature with a nanny. Women in the Agency tended to stay single, because there weren't many men willing to follow them around the world, playing tennis in the embassy compound in Ulan Bator while their wives disappeared for weeks or months at a stretch without word, afterward unable to tell them where they'd been. Women who were determined to wed tended to marry other case officers, but rarely with lasting success: The pressures of the job took too much out of marriages. One woman, now an instructor at the Farm, had set a record by marrying and divorcing *four* case officers in a row.

The men seemed to have less trouble finding women willing to follow their mysterious husbands from country to country. The newlywed wives usually described themselves as "really excited" by the prospect. But the rest of us knew that CIA men tended to take off their wedding rings as soon as they assumed an alias, as if the adoption of another name unburdened them of their marriage vows. The CIA protected the secrets of its officers' indiscretions as vigorously as it did the details of its covert action programs: "What goes on in the field," we were told, "*stays* in the field."

After Iris and I finished our coffee, I walked back from the cafeteria to the block of shared offices where the students kept their computers and papers. I found Stan at his desk getting a head start on the evening's homework. I kissed him and rubbed his neck as he leaned down to open his safe, trying to massage the rubbery knots of tension from his shoulders.

Out of the blue, Stan said: "Step back."

"Excuse me?"

"Step back. You don't need to know my combination."

We all had exactly the same things in our safes: our textbooks, reports we had written on the same exercises, petty cash. I hadn't meant to see his combination, but suddenly I wanted to know it.

"Selena, *back off*. I said that you don't need to know the combination to my safe."

"What's the big secret? What do you think I'm going to do, sneak in under cover of darkness and steal your favorite pencil?" I didn't budge.

"*Get back*. You don't need to know the combination to my safe. We're professionals. Part of our profession is good security—all the time. If you don't make a habit of good security, it doesn't become second nature. If it doesn't become second nature, you might slip up one day when it counts. Would you want a surgeon who thought it wasn't so important to *count* the sponges each time? Who thought, Ah, hell, I think I got 'em all?"

"Stan, you're being a patronizing prick. Don't talk to me like that. Screw you *and* your pencils," I said. I walked away, stung.

He knocked on my door a few hours later. "I stand by what I said, but I said it like a jerk. We're both overtired. Let's not take it out on each other. I'm an asshole, but I love you."

I didn't want to fight either. I pulled him toward me. We spent the night close in each other's arms.

The next day was a Friday, and on Saturday we drove back to Washington and Stan took me to the National Zoo. The scented gardens were in bloom. The animals were gay and fractious, swinging merrily from their vines, roaring and galloping, swatting flies with their tails, displaying their insolent rumps.

"Come on," he said. "The otters are my favorites." He dragged me by the hand, almost trotting himself, to the otters' den, where a male and a female were sunning themselves on a rock.

The female was trying to snooze in the afternoon breeze, but the male would have none of it. He didn't seem to be amorous, as far as we could tell, but he seemed desperate for her attention. He capered madly to impress her. He tossed twigs in the air and caught them, nudged her with his nose, poked her with his flipper-paws, danced on his hind legs.

Stan put words in the animal's mouth: "Look at me! Look at me! Wanna swim? Wanna roll around in the mud? Mud's great today! Real warm! C'mon, wake up! Look at me! I'm cute, aren't I? Clever, too! C'mon! Let's toss twigs!"

Finally, the female rolled over, swatted her mate soundly, then trundled off to another rock to get some peace and quiet. From then on, whenever Stan wanted my attention, he would pretend to be an otter clapping his paws.

By now he had lost more than twenty pounds. His serious clothes were loose. He didn't have the bones for handsomeness—his nose and eyes would always be too small—but one could see that if he continued to slim, his doughy ungainliness would be replaced by a pleasing sturdiness. His face no longer looked overstuffed; his chin was shrinking into proportion with his features. His thighs still looked thick, but he no longer lumbered in quite the same effortful way. He was still pale, but the nightly exertions at the gym seemed to have put a bloom in his cheeks. That weekend he didn't shave, and the dark red shadow on his face subtly transfigured him. His earnestness was obscured; he looked instead like a man with passion and a complicated pirate's soul. I found that exciting. The otter never managed to attract the female's attention, but when we went home, Stan had mine, all of it, and afterward I rubbed his belly and told him that he was a *very* good otter indeed.

Days later, the Deutch scandal made the headlines again. The former Director of Central Intelligence had placed his private diary on an unsecured computer in his home, and in that diary he had detailed the most sensitive of the CIA's covert action programs. He had then used that computer to surf the Internet and to exchange e-mail with foreigners—one of them a Russian, no less. His unsupervised teenage son, poor horny lummox, had used the *same* computer to frequent the Web's more exotic pornography libraries, unaware that he would not only be caught by his parents consorting with amateur housewives, which I'm sure was bad enough, but that his fetishes would become the subject of a federal investigation.

Every two or three weeks, a new development in the story made the front page of *The Washington Post*. The investigators suspected that Deutch had hoped to cover up the evidence by deleting the incriminating files—which, as he should have known, can never truly be done except when you *really* need to get the document back. His allies at the Agency had sought to sweep the whole business under the carpet and would have succeeded but for a whistle-blower in the Office of Security, who brought the matter to the attention of certain very interested chairmen of the House and Senate Intelligence committees. The scandal exploded.

Dr. Deutch had been a chemistry professor at MIT before becoming Director of Central Intelligence, and his tenure at the Agency had been wildly unpopular. He was reputed to be both arrogant and ignorant of the CIA's culture. My colleagues said that he had been considered an outsider, some kind of *intellectual*—and when they used this word, it did not seem to be a term of esteem. The scandal proved what everyone had always suspected: Despite his fancy degrees, the man was a moron.

Deutch's parents had grown up in Germany, as my grandmother had, and, like her, had fled the Nazis in terror. My grandmother—not surprisingly, given her life story—could discern subtle anti-Semitism in a bowl of noodle soup. "This Deutch business reminds me too much of the Dreyfus affair," she said.

I reassured her: "No, Grandma, what he did was really very serious." I added, "If I had done the same thing, they'd be just as hard on me."

Stan told me that Deutch had never wanted to be Director of Central Intelligence. He had been aiming for secretary of defense, and his appointment to the CIA was a consolation prize. Not much of a consolation, Stan added, given that Deutch had always disliked the Agency. Deutch found espionage distasteful and thought the organization was comprised of congenital liars. I don't know how Stan knew this. Stan always knew the most intimate gossip about the Agency's senior ranks. He knew who was in, who was out, who was up, who was down, who was sleeping with whom; he knew who really pulled the strings and who was just a figurehead. He calculated out loud, deciding which instructors were important to cultivate and which ones weren't worth the time. "Did you see the way Hertz wouldn't give up the podium for Simpson this morning? Power struggle. Hertz is going to crush him. Hertz has Panther's ear—did you notice them together in the cafeteria last Wednesday when he came down from Headquarters?" Linus Panther, the head of the Clandestine Service, was pretty much at the top of the Agency's food chain.

I hadn't noticed, no.

While we were lying in bed one night at the Farm, I asked Stan whether Deutch's actions were truly as reckless as they'd been portrayed—was it really possible that a hostile power had penetrated his computer via the Internet? Or was that just scaremongering, as my grandmother suspected? "You better believe it," Stan answered grimly. "Likely, even. When you log on, your computer belongs to the whole planet. You might as well just take off your panties and spread your legs."

I thought about the messages I'd sent my mother and my sister when I'd told them how I'd flunked surveillance detection and was afraid of losing my job. It wasn't much of a gaffe—it was a handful of messages among billions in the ether. I hadn't said anything that important, but I'd sure never do it again.

∞

Stan was a hobbyist; he collected stamps, coins, even Oriental rugs. In all of these enthusiasms he was an expert. His passion, though, was fish—not tropical fish but goldfish. As a child he had tended an extensive aquarium, carefully measuring the temperature and saline levels of the water, sending away for newer and more exotic species by mail order. He had once owned two rare Japanese goldfish, named Milton and Sheldrake. They had accompanied him across the country to law school and back, living a dozen years before dying peacefully of old age. He hadn't owned fish in ages, he told me, but he missed watching them in their tank. "Watching fish swim is so calming that it actually changes your brain waves," he said. "I saw an interesting study."

I surprised him one day with two baby goldfish from the Fish 'n' Feather near the Farm. I bought a little tank and lined it with bright blue aquarium gravel and plastic plants. I stuck a plastic toad that appeared to be playing a banjo in the tank, although it refused to stay moored and bobbed insistently at the surface. I left the aquarium in his room as a surprise.

When he saw what I'd done, he hugged me tightly. He sat at the foot of his bed and watched them for almost an hour in a delighted, childish, innocently pudgy way. He named them Milton and Sheldrake the Second, and took exceedingly good care of them. Over the following weeks he bought a bigger tank, an oxygen filter, and a tank light. He threw out the bright blue gravel and replaced it with natural sand. He replaced the plastic plants with live ones and retired the banjo-playing toad to the closet. I was tickled that I'd made him so happy. I think we both imagined that raising goldfish together was the first step.

∽

Sometimes, when there is no other way to get close to an especially interesting target, a case officer is forced simply to approach him in public as if by chance and strike up a conversation. In our next exercise, the instructors would play Swedish arms dealers whom we knew to have dealings with Iraq. I was told that mine stayed at the Ramada Inn whenever he visited Turkrapistan; surveillance teams had observed him taking his breakfast in the dining room at roughly eight each morning.

I was to find an excuse to approach him, and since we had no idea if he would welcome an overture from the CIA, I was to do so without raising his suspicions. My goal was somehow to befriend him and, if I judged him receptive, reveal my affiliation and persuade him to return to Iraq on the CIA's behalf. I was to do this within four meetings. The target would be a man I had never seen before; this was often the case in the field. I was to look for someone in his early fifties, heavyset, with a salt-and-pepper beard and a ruddy complexion. That was all I knew.

I arrived at the lobby of the Ramada Inn at the appointed time, having spent several hours assuring myself that I wasn't under surveillance. I saw him immediately; he was sitting alone in the dining room reading a paperback. Oh thank God, I thought. *I've* read that book. I strode over. "Hey! You're reading *A Tour of the Calculus*! What a coincidence. I'm so glad I saw you. I just finished it last night, and I am *so* confused about the mean-value theorem. It's driving me crazy! Do you understand it?"

"I haven't reached that part yet," he answered, putting the

book down on the table and regarding me with real pleasure. "I'm only halfway through. But it's a terrific book, isn't it? I really love the author, he's so poetic—"

We launched into an animated discussion of this book, other books, the teaching of mathematics in high school, literature in the late twentieth century. He was a soft touch. Some instructors were like that, and others were real brutes. I'd heard this was supposed to be a tough exercise; many of the instructors played this role close to the chest, refusing to engage in conversation, pretending to be annoyed by the intrusion. This one was doing all the talking, though, and it almost seemed he was hinting that he'd like to invite me to dinner, although that would have been far too easy: The exercise book said explicitly that finding an excuse for another meeting was *my* job.

"So," he said after we'd been chatting for a quarter of an hour. "What do you do?"

I went along with the scenario from the exercise book. "Me? I'm a diplomat."

"Really? What interesting work! What are you doing here?"

"Oh, I'm posted here."

He looked a little lost. "Here? What do you mean? Where do you work?"

"Oh, I'm sure you've seen the building, it's right by the Ministry of Defense, on the Street of the Martyrs of the Revolution, you know it? What about you? What part of Sweden are you from?"

Now he looked even more perplexed. "Sweden?"

Had he forgotten who he was supposed to be? The instructors played multiple roles, and sometimes they didn't read the exercise books carefully. "Yes—Sweden? That is a Swedish accent you have, isn't it?"

"No," he looked at me, a baffled expression passing over his mild features. "It's not."

"I see—" I had a horrible feeling, a glimmer. "Where would you be from, then?"

"Uh, Baltimore?"

Son of a motherless goat!

Panicking—I was now late for my *real* meeting—I made my excuses as quickly as I could. But where was the real instructor? *There* he was, in the other corner. Salt-and-pepper beard; portly. I rushed over frantically and struck up a conversation. I asked him where he had bought his watch, told him I wanted to get the same kind for my father. When I looked up, I saw the first man staring at us, eyes round with bewilderment.

Of course, most of the longtime residents in the area knew perfectly well that they lived near a CIA training facility. One well-situated fence post in the nearest town bore over sixty inch-long chalk marks, and if you kicked over a rock in the countryside, you'd likely as not find a detailed diagram of the PFLT's hillside training compound. So maybe he figured it out eventually.

The merry instructor who played the Swedish arms dealer didn't hold my gaffe against me. He wrote a lovely review of my performance, calling me a natural, even including a little poem he'd composed about the mishap:

> There once was a buxom young lass,
> The belle of her espionage class,
> When she asked some poor dweeb
> If he might be a Swede,
> He thought, "She's got her head up her ass."

I showed the poem to Stan. "What a fucking idiot," he said.

"Oh, come on, it's funny."

"It might be funny, but he'll get himself fired if he sends something like that to the wrong person. He's an instructor; he's in a position of power over you, and he's sending you poetry about how *buxom* you are? Moron. And doesn't he know you have a boyfriend?"

"I suppose. I still think it's funny."

∽

Stan and I were driving back to his apartment from the Farm the following week when I took a wrong turn. We ended up in the vicinity of my friend Byron's house, and when I realized where we were, I asked Stan whether he'd like to call Byron and his wife and ask them out for a drink.

Byron worked on the Hill as a lobbyist for the National Apartment Dwellers Union—or something like that—it had to do with apartments, anyway. He was a handsome black man, entirely African in appearance, *and* an Orthodox Jew. He had his mother's name as well as her blood—Byron *Lefkowitz*—and the congressmen to whom he introduced himself on the phone were often taken aback when he pitched up at their offices in the flesh: "*You're* Lefkowitz?"

His wife had been a professional ballerina once, but she stayed home now with their two young daughters. I was fond of their family but hadn't seen them for almost a year because I'd had no time, and besides, I felt weird lying to my friends about where I worked.

Stan said sure, he would be delighted to meet friends of mine, so I called them. Byron answered and sounded happy to hear from me, said it had been too long, he would love to meet Stan, what great news that I'd finally met a nice guy, and why didn't we come over right now? His wife was preparing a barbecue— she'd bought way too much food—and no of course it wouldn't be an imposition, not in the least. We agreed. On the drive over, Stan and I rehearsed the details of my cover and his, arranging a story to explain how we had met—in a wine-tasting class, we decided, in Washington.

As we drove I debated whether to tell Stan that Byron and I had once had a one-night stand. It hardly seemed relevant now, but I felt that if the position were reversed, I'd want to know, so I told him.

"You've *slept* with this guy?"

"I'm sorry. Maybe I should have mentioned that sooner. It was years ago. I don't even remember it now. I don't think about him that way anymore, don't worry. He's really changed—he used to be a fun, happy-go-lucky guy, but now he's become almost oppressive about this Orthodox Jewish stuff, especially since he got married. He doesn't even eat out anymore unless it's at a kosher restaurant. Does it bother you? We don't have to go if it does, we can still cancel—"

"No. It's fine. Let's go."

Stan was charming at dinner. By the end of the evening he had Byron's wife eating out of his hand. He complimented her on her yellow sundress with thin spaghetti straps and asked if she had ever danced his favorite ballet, *Coppélia*. He did magic tricks for the two girls, delighting them by making coins appear from their ears and disappear just as mysteriously. He spent a half-hour earnestly discussing the new HUD regulations with Byron. Afterward, Byron and I played with the girls on the lawn while Stan and Byron's wife did the dishes and watched us from the kitchen window. The girls begged Byron to perform a headstand and he obliged, kicking his toes into the air. His T-shirt dropped around his shoulders and I noticed that he was as well built as ever. For a second I thought of Stan attempting similarly to invert himself, then shook the thought out of my head. It was like trying to imagine him dancing *Coppélia*.

We got through the evening without having to answer too

many questions about our imaginary jobs. We left early; we both wanted to get some sleep. We made all the usual promises about how we all had to see each other more often.

On the drive back, Stan was unusually quiet. "Is anything wrong?" I asked.

"I'm fine."

"You seem quiet."

"I'm fine. Really. I just don't feel like going back to the Farm tomorrow."

We kept driving.

Then he asked: "So how was it with him?"

"It was a long time ago—"

"No, I'm just curious—is it true what they say about black guys?"

"Like I should remember?"

"Were you drunk? I mean, how did it all happen?" He pulled into the left lane and passed a semi, pressing hard on the accelerator.

"Stan, why are you asking these questions?"

"Honestly? Honestly? Because when I think about someone else touching you, it makes me want to vomit."

"It was years ago! It only happened one time. It was *college*. He's not at all attractive to me that way anymore, not at all. Why are you behaving like this?"

"Me? I'm not the one who spreads my legs for everyone!"

I was too stunned to speak. We drove the rest of the way in pitch-black silence.

∽

Once we were home, Stan finally told me what I had come to suspect. To impress me, he had reinvented himself as someone much jauntier and more cocksure than he truly was, a man of experience and savoir faire. But all those women he'd alluded to, the ones who liked to be tied up and spanked, were in fact just *one* woman who liked to be tied up and spanked. He had been with her through most of his twenties; she was the one who had left him when he joined the CIA. "I tied her up and spanked her a *lot,* for what it's worth," he added forlornly.

He had loved a girl in high school, he told me. She was his first, and they had been lovers for three years. "She was beautiful," he said, "and she was a flirt, like you." When they graduated, he had proposed to her; she said she wasn't ready. He went to Cornell; she went to the big state university. One night she called to tell him she wanted to date other men. Destroyed, he told her never to call him again. Two months later, she called anyway; she was angry, she was drunk, she told him that she had slept with six men since they had broken up, then she told him that before she left she had aborted his child. Stan had never known she was pregnant. As he told me this, his arms were tight across his chest and his jaw was tense.

"A couple of times," he added, "I've gone out a few times with a woman, and things have seemed good to me, and then one night I walk into a bar and she's there on some other guy's lap. Then Margaret left me because I joined the CIA. I'd always thought we'd get married sooner or later. It's not that I don't trust women anymore, it's just that now I think I've got to cut the deck before I play."

Where had he found the confidence to pursue me as he had? "Are you kidding? I couldn't even bring myself to talk to you for a whole year. I watched you for months. I wanted you from the moment I saw you—you had the most beautiful smile I'd ever seen, and you were so flirty and sexy—and you didn't even know I existed. Then you started seeing that asshole, and for a while I gave up, but when you two broke it off I thought I might have a chance if I could only get near you. That's why I started smoking, that's why I started reading that god-awful Sanskrit literature, and that's why I arranged for our rooms to be near each other when we got to the Farm."

"You did *what*? How?"

He shrugged. "I'm good at getting things done."

But Stan couldn't understand how I could have had so many lovers before him, when I was so unique to his experience. "It doesn't make sense to me. You're so vulnerable with me when we make love—how could you share that part of yourself so easily?"

I had no idea how to take that, and no idea what to say.

The next week, Stan, Nathan, and a few other students went back to Headquarters to attend a three-day seminar on covert finance. Stan and Nathan drove together. The CIA had a number of complex methods of moving money around the globe, and the bookkeeping involved was particularly labyrinthine: Large sums of taxpayer money had on occasion gone missing between Bermuda and Berlin, with a great deal of finger-pointing ensuing, the specialists in covert bank accounts accusing the folks in covert credit cards of misfiling the relevant records, and vice versa. The cash that flowed through phony entities every year was a tidy sum, and senior management had of late become particularly concerned about the amount no one seemed able to locate. Laundering money was a fastidious business, and Stan thought it would be useful to master it.

While Stan was gone, I practiced handing over one of my assets, PLUMBBOB, to Kirk. Assets become extremely attached to their case officers, so the handover is a delicate moment. We were told to take pains to laud the new case officer as "one of the very best, someone with whom I would trust my life" and to make sure our colleagues were thoroughly briefed about the asset and his emotional needs. Kirk and I spent three days in a motel room with PLUMBBOB, curing him of his angst. When Kirk revealed to PLUMBBOB that he too was a military man who abominated the idea of women in the modern army, PLUMBBOB began to warm to him. Kirk was competent and workmanlike, but he lacked finesse, and I missed discussing the case with Stan at the end of the day. The handover complete, I bid PLUMBBOB farewell and left him with Kirk in the motel room, the two soldiers engaged in a discussion of Second World War field artillery. I noted with excitement that I might have time to fit in a short nap before Stan's return.

But when I got back to the Farm, Stan was waiting for me in the parking lot. I pulled up and sang, "Hey, sailor! Welcome back!"

"Hello, Selena." He gave me a single sharp glance, as if verifying my identity, then nodded in the direction of a vacant parking spot. His body was ramrod-straight, and he seemed to have grown bigger.

I parked and walked over to him. "What's the matter?"

Stan didn't move to embrace me. "Is it true?"

"Is what true?"

"Nathan spoke to Jade last night. Evidently, *everyone* knows you spent last night with Kirk."

"Nathan said *what*?"

"You heard me."

"You don't believe that, do you?"

"How could you do that to me? After all I've done for you?" He was shaking with rage. He looked as if he hadn't slept.

"Are you out of your mind? You're going to believe Nathan before you believe me? Nathan hates me. You know that. He can't stand to see a man and a woman happy together. God, I'm going to *kill* that little fucker!"

"That's your theory, huh?" He looked out over the parking lot, scowling in the sun. The other students were pulling in from their meetings. He eyed each of them in turn. His mouth was a narrow slit.

"Did Nathan try to *justify* repeating this rumor to you in any way?"

"He said he was telling me because he *cared* about me and he thought I deserved better. He said that everybody knew."

"Christ almighty! That little prick! Stan, I would never do that—never!—Kirk's an asshole. Nathan's a psychopath. I love *you,* and you can fucking well ask Iris where I was last night, because I was in *her* room until midnight. Go on! Ask her!"

His face softened, and he looked hesitant. "I don't know what to think."

"Think that I love you." I took his hands in mine and looked directly into his eyes. "It is *not true*. It will *never* be true. You have *got to trust me*. Please. Don't destroy us like this."

He looked at me, trying to read my thoughts. I felt tears coming into my eyes. Finally, his body relaxed, and he said, "I'm sorry." He put his arms around me and held me tightly. "Oh, God, I'm so sorry. I'm so sorry. I hate myself for being this way. Forgive me. I'm so sorry."

Stan seemed fragile for a while. Watching me brush my hair that night, he grew melancholy. "Is it just arrogance for someone like me to think I could keep a beautiful woman like you?" he asked.

"Yes," I said, "sheer arrogance."

∞

The next day, when I knocked on his door, I found him sitting in his bed, propped against his pillows, wearing his reading glasses, a thick paperback in his hands. The title of the book was *Overcoming Jealousy*.

"Where did you get that?" I asked.

He put his mechanical pencil down on the bedside table. A

blush passed over his pale skin; he didn't look up at me. "I found it at the bookstore," he said.

"Can I look?"

"Sure. Here."

I looked: The author was a clinical psychologist from California. The margins were dark with Stan's tidy, parsimonious script. The first comment I saw read: *Could I be so repulsive???*

I handed the book back to him. "What do you make of it?"

"I don't want to be a jealous man. It's not worthy of me and I know it's not fair to you."

I knelt down and pulled his head to my chest. I kissed his forehead, and his temples, then his mouth.

∞

The Turkrapistani foreign minister was coming in from the cold. Terrific news to be sure, but in practice it meant that the students had to wait up all night in the mock station, standing on alert for the word that he had crossed safely. We were taking him out in the trunk of a Ford Fiesta with phony license plates. The instructors always *hated* playing that role.

We were getting bored and antsy. First we played Truth or Dare, then we swapped Helen Keller jokes. Mark suggested a stupid game he'd learned during his interim assignment on the Iran Task Force called Tell Me a Secret. You had to ask one of the other players to tell you a secret about a country—France, China, Brazil—but the respondent had to answer *in the accent of the natives of that country,* and the reply had to involve a famous national dish and a covert military strategy. "Tell me a secret about Russia." Mark leered at Allison. "In Mother Russia," Allison replied, gurgling her *r*'s throatily, "we make borscht weeth peeg urine, to make troops strong like bull!" You had two seconds to answer. If you couldn't think of a response, or flubbed the accent, or forgot the national dish, you were eliminated.

"Selena," Allison said to me. "Tell me a secret about France!"

"Ah oui! In la France, we wedge zee brie in our ears! When zee German troops arrive, zey play zee *Tannhäuser* ovair and ovair, but zey do not understand why zee Frenchmen are nevaire afraid!"

I remained in the game.

For some reason, Stan just couldn't get it. Usually, he was the first out of the gate with these kinds of games, but this one stumped him. Maybe he was just tired, or maybe the others were picking on him. "Stan!" said Allison. "Tell me a secret about South Africa!" That flummoxed him. What the hell was the South African national dish? He made a game effort: "In South Effrika, we take our coffee strong and bleck, like our gardeners!" Instantly, there was a chorus of complaints: Coffee wasn't a South African national dish, and that wasn't a military secret. He was eliminated from the round.

We played round after round, and each time, Stan was eliminated on his first try. Vaguely tickled to see him humiliated, the other students began to tease him. "Stan! Tell me a secret about Nicaragua!" "Stan, tell me a secret about Sierra Leone!" He couldn't think of the dishes, he couldn't do the accents convincingly, and no matter what he said, the other students eliminated him, making loud *Gong Show* noises after his replies. He was getting more and more upset. I could tell he was too tired to see the funny side of it, and I felt bad for him. I wanted to comfort him, but I knew he would only be more embarrassed if I did it in front of the others.

At sunrise we got the word that the minister had died in the trunk. It happened from time to time. It was a shame. Allison was elected to write the we-regret-to-inform-you cable to Headquarters. The instructors loved giving us exercises like that, where the whole point seemed to be to make us lose a night's sleep.

"That's the way it is out in the field," they would always say if anyone complained. "Suck it up."

We went back to our rooms. Stan was foul-tempered. We'd stayed up all night for nothing, and he was smarting from the other students' ridicule. I put my arms around his neck and caressed his cheek. I stood on my toes and gently whispered in his ear, "All right, tell me a secret." I meant it to be a flirtatious invitation, but I think Stan thought I was laughing at him too. His face turned red.

"You want to know a secret?" he hissed. "I'll tell you a goddamned secret. My secret is I don't got time for this crap. I'm not just some jerkoff junior trainee like those guys. I've done *real* ops. I've designed operations that only four people in the world know about—me, the head of the Special Activities Branch, the DCI, and the president of the fucking European Central Bank! *That's* a fucking secret."

"What?" I said, shocked and confused, trying to figure out what the hell he was talking about.

He sat down and put his head in his hands. His face was lined with fatigue. "Never mind. I shouldn't have said that."

"What the hell do you mean?" I insisted. *"Who are you?"*

Stan slumped his shoulders and hung his head. All the anger had drained out of him. He took my hands in his. "I'm sorry. I shouldn't have said that to you. It's not true. I was just blowing off steam. Please don't repeat that to anyone else. I don't know what made me say that. I'm just overtired. Promise me you'll forget what I said."

"Stan, come on! How can I forget that? What did you mean, that you're not a trainee like the others?"

His eyes narrowed. "Selena, I will only say this once. I cannot talk to you about that. Don't ask me again. You have to live with the fact that around here, there are some things you can't even discuss with your girlfriend. You are to forget what I just said. You cannot mention that to *anyone* or we will *both* go to jail. Do you get it?"

I saw that he was absolutely serious, and terrified by his own lapse. I knew that nothing I could say would convince him to tell me another word.

"Okay," I said. "I've forgotten it. Let's get some sleep."

☙

Kirk, who had been a Marine, and Joe, the former Green Beret, had been arguing since they met about which service was more manly, and as we grew more fatigued, the dispute became less and less of a joke. Kirk claimed to have read some statistic that 90 percent of the CEOs of the Fortune 500 were former Marines. Joe was using his precious spare time to research the question. Every day he would show up with the biography of another executive: "Head of Procter and Gamble: *not a Marine.* Where are all your goddamned Marines?"

They were both driving us nuts.

I wasn't there the night it happened. They had given us the evening off for the first time in months so that the instructors could attend a mandatory workshop at Headquarters called "Toward an Intelligent Intelligence Community: Educating the Educators." Stan and I had already decided we wanted nothing to do with the others that night. We went back to his room to take a nap and then to play Trivial Pursuit, a game we contested as if we were France and Germany fighting for the Alsace-Lorraine. So we missed the whole thing, which was probably for the best.

Joe and Kirk and the rest of the boys went to the bar. They were celebrating something, a basketball victory, I believe, but mostly they were just happy to have an evening without work. A bit too much to drink was had, that much was clear, and the headiness of an evening off made everyone a little giddy. Since I wasn't there, I'll never know what really happened after that. I heard many versions of the story, and each one was so different, you would never know the same episode was being recounted. But what seems certain enough is that Joe started in again about how the Green Berets were the most elite and highly trained forces on the Planet Earth and the Marines were just cannon fodder; Kirk was about to come back with the same old thing about the Fortune 500, but Allison, who was sitting with them at the bar, just couldn't take it anymore. "Oh, for God's sake," she said disgustedly. "Why don't you guys just whip it out to see who's bigger and settle this once and for all."

She was being sarcastic, but Kirk thought this was a terrific idea. He immediately dropped his pants and whipped out little Kirk with a magnificent *"Semper Fi!"* Not to be outdone, Joe dropped his shorts too and began shouting something incoherent about Pearl Harbor. Kirk apparently took matters in hand and clambered onto the counter, hollering, *"This is my rifle, mother-fuckers!"* Joe was on the verge of demonstrating that it *was* possible to urinate from where he was standing all the way to the pool table when someone convinced the two of them that maybe they should put the damned things back in their shorts, and I guess someone else took them back to their rooms and hosed them down, and they were both back in class the next morning, a little worse for wear. When I heard about it the next day I was sorry to have missed the show, although by some accounts (again, the story varied depending on who was telling it), there was not quite so much to see as one might have hoped. "White guys," Iris sniffed.

But that wasn't the end of the matter.

About a week later, the buzz started. Someone—the culprit was assumed to be a woman—had taken it upon herself to call the head of the Human Resources Department to complain that she had felt *harassed*. Apparently, someone thought that the sight of these guys waving their dicks around and yodeling amounted to a *hostile work environment*. And whaddya know, Human Resources took this seriously. Very seriously. You just knew that they were thinking about Tailhook and imagining the jokes on Leno.

That's when Joe and Kirk began their descent into their own personal hell. The internal investigators started hauling students away to get to the bottom of the matter. Interviews were conducted. Cleared attorneys took affidavits. There was talk of convening a special disciplinary panel. The word *lawsuit* was in the air. Someone started a rumor that the Senate Select Committee on Intelligence was going to hold hearings. People started calling it Dorkgate. Joe, once the soul of conviviality, grew pale and quiet. Kirk spent a lot of time with the punching bag in the gym.

Everyone had an opinion. The class became bitterly divided among those who thought they should be sacked immediately for their lack of judgment and those who could see the lighter side of it. I was in the latter camp; in fact I couldn't stop sniggering every time the subject came up. Stan was in the former: "This is not a fraternity house, this is the C-I-fucking-A! They exposed themselves in public! In front of their co-workers! On federal property! What kind of morons *do* that?"

"Well, I can't defend that . . . but don't you think they've been punished enough? I mean, think how embarrassed they must be . . . and in the history of CIA screwups, this isn't exactly the Bay of Pigs."

"It's a judgment issue. If these people don't know their *own* culture well enough to know that's not going to go down well, what are they going to do in the field? Would you want to be out with those clowns when they pulled a stunt like that in Tehran? Would you want your *life* to depend on people who can't figure out that that's not a good idea?"

No, I wouldn't. I realized he was right—I couldn't really hold up my side of the argument—but my heart went out to them, especially to Joe. I would always remember how kind he'd been to me during paramilitary training. His judgment may have been a little off that night, but I thought he was exactly the kind of man who would run into a burning building to save a child, no questions asked.

For weeks, it was the sole topic of conversation—not just among our class, but apparently among everyone in the intelligence community. *Everyone* wanted to know what had really happened that night. The guys' friends swore that nothing had happened at all. By God, this was a mountain made of a molehill, a tempest in a teapot—hell, the Ladies' Sewing Circle would have felt perfectly at home hosting its annual quilting bee in that bar. Their enemies recounted a tale of degeneracy and obscenity that dwarfed the Profumo affair, claiming, among other things, that Joe had relieved himself on a statue of Bill Casey and Kirk had needed to be restrained lest he rape a terrified finance officer. Few people could back up these claims by reference to identifying anatomical features or specific dimensional details, an avenue for the establishment of the truth that I, for one, in my passion for veracity, investigated thoroughly.

We all wanted to know who'd squealed. Jade was the chief suspect, although the finger was pointed at almost everyone sooner or later. Allison collapsed under the weight of suspicion; she was held to be a likely culprit because she had once worked in a rape crisis center, which most of the men took to be an assertion of a feminist radicalism no less arduous than Andrea Dworkin's. Condemning her, I understand, after some kind of secret trial, the men stopped speaking to her, which proved to be too much for her to bear. She was found shaking in her bathroom, weeping, covered in psychosomatic hives.

Joe and Kirk walked around dazed, looking like deer caught in the headlights. Nothing in the Marines *or* the Green Berets had ever prepared them for this.

I had just returned from a meeting with an asset when we were summoned for an urgent unscheduled meeting in the auditorium. The head of the Clandestine Service himself, the venerable Linus Panther, had traveled to the Farm from Headquarters, descending upon us like Judgment Day to deliver himself of a stern rebuke.

He began by staring us down wordlessly for a full thirty seconds. With his bushy white hair, he looked like an enraged Q-tip. I suddenly felt squirmy and embarrassed, the way I did in the fourth grade when the principal came down to talk to the girls—only the girls; the boys were allowed to leave—to say that *someone* had been chucking balls of wet, wadded-up toilet paper at the ceiling of the girls' bathroom, where it was *sticking,* and that while we might think this was funny, it was *seriously inconveniencing* the janitor and that when the culprit was found—and she *would* be found—she was going to have some *serious explaining* to do. Of course I was the one who had been chucking the toilet paper, along with my friend Sally Duxbery, and we never did get caught.

Panther finally spoke, tremulous and affronted as a Baptist preacher confronting Original Sin: "Many of you know about the *incident* in the bar three weeks ago."

We all bowed our heads and tried to look as if we had no idea what he was talking about.

"And I *gather*—" his voice rose, like Moses urging the smashing of the idols "—that some of you may even find this incident *amusing.*"

I composed my features into an expression that said, I hoped, *No, not me, not me. I'm outraged. I too am so very very disappointed by the behavior of a few, and it is only a few—*

"Well, let me explain something to you. Not *one* of you has graduated from this course yet. *Not one of you.* Do you understand me?" We all nodded vigorously.

"You are being trained to represent our country overseas and to hold the most sensitive and responsible jobs *in the United States government*. If you think for one minute that you can represent our country adequately with your pants around your ankles, you do not *deserve* the honor of being here. Your graduation barbecue is *canceled*." He paused again for emphasis. "No one should be amused that there are people in this room who have the *morals of a goat!*"

We were excused. From then on, we were infamous. We were the Class with the Morals of a Goat.

Two weeks before the end of the course, Joe and Kirk were relieved of their positions. When the news came, they were hustled off the base within an hour, given only enough time to pack their things. I never even had the chance to say good-bye.

Panther relented and sent word that we would be allowed to have our graduation barbecue after all, not that anyone cared, since by that point we all hated each other and just wanted to go home. But before the graduation, Hal Hertz, the course director, called us back to the auditorium for one last warning. He had got wind of a rumor that some of the students planned to find a goat somewhere and bring the thing to the barbecue. "Well, gang, let me tell you this," he, said, his dark eyebrows narrowing to the midpoint of his long, thin nose. "Come graduation day, if so much as the *snout* of a goddamned goat is found on these premises, if so much as a goat *whisker* makes its way *near* that goddamned barbecue grill, you will *all* be fired on the spot. *And if you think I'm kidding, gang, just try me.*"

∽

The closer we came to finishing, the longer the hours got and the more Stan and I longed for it to be over. We never got more than a few hours of sleep at night. The pressure never eased. We counted the minutes until we could leave. Time seemed to be expanding. The days were endless and the weeks almost infinite. Stan told me that a colleague of his from Headquarters had warned him: "You know how most things, even if they suck, one day you'll feel nostalgic for them? That's not true about the Farm. That place will make you feel sick and anxious for the rest of your life. If you have to go back there for a conference or anything, your heart will sink when you drive in."

I believed it.

We fantasized about what we would do when the training was done. Language training sounded great. Nine-to-five days would be a vacation. We imagined our new apartment. I wanted to plant a summer garden on the balcony, with fresh tarragon and thyme. I imagined Lou and Caesaria chirping, fuchsia hanging in the garden, bougainvillea climbing the walls. For some reason, whenever I imagined this new home, it was improbably transmogrified in my mind into one of those glorious sun-splashed Spanish villas you see in *House & Garden,* with a vista that stretched over a whitewashed balcony toward the limpid sea beyond.

We would have a week of administrative leave when the class finished. Maybe, Stan proposed, we should get into his car, his old convertible Chevy, which rattled like a Calcutta taxi, and drive somewhere far away. Neither of us had ever been to Kentucky. It sounded romantic—Kentucky. We could spend a week talking about anything but espionage. We could bring watercolors and paint, or we could just be outside and stroll hand in hand through the bluegrass, which I imagined, literally, as blue.

Or maybe we would fly to the Caribbean. It would require doing a bit of paperwork, because technically it was foreign travel and we would need permission, but I liked the thought of paddling in a turquoise sea, watching the fish sparkle through a glass-bottomed boat. I would wear a white bikini and Stan would pet me while I stretched like a cat in the sun, and he would tell me how pretty I was. As we drifted off to sleep at night, we would discuss our plans and count off the number of days left. "Twelve days." "Eleven." "Single digits."

Finally, we entered the last week. "This week," explained Hal Hertz to a visiting congressional delegation, "tests the candidate's ability to resist sleep deprivation." Every time we thought nothing else could come down the pipe, they threw another crisis at us. At two in the morning, a Libyan refugee walked into our mock embassy claiming to have information about the PFLT's chemical weapons laboratory in the Greater Turkrap Mountains. Six hours of debriefing, then eighteen more hours of writing the reports.

They showed up with monstrously detailed but imperfectly memorized floor plans of the facility in question, these defectors; we spent hours trying to understand and sketch the details. The instructors amused themselves by dressing up as real refugees—in old, stinking furs, or reeking of vodka—and pretending to speak only Pushtu or Amharic. They picked up letter openers from the desk and threatened to plunge them into their own hearts if we didn't promise them asylum in the United States. Our assets failed to show up for scheduled meetings, forcing us to revert to the backup, wasting the hours we had spent assuring ourselves that we weren't under surveillance and making us do it again. We received word from another source that our most reliable informant was a dangle. Nan was complaining; an instructor overheard her and said, "Get used to it, Nan. This is the way it is in the field. *Always*."

On the final night of training, having slept no more than three hours the night before and each night prior for the past week, the mock station's prize asset, the assistant to the Turkrapistani defense minister, told me in our clandestine rendezvous that Turkrapistan had the Bomb and was planning to use it. I sprinted back to the office to tell the rest of the station. The news meant even more work: Something this urgent had to be disseminated in a special, attention-getting format used only for nuclear emergencies, and since we had heard Wally's lecture on the subject months and months before—and hadn't paid attention anyway—none of us remembered how to do it. We would have to teach ourselves from the manual. "Is this really that critical?" Kevin asked. "Couldn't we just send it in the normal way?"

"Kevin," I said irritably. "They're planning to drop a fucking nuclear weapon on Manhattan—what could be more fucking critical? Are you waiting for Mars to attack?"

He saw my point. We dutifully did the research, wrote up the report, and sent it out in the right format. When it was finally over, the next morning—the class ending with a final sentimental broadcast from the TBC, the impending nuclear holocaust defused, thanks to our timely reporting—no one felt like celebrating. We wanted only to sleep, but most of us were too wired from caffeine and days of sleeplessness even to do that. We lay in our beds and twitched.

I found out the next morning that I had passed. My adviser told me in his office the next day that support for me among the instructors had been unanimous. "Toward the end," he said, "your record in detecting surveillance was perfect. The teams had no trouble at all with your demeanor or your driving—you actually did better than most of your classmates. You overcame a lot of handicaps, and everyone was impressed by your determination. You didn't let anything beat you. Congratulations." He handed me my final performance appraisal to sign; it was, despite all my fears, exemplary.

I was at last an envoy of our government's clandestine arm, fully qualified to recruit and handle spies for the United States. I would learn where I would be posted before the end of the week. I knew that I owed my success to Stan. I was too tired to be triumphant, but I was quietly relieved and terribly grateful to him.

Following graduation, we were supposed to have a week off to put our neglected personal lives back in order, but directly after congratulating me, my adviser handed me a note telling me to report to the Special Investigations Branch the following Monday at eight in the morning. *Goddammit,* I thought, looking at the message. *Can't they just give me one fucking day of peace?*

I knew instinctively that the note meant something bad, but I had no idea what. Nor did I know what the Special Investigations Branch did. It specialized in security or employee discipline—that much I surmised from the name—but beyond that, I had no clue. My adviser didn't know what it was about; he said Hal Hertz might. I went to Hertz's office and knocked on the door. He kicked it open with his foot, saw it was me, nodded, and slammed the door closed again. I listened for voices in his office but heard nothing. Finally, after I'd passed about ten minutes standing stupidly in the corridor, he erupted: "Come in! Now!"

He was sitting over a stack of paperwork, at which he continued to stare when I entered, acknowledging my entrance only with a curt pump of his glabrous head. The sharp angles of his skull and his long, flared nose made him look like a bird of prey. When he looked up at me, it was as if I were an unwelcome intrusion.

I asked him if he knew why the Special Investigations Branch wanted to see me. He began rhythmically stamping EYES ONLY on the folders on his desk. "Beats me." He shrugged. "We're just passing on the message." I was sure he knew what the appointment was about, but obviously I wasn't going to get anywhere with him. I resigned myself to waiting, and wondered if I had done something wrong. I told myself that this might be a routine reinvestigation—the kind they scheduled for all of us every few years. Or perhaps this was about someone else.

When I left his office, I heard Jade's harsh, bronchial voice. She was telling everyone within earshot that Iris had failed.

∽

Iris was dumped unceremoniously from the Clandestine Service—on graduation day, no less. Her adviser said, "It seems to have been an attitude issue. Some of the instructors felt you didn't accept criticism well."

I found her on the staircase near the auditorium. She was trembling. I knew that if the others saw her cry it would be an unbearable humiliation. I put my sweater around her shoulders and hustled her to my room, where she would be safe.

"Did you have *any* idea this was coming, Iris?"

"None. Not at all. None. None."

She finally began to cry, in great heaving sobs. I gave her a tissue, then another, and let her weep. Her breath became ragged, then the sobs quieted. "Which one of them put the knife in my back?" she asked.

"It's probably not a good idea to torture yourself wondering about something you'll never know the answer to."

"How could they have let me get to the last day without warning me?"

"They're assholes. Complete assholes."

"What do you think I did wrong?"

I stroked her hand. I told her how sorry I was. I told her they had made an appalling mistake.

"What am I going to do now?" She had quit her job to join the CIA; she had sold her house; she had even given away her dog. She couldn't list what she'd been doing for the past eighteen months on her résumé, because it would compromise the cover entity she'd been using. She supposedly worked for a company called Mayquest. If she revealed that Mayquest didn't exist, everyone else who supposedly worked there would be blown. But if anyone called Mayquest for a reference, they'd get that same CIA flack who, having no idea who Iris was, would say, "She's in a meeting. I'll have to have her call you back."

Iris was barred from attending the graduation ceremony. She was given only that afternoon to adjust to the news, compose herself, pack her things, and get off the CIA's property. It was an article of faith at the Agency that people who had been fired must be separated from classified material as quickly as possible, lest they be tempted, in their spite, to help themselves to a few state secrets and sell them to the highest bidder. I helped her pack.

I got dressed for graduation and went to the auditorium. I found my assigned seat and sat down next to Mark, the former stockbroker who would have let a plane explode to protect GONZO. He offered me his hand. "Congratulations," he said. I could tell by the way he looked at me that he was preparing a little speech. "You know," he said. "I want to tell you something." *Here it comes,* I thought. *Bring it on, killer.* "When I first met you, I didn't trust you. You seemed to think you were smarter than everyone else. I'm just telling you so you know, okay? You should really know what kind of impression you give other people. I'm just telling you this as a friend, Selena. Because after watching you all this time, I've realized you're okay. You might have more higher education than the rest of us, but you busted your ass just like everyone else. You're a good officer, and I'd be happy to serve with you anywhere."

"Thanks, Mark. You too. Congratulations."

"Great to be done, isn't it?"

"I feel sad for Iris," I answered.

He looked surprised. "Don't worry about it. She wouldn't want you to let that ruin your evening."

The Director of Central Intelligence arrived and handed us our diplomas, which were given to us in alias and taken away immediately for storage in a secure facility. The auditorium was filled with Agency brass—the Deputy Director for Operations, the executive director, Betty Argus, Hal Hertz. They sat on the dais before a row of flags—the American flag, of course, and a flag with the Agency seal, and a few other flags of indeterminate provenance: One seemed to be from the Department of Energy. The executive director was wearing his military regalia. I noticed a run in my nylons during the ceremony. I tried to scrunch it inside my shoe.

The speeches involved a mixture of bromides and congratulations and many descriptions of the Agency as the finest intelligence service in the world, and a family. The Deputy Director for Operations told an anecdote about a case officer who had run over a bandit in Zimbabwe with his Range Rover.

All I wanted was to go home.

At the reception afterward, the Director of Central Intelligence shook my hand and clapped me on the back. "Well done," he murmured through an unlit cigar, his florid skin creasing, his face at once avuncular and vaguely voluptuarian. "We're expecting great things from you. You've got a lot of talent, that's what I hear." Gliding on his heels, he passed to the next student and said precisely the same thing.

Of course Stan had also passed. His adviser had told him he was the most talented student the instructors could remember. He had reached his lowest weight in five years. Catching a glimpse of him as he strode into the auditorium wearing his best single-breasted suit, I realized with surprise that he looked handsome.

We found each other after the ceremony and went back to his dormitory room. "It's an anticlimax," he said.

"I can't believe what they did to Iris. I can't believe she didn't graduate with us."

We lit a scented candle, and I lay in his arms quietly as the smell of freesia filled the air.

We'd had so many plans, but we were too tired to realize them. We'd given up on the idea of a Caribbean vacation a while ago. Now, we admitted to each other that we didn't have the time or the energy to drive to Kentucky, either. We spent the weekend watching television in bed. We ordered in Chinese food and pizza. I slept most of the time, wearing Stan's T-shirt and his underwear, because I hadn't done laundry in almost two months. I was anxious about my Monday-morning appointment at the Special Investigations Branch. Stan thought it was probably nothing, but I had a bad feeling about it. Stan watched reruns of *Red Dwarf* and *Deep Space Nine*. We let the take-out boxes and cartons stack up at the foot of the bed, like Aztec ruins, and stepped over them gingerly when we got up to use the toilet.

CHAPTER 7

———✦———

The receptionist at the Special Investigations Branch placed me in a waiting room with three steel folding chairs and a small utility table. An old copy of *Newsweek,* coffee-stained and coverless, lay on the laminate tabletop. A framed award plaque hung at a skewed angle on the wall. MERITORIOUS UNIT CITATION, it read, and listed six unfamiliar names underneath. I studied it for hints but found none.

A middle-aged woman walked past the door, acknowledged me by name, and told me to wait another minute. She slipped off and I heard low voices. When she returned, she told me to follow her. Frayed posters on the corridor wall recalled the need for vigilance. YOU HAVE ACCESS, read one. YOU COULD BE A TARGET.

INTERVIEW ROOM was written on the door. The woman opened it and stepped aside so that I could walk in. The small room was air-conditioned to a light chill, bare but for four metal folding chairs and a long wooden table. A small hole in the wall, concealing a camera, pointed toward my chair. The woman carried a thick dossier and a notepad, both held at an angle so I couldn't see the writing. Her name was Janet, and crow's-feet serrated the skin around her eyes and mouth. Her pale foundation makeup collected in those creases and absorbed the fluorescent light of the room.

"You're probably wondering why you're here," she said.

"Yes, I am."

"Why do you think you're here?" She had very pale eyes, with pinprick pupils.

"I have no idea."

Janet cleared her throat and reseated herself, smoothing her suit skirt. "I will begin by explaining what this office does. This is the Special Investigations Branch of the Central Intelligence Agency. By statute, we hold the authority to investigate Agency employees when their behavior raises concerns relevant to national security." She pulled a leaflet of Agency regulations from a dossier she had carried with her into the room and opened it; she thumbed to the middle and pointed with her pen to a subsection highlighted in yellow. She showed me the words she had just used, verbatim.

She continued: "If concern were to arise over an employee's loyalty to the Agency, for example, or substance abuse, or unreported contact with foreigners, the investigation of these allegations would fall under our purview."

I nodded, and felt spiders of anxiety crawling up my back.

"We have sources and informants throughout the Agency," she said. "We have many methods of getting information."

I anchored my hands on the chair so that I wouldn't fidget. The instructors had advised us to do this in our classes on interrogation.

"We have several concerns to discuss today," she said. "At issue are your security clearances. As you are certainly aware, security clearances are granted only to men and women of unquestioned integrity and allegiance to the United States. Lack of loyalty to the United States, inability to protect classified information, or unwillingness to do so would be grounds for their revocation."

She leafed through the booklet and found this stipulation there as well; it too had been yellowed with a highlighter pen; it read exactly as she had said.

"Selena, the Special Investigations Branch has received a report from an informant that you are sympathetic to Jonathan Pollard."

"That's *ludicrous*. Who said that?"

"Our sources are confidential."

"Your sources are *wrong*."

"Can you explain why this has been brought to our attention?"

"Presumably because I'm Jewish."

"I was unaware that you were Jewish. This has nothing to do with that. This is about whether you admire the actions of a convicted traitor."

"No. I don't."

"Could you state, for the record, whether your loyalties lie with the United States?" she asked.

"Yes. *For the record,* my loyalties lie with the United States. Entirely. I believe in the principles upon which the United States was founded. I believe in the Constitution and the Bill of Rights. I am completely loyal to the United States."

Janet took notes on a sheet of yellow legal paper. "What about your loyalty to the Central Intelligence Agency?"

"Yes, I am loyal to this Agency."

She took more notes. I couldn't see what she was writing.

"I have noted for the record that you dispute this allegation against you."

"Good. But be careful to note that the suspicion I may be a Jew is correct."

She looked at me sharply, her face frigid. "Selena, the Special Investigations Branch has received another very serious allegation about you. We've received an allegation that you have deliberately compromised classified information."

Keep still, I told myself. I felt a blush of anger and confusion reddening my face. *Keep your hands on the chair.* A light sweat moistened the small of my back despite the chill of the room.

"That's crazy too. Who the hell is *telling* you this?"

"Our sources are confidential."

"Your sources are *full of shit.*"

Her pale blue eyes iced over and her small pupils shrank until her eyes looked like glassy buttons. "We cannot work together if you use profanity."

"It's *completely* untrue, and it's absurd."

She took more notes, "I have noted for the record that you also dispute the allegation against you."

Acid rose in my throat. "I do not know what the allegations against me *are.*"

Janet cleared her throat again. "We have evidence that you have placed classified information on an unsecured computer system."

For a second, I had no idea what she was talking about.

And then I realized

—*oh, shit*—

that I was in big trouble.

She was talking about the e-mail I had sent to Mom and Lilia.

I had no choice but to admit it immediately: If she knew enough to ask, she knew enough to demand to see my computer, and if I refused, she would have it subpoenaed. I figured this out in seconds. I could only make the situation worse by lying. At the Farm, we had been taught to survive a hostile interrogation: *Admit nothing, deny everything, make counteraccusations.* In training, I never gave anything away, even when they chained me to a tree for days without food and threatened to put a bullet in the base of my skull. That's the difference between training and real life.

I told Janet what I could remember; she took more notes. She said to wait for her while she spoke to her colleagues and left the room. I sat in view of the pinhole eye, my stomach churning. To stay composed, I tried to count backward from a thousand by sevens. The sweat on my back dampened my blouse, sticking me to the chair. Janet returned with her partner, a gray-haired, plump bird of a woman in a calico-print dress. Granny glasses hung from a chain around her soft neck; she had a round, pink face. "I'm Nancy," she said. "I'll be working with Janet on this investigation."

"We need you to bring your computer to us before Wednesday at noon," Janet said.

"What will happen?"

"I can't say anything about that until this investigation is concluded. There are a number of serious issues here."

Nancy spoke; her voice was gentle and sweet. "I understand you've been very cooperative. That's encouraging to us. Your cooperation works in your favor. We do want to *help* you get through this, Selena. We want to help you resolve these issues."

My eyes began to glisten; it was the kindness in her voice. I knew it was a good-cop-bad-cop routine, but it didn't matter. Knowledge of an interrogator's methods is no proof against them.

"You can go home now. We know this has been a rough morning for you," Nancy said. "But I want you to be careful driving back. The weather's awfully bad out there. In fact, I want you to call me when you get back to let me know that you're all right. It's my *Mom* instinct. I worry about these things."

She looked like a Mom, too, as if she might have pictures of her children, in graduation capes and prom dresses, on her desk in a heart-shaped frame. I knew what her display of solicitude meant. I'd been trained to behave the same way. Build rapport with your subject. Give to get. We practiced down at the Farm, with the instructors dressed up as defectors from North Korea and Iraq. *Remember his humanity,* the lecturer said. *This is a disturbed human being. He's scared. He doesn't know if he can trust you. Express concern for his welfare. Offer him a beverage.* I knew what Nancy was doing, and it worked all the same. I wanted her to help me resolve these issues. *Someone in trouble is like a baby duck. He's vulnerable and lost. Baby ducks imprint on the first thing they see. He'll look at you and think: "Are you my mommy?"*

"I appreciate your concern. I'd like to discuss this with my family. Is that permitted?" I asked.

"No." From both of them at once. Emphatically.

"Why not, exactly? Is the fact that you've opened this investigation in itself classified?"

"Yes, of course," said Janet. "You may not discuss this with anyone. That's how an investigation becomes contaminated." She spoke as if my life were a urine sample.

"Can I discuss this with my boyfriend? He's Agency too— he's cleared as high as I am."

"No." Janet answered. "We are very serious about this. You may not discuss the details of this investigation with *anyone.*"

"What *can* I say to him? He'll notice that something's wrong. I live with him."

"You can say that you are under investigation by the Special Investigations Branch but are not at liberty to discuss the details."

I shook their hands and thanked them for their time.

�∞

Nancy was right—it had begun to pour. I lit a cigarette and drew on it so hard that I choked. I looked for my cell phone and burned myself on the lit cigarette. I pulled out past a mist of security guards in yellow rain slickers, then dialed Stan. For a second I was unable to speak the first word.

"What's the matter?" he asked.

"I can't tell you."

"Come home right now. *Drive carefully*."

I crawled through Beltway traffic in the blinding rain. My idiotic confessions to my mother whirled around and around in my mind. *Mom, I missed an entire surveillance team and led them right to our asset.*

Stan was waiting for me downstairs. He rushed to me and grabbed my wrists. "What happened?"

"I can't discuss it." Despite everything, I took a small pleasure in having a secret.

We took the elevator up to the seventh floor; he protected me with his arm as if escorting me from the scene of an accident. I put my bag down on the couch and asked him to pour me a drink.

He poured me a tumbler of scotch and then another. I sat on the floor. Outside, the Beltway sounded like a mosquito's drone. Within two hours I had told him everything.

"Calm down. Deep breaths. Calm down. It's going to be okay," he said. I searched his face for assurance.

"How could they have known?"

"It could have been anything. Maybe the FBI pinged on the word *surveillance* while they were scanning your ISP looking for a terrorist. The NSA has hundreds of analysts whose job is to go through that stuff. The Agency has all sorts of ways of finding things out. It's the most powerful intelligence apparatus in the world. Maybe someone who visited you looked on your computer."

Stan shook his head, and I could feel his disappointment in me and his frustration. I had let him down. I was too sloppy, too careless, too immature. He seemed somehow much older than me now, and formidable. He sat across from me on the floor, lowering himself into my field of vision. He placed one hand on each of my shoulders and looked me directly in the eye, his expression grave. He dipped his chin to magnify his gaze, then squeezed my shoulders like a captain bracing a terrified new recruit for his first descent into the combat zone. "It was a stupid thing to do. Dead stupid. But they're not going to fire you. You were a trainee. You made a mistake. Everyone makes mistakes, and at least you made this mistake in training and not out in the field."

"How should I handle it?" I asked.

"You've got to cooperate with them *completely*. Don't try to cover anything up. The cover-up is what gets you into trouble in this town, not the crime. You need to be absolutely contrite and humble. You need to tell them you fucked up, and you need to take responsibility. You'll be disciplined—they're going to slap you, hard, but you'll get through it."

I asked him how he knew.

"I know this place. What exactly did you put in those letters?"

"I told you—that I'd flunked surveillance. I think I said I'd probably get all my assets killed—"

"Oh, for God's sake. Why didn't you just take out an ad in the paper saying 'My name is Selena M. Keller and I work for the Central Intelligence Agency' while you were at it?"

My eyes filled with tears; he looked at me and sighed. "These things happen around here—it's the CIA. Calm down. You'll get through this. We'll get through this together."

I put my head between my knees. Stan reached out for me; he took my head in his hands and pulled my body against his chest, then folded me in his arms. He stroked my hair gently. "It's gonna be okay, baby. It's gonna be okay."

We both fell silent for a minute. I felt woozy from the scotch, as if all the blood had drained out of my body, leaving nothing but my crumpled skeleton. My stomach was on fire with acid. I took his hand and pressed it against my cheek. "Fuck," I said to no one and nothing. "Fuck. Fuck. Fuck." Feeling ashamed that I had dragged him into this along with me, I said, "Thank you for being here for me."

∞

Why did I write those letters? It's simple: *I just didn't think.* Screwups always say that. "You drank eleven margaritas and then you tried to *run* that dang chain saw?" *I just didn't think.* "You put your hand in the polar-bear cage and tried to *pet* all that fluffy fur?" *I just didn't think.*

There's a special hell reserved for people who do something stupid. Your mind traces and retraces the moment you did what you can never take back, no matter how much you will it. If only you could reverse history by replaying the scene in your mind, over and over again. Each time you give the story a different ending, and each time you realize the ending will *never* change. How many times did Bill Clinton think how it might have been: *No, Monica, absolutely not. I'm a married man, I'm twice your age, and I'm the president of the United States.* How many people before me, how many after, have rued a carelessly whispered word, an indiscreet letter, a confession in a moment of passion or tenderness?

I wasn't alone. *Dr. Deutch—John, if I may?—wherever you are, I know how you feel.* I'd seen the pictures of him in the news, the haunted eyes, the shadows of shame darkening his face. His friends told the press he was destroyed, crushed, humiliated beyond words. His enemies said they always knew the man couldn't be trusted. That hurts more than anything, the gloating of your enemies. *How well I know, Dr. Deutch. How well I know.*

∞

I turned in my computer as they'd told me to. I asked Janet how long it would take to investigate and adjudicate my case. She told me it could be months. Why months? I asked. Because we have to convene committees, interview your classmates, write reports. Over the summer, we take annual leave.

Two days later, everyone received their assignments. Nathan was to go to Istanbul. Jade was slotted for Kinshasa. Mark was going to be wintering in Delhi. Nan was going to Peshawar. It hardly even gave me any pleasure to think that she would probably be dead within a week, either at the hands of Islamic terrorists or from secondhand smoke.

Stan would go to Moscow—the Yankee Stadium of espionage. He was to begin his six-month Russian class immediately.

I was told I would file papers about Canada until further notice.

∞

Canada was wedged between Luxembourg and a broom closet. No one knew where it was, and one woman I asked denied that there was such a place. I came in about twenty minutes late, but nobody seemed to notice. My new supervisor, Bob, nodded his head gently when I introduced myself, as if he wasn't quite sure what I was doing there. He told me he would be glad to have another body around and that he was there to help me grow in my career. "Just hang out here for a few minutes," he said. "We're about to have a staff meeting."

I looked at the books on his wall. *Canada: A Statistical Abstract. The Hidden Waterways of Northern Canada. Oh Canada! Oh Quebec! Requiem for a Divided Country. The Canadian Statesman Speaks.* I remembered the marble cool of the Columbia University library, reading the *Mahabharata,* the calm of the Sanskrit syllables, and I remembered thinking that surely there was more than *this* to life. I thought about that night train to Marrakech, the scent of jasmine stirring the hot desert air. I wanted to die.

Half a dozen Canada staffers assembled in his cramped office. Our supervisor addressed us. Our requirements, he said, had come straight from the cabinet. The secretary of agriculture was in a thoroughgoing lather. The White House was worried about a fresh Canadian parry in the salmon dispute.

Bob was a middle-aged man with a sandy fringe of thinning hair and a slight paunch; he wore a cardigan over his oxford shirt in the manner of Mr. Rogers. The only other seated participant was the desk officer. She was a large woman, very large; when she nodded in agreement with the chief, her chin disappeared into folds of flesh. A wizened grandmother stood directly behind her. "Virginia's our institutional memory," Bob had told me when he introduced me to her. "She's been here since forever." Across from me was the Reports officer. Her face was hidden behind heavy black bangs. She was our Canadian regional specialist, an expert, Bob said, on all things Canadian. She offered a shy half-smile at the compliment. To my left was our Chief of Operations, a gnomelike man with a bushy red beard, pockmarked skin, and a nose that glowed with spider veins. I wasn't sure if I was imagining it, but it seemed to me that he smelled of gin.

"This is going to be an election issue," the chief said. "There are a hundred thousand jobs at stake in Alaska and the Pacific Northwest. We can't afford to drop the ball here. Our customers need some solid reporting on this and they need it *yesterday*." The CIA always called the people who read its intelligence reports its *customers,* as if it were trying to sell them a shoe shine or roof repairs. "Every man in Toronto has to be focused on this. We need at least three developmentals by Labor Day. Is everyone clear?"

I nodded, and wondered if I would still have a job come Labor Day.

∽

Officially, we did not spy on Canada. But desperate times call for desperate measures, and the migratory patterns of the Pacific salmon had changed. Under international law, countries have the exclusive right to fish their own waters; international waters are open to all and sundry. But salmon are strange fish: Coho salmon are spawned in Canadian waters but migrate as adults to warmer American waters. American sockeye do the opposite. Thus the United States–Canada Pacific Salmon Conflict: Which are American fish? Which are Canuck fish? Fish don't come stamped with their country of origin. So who has the right to harvest them? The United States and Canada split the difference in 1985 with a treaty that allowed American fishermen to harvest a certain number of Canadian coho; in exchange the Canadians were permitted to catch some of our sockeye. The quota system worked well enough until, for reasons not fully understood, American salmon, like American draft dodgers, decided they'd had it with swimming to Canada. Suddenly, the Americans had *all* the fish and Canadian fisherman found themselves confronting economic ruin. The Canadians wanted to renegotiate the treaty, but naturally we were hesitant. We were, after all, getting all the fish.

Not long before I'd set up shop in my new cubicle, an enraged mob of Canadian fishermen had trapped the Alaskan ferry *Malaspina* in the port of Prince Rupert. A radio call went out over the Canadian airwaves. "Show these big boys that we're not putting up with their crap!" the organizers urged. Hundreds of fishing boats joined the blockade. The Canadians burned an American flag for the cameras; the outraged passengers on the *Malaspina* condemned the Canadians as terrorists. For three days, the fishermen defied a Canadian court order to free the ship. After a personal plea from Canada's fisheries minister, the *Malaspina* was released, but tensions remained high: The United States Senate approved a resolution allowing the use of force, if necessary, to protect Alaskan ferries. American and Canadian diplomats sequestered themselves in British Columbia, trying to damp the hostilities.

"Selena," Bob said to me after I'd been in the office for a day. "You know who Ted Stevens is?" The name sounded vaguely familiar, but I couldn't place it.

"That's *Senator* Ted Stevens," he said, answering his own question. "From Alaska. Chairman of the Senate Appropriations Committee." He didn't need to elaborate—the committee approved the CIA's budget. If the good people of Alaska didn't have something to show for their investment in the CIA, my supervisor's expression intimated, there would be hell to pay. We needed to know the Canadian negotiators' bottom line: If pressed to the limit, how many salmon would they let us harvest?

I was told to study the case of RAINBOW, a twenty-nine-year-old conservation scientist acting as an adviser to the Canadian negotiating team. RAINBOW grew up in a small fishing village not far from the Fraser River, the great coho-salmon spawning grounds. His father and two older brothers were salmon fishermen. The decline in the coho-salmon catch had brought the family to the brink of bankruptcy. The case officer developing him, Lucius K. ROSENBLATT, was posing as some suit who worked for Chicken of the Sea. He had recently discovered that the RAINBOW family fishing boat was soon to be repossessed. RAINBOW was encouragingly indiscreet and had already provided clues to the Canadians' negotiating strategy. ROSENBLATT had sent us grainy surveillance photos of our developmental, taken as he arrived at their lunch meetings. RAINBOW was thin and drawn; he had a young, pale, earnest face. He was wearing a bulky parka and a tattered knit cap with a tassel. He looked worn. That was encouraging. Happy people don't commit treason.

∽

A week passed with no news, and then another. My supervisor found me one day at my cubicle with my head in my hands. He invited me to come to his office for a chat. I followed him. He had a kettle of water on his desk; he offered me a cup of chamomile tea.

"How are you holding up here?" he asked.

I didn't know whether he knew about the investigation yet.

"Fine, really well, this is a wonderful division. Great people."

He asked me to shut the door. "I know you've been having a little brouhaha with the security folks," he said. "I wanted to talk about that. See how you're really doing."

"They told me I couldn't discuss it with anyone."

"That's okay. We don't need to talk details." Bob squeezed the teabag with his spoon and placed it on his saucer. "But I'd like to share an experience of my own."

He sipped his tea, and little tea beads gathered on his mustache.

"When I came back from my third tour in Latin America, I walked into my office one morning and found the Feds waiting for me. Four of them. Complete surprise."

He paused and put his fingers together in a steeple.

"Congress had gotten wind that an asset we'd used was a torturer. Nasty customer. Now the Feds were investigating the charge. It was me who'd recruited this fellow, three years before. These guys from the FBI barged into my office, three years later, and they were acting like *I* was the torturer. There was no presumption of innocence, no assumption that we were all working *for the same side*. Their arrogance was unbelievable. I said, 'Am I under arrest?' And they said 'We don't know yet.' Worst moment of my life.

"I'd done everything exactly by the books—I ran everything past Legal when I recruited this guy, I got all the right approvals, but suddenly I was in trouble, just out of the blue. My stomach was at my feet. And these guys, they didn't even know how to read one of our cables—they didn't know anything about how we do our jobs, but they were acting like I was a criminal. It was one of the worst experiences of my life."

"What happened?"

"They investigated it for a year, and I was warehoused on the desk like you are now, and I couldn't even tell my wife why. So I sure know what you must be going through."

I nodded my head slowly. I wasn't sure what reply he was expecting.

"I'd wake up every day and feel like a fish caught in the net. The worst part was just not knowing—not knowing what would happen, wondering if I was just some sort of political pawn. Not knowing is a terrible thing. In the end they couldn't find anything to pin on me. But I learned that around here, someone is always watching, no matter what you do. You've always got to think about how it's going to look, how it's going to look to Security, to Congress, on the front page of *The New York Times,* how it's going to look if you get caught, how it's going to look if you don't take the risk because you're afraid of getting caught, but you don't get the intelligence, either."

"What happened to you after the investigation?"

"I learned the lesson, I guess. Everyone learns the lesson around here, sooner or later. A lot of us have been right where you are right now."

"How did you get through it?"

"Jesus helped me. He was my best friend. He'll help you, too."

He took another sip of tea and looked at me with kind, watery eyes.

∞

Every morning when the alarm went off, a wave of anger and anxiety would wash over me as I remembered that I was under investigation. At night I would stare at the ceiling while Stan made soft chuffing noises in his sleep. The thought of Janet reading my personal correspondence infuriated me. All of my sister's letters to me were on the hard drive. There was a memo from my thesis adviser complaining that my analysis of *Manjusri* was derivative, my literature review inadequate, and my grasp of Pali superficial. The thought of Janet reading that bothered me more than if my computer had hidden my most secret sexual fantasies.

I told Stan that it was driving me crazy, the thought of Janet and Nancy shutting the office door and reading that letter from my adviser out loud.

"Yeah? Really? Geez, I guess that would be awful, I mean you *did* win the Crewdson thesis prize and all, in the end. That's really unfair, that they might not realize how good your Pali got." His voice got hard. "Selena, you get sent to Moscow, or Beijing, you will have hidden video cameras in every room of your apartment—including the bathroom. People who do not care about you, people who hate you with a passion, will watch *everything you do*. They'll put a picture of you giving your boyfriend a blow job on their walls and they'll whack off to it. That's what this job is *about*. You'll have no privacy whatsoever. If you can't deal with that, you're in the wrong job."

"But this is having my privacy invaded by my own side."

"Selena. Selena. If you're a spy, privacy has to be about something else. It has to be about what's in here—" He pointed to his head. "Because someone is going to be watching you for the rest of your life. Someone is going to be watching, whatever you do. Our side, their side—it doesn't matter. You need to think about every single action, every expression on your face—not just what it is, but what it would look like to someone else. You need to assume that someone's watching, even when you have no idea how."

July became August, with thunderstorms and polluted, stifling air. Each day was the same as the last: no news, long drives in to work with Stan, the traffic bumper to bumper as we crawled across the concrete overpasses and past strip malls, and endless files about fishing rights to review.

Files, fish, filing, fish, filing, fishing, filing, filed.

I ran into my classmates in the long halls; we said hello to each other politely. I could tell they were puzzled that I was working on Canada, but the bureaucracy works in mysterious ways, and no one was that surprised that I had a bum assignment: Someone had to get them. As far as I knew, the fact that I was under investigation was not yet public knowledge, although it would be, sooner or later.

Lilia called one evening. "Hey, secret sister!" she said brightly. "Depose any democratically elected governments lately?"

"Jesus, Lilia, not on the fucking phone!" I regretted my tone. She couldn't possibly understand. I apologized. "I'm just under some stress at work."

"What's going on? Can you tell me?"

"I can't talk about it. I really can't."

Lilia was quiet on the other end, as if she were very far away and my words had taken a long time to reach her. At last she spoke, her voice subdued: "We're getting a little worried about you. You sound like the Manchurian Candidate or something. Dad is planning an intervention."

"Lilia, please . . . please don't ask me to talk about this. Please. Don't worry. Everything is okay. I promise there's nothing wrong."

CHAPTER 8

I ris had landed on her feet. Within a week of being escorted off CIA property by armed guards, she'd found herself a new job as a marketing strategist for Coca-Cola in Europe. She was supposed to spend a year in Washington learning the bottling business, but eventually, they had promised, she'd be working in the Paris office. She'd found a new apartment in Georgetown. She'd left Brad. She wanted a clean break, she said, and a man who could tell her what he'd done all day at the office.

Iris was partial to a serene tea salon in Georgetown run by a family of Asian immigrants. I joined her at Ching-Ching Cha on a sultry Sunday morning. The room had high ceilings and a skylight. Clay pots and canisters with Chinese lettering decorated the walls; ceiling fans gently stirred the air. The effect was intended, perhaps, to recall an opium den in colonial Burma, although nothing I had ever seen in Burma looked like this. The room felt cool and calm even in high summer. A grave Mongolian met us at the door with a low bow. He showed us to our table, reminding us to remove our shoes before stepping on the bamboo mats. Iris slipped off her gold lamé sandals to reveal her slender feet and immaculately polished toenails. I followed suit.

The Mongolian returned and offered us hand-lettered menus.

After considerable deliberation, we decided to share a pot of Dragon Phoenix Pearl, thus named, the menu explained, because its leaves rose from the hillsides like a dragon and the women who picked it resembled dancing phoenixes next to the dragon's slender body.

The waiter floated away. We were the only customers in the room.

Iris chattered happily about her new job and her expense account. "All gold, baby," she boasted. Brad was making a pest of himself, "calling, calling, calling, like he's on fire and I'm 911." Her sister was getting married. "We're reckoning this is her *first* marriage. He'll be about as useful to a woman as—" She broke off in mid-sentence, suddenly losing interest in her sister's fiancé. "Let's talk about you. Where are they sending you? You know yet?"

I looked at the ground. "I'm on Canada for the moment," I said, hoping that if I said *Canada* in a low enough voice, she'd think I'd said "any country other than Canada." She heard perfectly, unfortunately.

"*Canada?* You've got to be kidding me."

"It's only temporary. Security is trying to clear some things up."

"Uh-oh," she said.

Despite myself, I began to puddle up. I felt self-conscious when the waiter came back with our tea. "Allergies," I said to him. "Ragweed."

The waiter nodded mutely.

"I can't tell you about it," I said. "I would if I could."

"I know," said Iris.

"I would tell you—you know that."

"Of course you would, honey. But if you just want to talk to this old teapot while I sit here and file my nails, I doubt I'd hear a thing."

Iris still had her security clearances, I rationalized. I told the teapot everything. Iris sipped from her cup as I spoke, holding it in both hands. When I finished, she set it gently in its saucer. "Everyone talks to their family about problems at work," she said. "Half the guys there use the fact that they're Agency as a pickup line in bars. It's not like you're the only one. Why you?"

"I got caught."

"But why were they *trying* to catch you?"

"I guess someone said something about me."

Iris inhaled slowly and fixed me with an even gaze.

"Maybe Jade," I said. "She's crazy enough to denounce *herself*."

Iris crossed her hands, extended her forefingers, and put the long digits against her lips.

I continued, "Maybe Nathan. Anyone who had a problem with me."

"Who do you really think did it?" she asked.

"I don't know. I'll never know. Why? Who do you think it was?"

"If I say what I think, will you be angry with me?"

I felt vaguely apprehensive. I wanted to tell her to stop, but I told her to speak her mind.

"You know what I'm going to say, don't you?"

I swiveled my head from side to side.

"I'd say it was your man."

I must have looked shocked, because Iris put her hand on mine. Her skin was soft. "My God, why would you say something like that?" I said. "He wants to marry me, for the love of God."

Iris took a shallow breath and exhaled audibly. "Selena, you come from a *nice* kind of folk—folk who go to the symphony. Where you come from, when a woman steps out on her man, y'all visit Lionel Humberdolt, Esquire, and then you divvy up the house and the furniture and the kids, and you still go to your Passover seder together so no one gets too sad. You're an awful smart girl and I love you, but you don't know folks. My uncle put a knife in my aunt's thigh when he thought she was messing on him, then dragged her around the house by her hair, hollering, 'You bad bitch, I'll put you down.' That's the kind of man Stan is, deep down, under all the white. When he came back from Headquarters that time, he was saying to himself, 'Kirk and that girl made a fool of me.' Next thing you know, Kirk's out of a job, your best friend's out of a job, and you've been reported to security. I'd say Stan ain't the kind of man who lets a woman make a fool of him."

I took my hand away from hers. "Iris, Stan *loves* me."

"Love's not always a beautiful thing."

We sat silently under the spinning ceiling fans. I could feel my heart beating in all my veins, behind my knees, in my shoulders, in my belly. After a minute, Iris's cell phone rang; she answered it and in a flirtatious voice made a dinner date with someone named Max. She told him he was sweet as sugar and hung up.

ROSENBLATT had diligently gathered background information—biodata, as we called it—about RAINBOW. His file was growing thick with reports from their lunch meetings. They had taken a snowboarding trip together, and now that the weather was fine, RAINBOW had accompanied our case officer on a series of weekend fly-fishing expeditions.

I had been asked by my supervisor to study the RAINBOW file and draft a cable with an appropriate recruitment scenario. ROSENBLATT believed RAINBOW was nearly ripe.

I studied RAINBOW's Personal Record Questionnaires. He had been born in Finn Slough, population 352, a fishing village named for the Finnish immigrants who had settled the town in the late nineteenth century. The Slough, on the banks of the whimsically named Lulu Island, lay on the north arm of the Fraser River. RAINBOW's dour great-grandfather, who had immigrated to Canada after taking leave from an Astoria coal mine in Washington, had taken in the island, with its lush green meadows and melancholy northern skies, and pronounced the place a New Finland—a promised land. The town's main road still bore the RAINBOW family name. The miner's four diligent sons had become commercial fishermen, their seventeen children had followed suit, and indeed every member of RAINBOW's extended family earned a livelihood from the water. RAINBOW had grown up in the floating wooden scow house his grandfather built. His childhood had been organized by the rise and fall of the Fraser's tidal waters. In the summer he caught frogs and tended the family's garden and potato fields; in the winter, he attended the modest local public school.

RAINBOW was, to his family's surprise, unusually good with numbers and figures. When his teacher proposed that he attend the University of British Columbia, his parents and older brothers mortgaged the family fishing boat—the *Mikko Hinhalla,* named after his great-grandfather—to make it possible. RAINBOW was the first member of his family (and one of the first residents of the Slough) ever to receive a university degree.

He had studied fish conservation at the university, graduating with a respectable 3.6 grade-point average. There, he had become active in environmental politics. Passionate about preserving the river that had sustained his family's way of life for generations, he had accepted an internship with the Canadian Ministry of Fisheries after his graduation, where he discharged his duties so effectively that he was offered a permanent post. Although he loved his work, he found Toronto enormous, impersonal, alienating. He was deeply shy with women, and C/O ROSENBLATT perceived in him a terrible loneliness. When

C/O ROSENBLATT invited him on weekend excursions to the countryside, RAINBOW accepted gratefully. The two men drank beer and swapped fish tales. As they cast their lures into the river, RAINBOW told C/O ROSENBLATT about the difficulties his family faced because of the decline in the salmon stock. His brothers, all of whom had small children to feed, had fallen on hard times. RAINBOW recalled that when he was growing up, it hadn't been unusual for his father to catch as many as five hundred fish in a day. His brothers were lucky now to come home with half that. RAINBOW's terrible fear was that the bank would repossess the *Mikko Hinhalla*. Since the boat had been mortgaged to pay for his education, the prospect filled him not only with anxiety but with agonizing guilt.

Clearly, I wrote in the cable, RAINBOW had ample economic motivation to commit espionage. C/O ROSENBLATT had done an excellent job in establishing rapport with the target and engendering his trust. There was no way on earth RAINBOW would give us the information we wanted if he knew it would be used to bolster the U.S. trade negotiators' position, but RO-SENBLATT was pretending to be an executive with Chicken of the Sea, which gave him the perfect pretext for talking fish.

I sketched out the scenario: C/O ROSENBLATT should tell RAINBOW that he would like him to write a series of confidential reports about Canadian salmon policy, with special reference to the U.S.–Canada salmon dispute. He would pay him $5,000 U.S. for each report, "but only if it really adds value, Dirk. My bosses won't pay for anything they can read in the papers. They need to be a step ahead of the competition—they need to know what's going down *before* the guys at Bumble Bee do." To make the offer still more attractive, C/O ROSEN-BLATT could tell RAINBOW that his company was studying plans to open several new canneries in British Columbia, near RAINBOW's hometown. "It could mean tens of thousands of new jobs for the folks back there, but they won't have the confidence to do it unless they really feel like they have a handle on this salmon situation. They can't afford to be caught short, you know what I mean?" C/O ROSENBLATT, I added, should immediately ask RAINBOW to sign a confidentiality agreement. "This is pretty much industry standard," he should say, motioning at the contract that would swear RAINBOW to eternal secrecy. "We've got to keep our backsides covered. Salmon's a ruthless business, and those guys at Bumble Bee are real sharks."

I wondered what objections RAINBOW might offer. What if he said he thought it was inappropriate to pass along government secrets? "Dirk, I love the way you're still so idealistic," C/O ROSENBLATT might say, "but let's face it—lecture fees and consulting, that's how everyone in government pays the bills. They can't really expect you to live on what they're paying you. They know you have to survive. You know, Norman Schwarzkopf gets $50,000 per *lecture*. It's just the way the world works these days." I added that he should tell RAINBOW how glad he was to be able to help him out. "I consider you a personal friend, Dirk. I hate the thought of your brothers having to sell that boat—I mean, how many years has that been in the family? It's not right to let that go. It's just not right." I imagined him lowering his voice conspiratorially and placing a manly hand on RAINBOW's shoulder. "I'll level with you, Dirk—I had to pull a lot of strings to get this deal for you. Frankly, they wanted someone with a bigger name, and they thought five thou was pretty steep. But I told 'em, 'I have confidence in Dirk. He knows salmon better than anyone else alive, and he's got a work ethic like you wouldn't believe. He'll pull through for us. I'll stake my job on it.'"

I finished the cable and sent it to Bob for approval. He liked it. "Great stuff. Send it out," he said. "Kudos."

∽

Iris hadn't been quite right about the folk I grew up with. Admittedly, I had seen the inside of a symphony hall. But my family sure didn't go to Passover seders together. My mother and father hadn't had a civil conversation since I was eleven. One evening, when I was in the sixth grade, the phone rang at our house. My mother answered. She turned pale when she heard the voice on the other end. She said, "How *dare* you!" then slammed the phone back on its cradle. Then she grabbed my father's key ring and went outside where his taxicab was parked on the street. She put on the seat belt, put the key in the ignition, put the car into drive, and stepped on the accelerator, smashing the car into the brick wall of our two-story brownstone. Then she backed up and did it again. Then again. And again. The front of the taxi was crumpled like an accordion. When she came back into the house, her face was bloody from slamming into the steering wheel. The cab was destroyed, and my father never spent another night under our roof.

So I did know something about folks. But Iris was just plumb loco about Stan. She didn't know Stan like I knew Stan. She didn't *like* Stan like I liked Stan. I would know if what she said were true. I would sense it. There was no way I could share a bed with Stan without feeling something like that. That's not the kind of secret lovers can hide.

Two days after my conversation with Iris, Stan's mother called. I told her he was out picking up the dry cleaning. Stan's mom had a broad Midwestern accent; she sounded like she baked Toll House cookies and drove car pool. She asked me how Stan was doing, and when I told her he seemed just great, she admitted that she'd been worried about him—the last time she had spoken to him, he'd told her he was under a lot of stress at the office. "I told him it's not a race to make partner, we're proud of him no matter what," she said. "Are they still taking depositions? Did they get the case relocated? He was so worried about that judge up in New York." She sighed proudly. I told her the deposition phase had been wrapped up, but there was no decision yet on the jurisdiction. She asked if Stan was taking time to eat properly. I told her Stan was eating just fine.

That night, I dreamt it was the last week of high school. Finals were over; the next day was the senior-class picnic. I saw Adam Goldenberg in the hall outside the machine shop. He was headed to Harvard in the fall. He was pleased with himself. Lee Cheng was going to Swarthmore. Jennifer Stoloff was taking a year off to work on a kibbutz, then returning to study at NYU. An enormous banner fluttered over the south staircase: CONGRATULATIONS SENIORS!

My homeroom teacher passed me a note from the guidance counselor. I was to see him *immediately*. I knew this couldn't be good news. I went to his office. Mr. Wasserman was abrupt. "Selena," he said, "I can't seem to find on file any record of your having taken, much less passed, Russian. Russian is a graduation requirement, you know."

"But—"

Stan's enormous face loomed over the desk at me. "You *do* speak Russian, don't you, Selenuschka?"

I realized that I had never once attended my Russian class. What had I been thinking? Maybe I could bluff it out? *"Da,"* I replied. *"Da, da."*

Stan began yelling at me in voluble Russian. He pounded his shoe on the table. I couldn't understand a word but somehow knew exactly what he was saying: *How could you do this to me? We will bury you!*

Stan gently shook me awake. "It's okay," he whispered. "You were having a bad dream. You were whimpering." He held me tight. "Go back to sleep. Everything's okay." He ruffled my hair and kept murmuring. "You're going to dream about fat little puppies who tug on your shoelaces. I'm a puppy and you're a puppy, and we're all curled up in a big feather bed and we're happy 'cause we've chewed up all those yummy shoes . . ." He kept whispering this tender nonsense, and I fell back asleep, dreaming the dream he had told me to dream.

∞

In early September, in honor of the one hundred eighty-eighth anniversary of the Battle of Borodino, Stan decided to prepare a Russian feast. His Russian teacher had lent him an antique illuminated cookbook entitled *Cuisine of the Czars.* He carefully sliced the eggs and garlic for the *salat iz yaits* and folded them with sour cream and scallions. For the *forshmak,* he soaked herring in milk, then chopped it finely and fried it in butter with caramelized onions, adding eggs and potatoes and pepper and then turning the mixture into a casserole. As it baked, he applied himself to fixing a lamb and raisin *plov,* spiced with cinnamon and saffron and studded with plump dates. Exotic aromas filled the apartment. For dessert, he made *Gourevskaya kasha,* a concoction of semolina, cream, nuts, and sugared apricots. He told me that he had searched in vain for kvass, the fermented beverage that would ordinarily accompany such a meal, but having failed to find it, served the meal with a 1998 Bordeaux.

The Special Investigations Branch had sent me an e-mail that morning. Janet had told me to describe my relationship with Paolo, who lived with my sister and was the father of her children. The message asked if he was a U.S. citizen. At dinner, I asked Stan why they cared.

"They have to figure that if he's living with Lilia, everything on her computer's been compromised to him, too. Way bigger deal if a foreign national had access to the information," he said, matter-of-factly. He speared a largish hunk of lamb and popped it into his mouth.

As we did the dishes after dinner, I asked him.

"Stan?"

"Da!" Stan had taken to replying to me in Russian. He took his Russian class very seriously. He played his Russian tapes in the bathroom when he showered in the morning and on the tape deck as we drove to work. I was beginning to know the tapes by heart myself. *Vam vyplachivayem vysokuyu tsendu dlya tekhnicheskikh usloviy modifikatsiy v esminets Sovremmenovo klassa,* the speaker enjoined over and over. *Vam vyplachivayem vysokuyu tsendu dlya tekhnicheskikh usloviy modifikatsiy v esminets Sovremmenovo klassa,* Stan repeated in his heavy American accent. His Russian teacher was thrilled with his progress, pronouncing him the best pupil he'd ever had.

"Stan, you didn't do it, did you?"

"Do what, my little Selenuschka?"

"Turn me in. To Security."

"Yup!" he said cheerfully, wiping the good china with a dishcloth.

"Seriously, Stan. Did you?"

"You bet. Also told them about the unmarked bills you keep in the broom closet—thought that you could slip that one past me?—and that meeting in Mexico City with Igor, and those weird phone calls we get from that Chinese guy who wants to know whether the dry cleaner is careful with silk, and—"

"I'm sorry, I'm so sorry, but I'm serious. I need to know."

"Selena," he said, putting down the dish towel and looking directly at me. "Listen. *I want you to be the mother of my children.* Can you seriously imagine that I would sneak off behind your back, go to Security, and deliberately harm you? Can you seriously imagine that I would jeopardize our future together? Can you seriously imagine that I would spend the evening cooking you a meal fit for Catherine the Great, all the while watching you twist in the wind? Is that consistent with anything you know about me? Is that consistent with how I treat you? Is that fair?"

I searched his face. His expression was completely convincing and honest.

But then, like all of us, he was a trained professional liar.

∞

A week later, the Cover division called me at my desk. I had received a piece of mail—my first ever—at my Department of Agriculture address. They told me I could pick it up at my convenience. I went downstairs right away. It was a postcard with a picture of the kind of beach you see on a postcard: white sand, turquoise sea, single palm tree, beach umbrella. It was postmarked Mexico, but there was no return address. On the back was written: "Life is better on the other side. Love, Paul."

I felt a sharper pang than I would have expected after all that time. I stared at the postcard, turning it over and over as I wandered back through the long, gray halls to my office. I imagined Paul, looking wistful as hell, on a lonely stretch of the Pacific, sanding the barnacles off the hull of his sailboat, the *Annette*. In my mind's eye, he was wearing a tattered pair of Levi's, no shoes or shirt, and a terrific tan.

I thumbtacked the postcard to the wall of my new cubicle, right above an elaborate list of instructions that Mary Jane, the Canada desk officer, had left for me when she went away on medical leave: I was to water her spider fern twice weekly, bring in doughnuts for the Friday staff meeting, make sure the coffeepot was unplugged at the end of the day (she had underlined this twice in red ink), and call maintenance about her defective window blind, which remained sullenly frozen at half-mast. "Good luck!" she signed off. She had drawn a smiley face underneath.

Still staring at Paul's card, I sat down and waited for my computer to boot up. The computer groaned; a little choo-choo train chugged across the screen for several minutes. At last I was invited to enter my secure password. A warning flashed across the screen: By using the computer, I was consenting to being monitored; my every keystroke would be logged.

I called up the latest cable from Toronto. The subject line was RECRUITMENT OF RAINBOW. ROSENBLATT's missive was rapturous, even by CIA standards. C/O ROSENBLATT had taken RAINBOW to Jumping Caribou Lake, about 250 miles north of Toronto, for a weekend of fly-fishing. He had left nothing to chance, packing a cooler of Pabst Blue Ribbon, sharp Cheddar cheese, and dried venison. "I brought something for you," C/O ROSENBLATT said when they unloaded the trunk of his Isuzu four-by-four. He pulled out a Battenkill fly-fishing reel and handed it to RAINBOW. "The company gave it to me as a Christmas bonus, but I already have two, so I thought you'd like it."

RAINBOW was delighted. "Are you sure?" he said, fingering the reel's frame. "Wouldn't you rather give it to one of your kids?"

"I can't get my kids to come fishing with me for love or money," said C/O ROSENBLATT. "Let's give it a whirl."

RAINBOW gave him pointers on tying his flies to the tippet, teaching him to hold the fly up to a pale, single-colored background. C/O ROSENBLATT admired his skill. They fished in manly silence for a while, wading through the gentle rapids and taking in lungfuls of loamy northern air. There wasn't another soul in sight. In the distance, the indigo of the water shaded into a cerulean sky, and the air was piney. RAINBOW caught half a dozen fat trout before lunchtime, and C/O ROSENBLATT caught three more—big ones, too.

Shortly after dusk, the men built a campfire and cleaned their fish. C/O ROSENBLATT began plying RAINBOW with beer and then broke out the Jack Daniel's. The fresh air and sunlight had left them tired and contented.

After dinner, C/O ROSENBLATT asked RAINBOW how things were going back home in the Slough.

RAINBOW looked pained. "Not good," he said. "Not good. I don't know how they're going to make it. One of my nephews just broke his arm when he fell off a jungle gym, and he's going to need physical therapy—and it's not covered by Medicare. I don't know what they're going to do."

C/O ROSENBLATT leaned in. "Dirk, I've got some great news for you. Wanted to save it for a moment like this, 'cause this is gonna knock your socks off. I just got permission from my managing director to offer you a little consulting job. I told them that you were the person we needed. We need someone with insight into what's going on in that whole salmon mess—someone who knows what the government is up to and where this whole thing is going to go. If you can write a thirty-page report for us, say, once a month, I can get you a cool five thousand per, if the information is good."

RAINBOW was so stunned he nearly spilled his Jack Daniel's.

∞

Exactly forty-eight hours after I received Paul's postcard, Janet called me at my desk. She told me to report to the Special Investigations Branch at two. She didn't say why.

I arrived on time. The receptionist ushered me into the interview room, opening the door wide, as if not wanting to get too close to me. She left me alone in the bare room. I sat on the metal folding chair, unsure whether to face the door or the small camera on the wall. I decided to face the camera. I crossed my legs and uncrossed them. I looked at my watch, and wondered how long Janet would make me wait. I rummaged through my purse, found some aspirin, and swallowed the tablets dry. I decided to sit with my back to the camera.

This, I thought, is how the chimps must feel when the Bad Man approaches their cage, brandishing the electric paddles.

Twenty-three minutes—that's how long it took for Janet to arrive. The door opened slightly. I rose halfway from my chair so I would be standing when she walked in, but the door remained where it was. I heard Janet's voice in the hallway asking someone to schedule Peterman for four-thirty, and I heard a male voice reply, "*That'll* be fun." The door opened fully and Janet backed into the room. I stood up all the way and began to offer her my hand when I saw that her right wrist and hand were in a plaster cast. I was unsure what do. She offered me her left hand, which I held clumsily with my right. I let go of her hand and sat down. Janet sat down as if her whole body, not just her hand, were fragile.

I hadn't seen Janet since the investigation began, almost four months ago. In my dreams she had been athletic, chasing me down on foot as I tried to flee. But she was older than I remembered her, and she looked tired.

"Thank you for coming by," she said.

"Thank you for having me," I replied. I wondered how she had managed to pull her wrist through the sleeve of her suit.

Janet cleared her throat. She pulled a pen out of her purse with her left hand and offered it to her crippled right hand. The right hand accepted it awkwardly.

She said, "I have conducted a careful audit of the information on your computer."

"I won the Crewdson thesis prize, you know."

Janet tilted her head slightly. "I'm sorry?" she asked. I waved the comment off. "Our investigative team has concluded that you have committed security violations. I am sure that this comes as no surprise to you. I have not yet formed a recommendation to offer the adjudication committee, and this investigation will be continuing."

I felt relieved and disappointed at once. It was as if my doctor had informed me that my disease was not, thank God, terminal—but my excruciating symptoms were incurable.

"Your case is more complicated than we expected. At this stage, your continued cooperation would be appreciated. There are certain evidentiary issues outstanding which we need to resolve."

"It's the *Dhammapada,* isn't it?"

Janet tilted her head again.

"It's my field notes on the *Dhammapada.* They're not really meant for a lay reader. I didn't bother to translate the source materials. Janet, I'd love to help you, but Pali took me almost four years to get the hang of. There's just no substitute for time and work. Pali's not only an inflected language, but highly metaphorical—it's a whole other way of thinking—"

She held up her good hand to silence me. "Selena, I don't have time for this. Believe it or not, I'm your new best friend." She fixed me with a long, unblinking stare. I wondered how long it had been since she'd been someone's best friend.

"Of course I'll cooperate."

"Good. As you know, a case officer is entrusted with truly extraordinary responsibilities. Out in the field, a case officer makes decisions—critical decisions—that will affect the security of every American. We must be confident that case officers are capable of assuming that responsibility." Her speech was measured and slow, as if she were narrating the introduction to a television drama. She continued, "I believe you might have information relevant to other investigations. If you share it with me, that cooperation will work in your favor."

"I'm not sure I can help you, but I'll work with you in any way I can."

"Thank you."

Janet tried to open the manila folder but couldn't. The thumb and forefinger of her right hand didn't touch, and she had no way to hold it while unhinging the clasp. After struggling for a few seconds, she handed the whole thing to me. I opened it and pulled out two pieces of paper. They were photocopies of the postcard Paul had sent me, both front and back. "Do you recognize this document?" she asked.

"Of course I recognize it. It's addressed to *me*."

"Is this the same Paul who resigned from your class of trainees?"

"I presume."

"We understand that you and Paul had an intimate relationship. Is this correct?"

"Yes."

"Do you have any idea what he meant in saying that it was *better on the other side*?"

"He meant that it was better not to work for *this* goddamned place."

"Have you had any other contact with Paul?"

"None."

"Do you know where he is right now?"

"No."

"Did Paul ever say anything to you that might indicate a counterintelligence concern?"

"No."

"Did he exhibit mood swings?"

"No."

"Did he have any unusual spending patterns?"

"I have no idea."

"Did he ask questions about classified information to which you had access?"

"Never."

"Thank you." Janet wrote a few words on her legal pad and winced. She stopped writing.

"Do you need me for anything else?" I asked.

"Yes. We understand that you live with another case officer from your class."

"Yes. I've had intimate relations with him, too."

"Can you tell us whether Stan has ever said anything to you that might indicate a counterintelligence—"

"Oh for God's sake!" I exploded. "Stan wants to be the *president of the United States.* His grandfather fought at Okinawa and lost his leg below the knee! The pitcher, the catcher, and the first baseman never came home, and he raises the flag outside the schoolyard every morning even if it's a thousand degrees below zero! *What are you guys after?"*

"Selena, if I were you," she said slowly, "I wouldn't worry too much about defending Stan. I'd say you don't owe him any—"

I'll always wonder how she meant to finish that sentence. But she stopped herself and said, "I know it's difficult to be asked questions like this about someone you care for. I can't tell you the reason we're asking this, because it would—"

"—contaminate your investigation."

"That's right. But I do want to assure you that we wouldn't be asking unless we had a good reason. Please remember we're in a tough business here. It's not paranoia to believe that people who wish harm to the United States would like nothing more than to have access to the things you and Paul and Stan know, or to believe that members of this Agency do not always act in accordance with the laws of our democratically elected government. We *all* have to put what's best for America ahead of our personal feelings. No one likes to be scrutinized the way we are here. But we can't afford to be naïve. Something you know—even something very small—could be the missing piece in a puzzle."

We looked at each other, and I looked at the photocopy of my postcard. At last I said, "I love my country as much as you do. Quite possibly more. But I know nothing, and I do mean *nothing,* that could help your investigation—or that would help you get yourself promoted by destroying yet another career for no good reason. I have nothing else to say."

Janet met my stare evenly. "Take some time to think it over. Maybe you'll remember something. Call us if you think there's something we ought to know. Remember that cooperation will work in your favor."

I handed Janet the manila envelope and the photocopies of Paul's postcard. When I left the room, she was still trying to put the evidence back where it belonged.

∞

I was a trained professional spy. My job—my métier, my calling, now my life's work—was to ferret out secrets. All my life, I had been good at it, better than I'd ever been at Sanskrit. My babysitter's diary had been thoroughly penetrated, numerous times. I had known all about my parents' divorce proceedings, known much more than they had told me, because while my mother was at work, I had systematically perused the court documents that she kept in the small filing cabinet in her bedroom. In college, I'd known that my Shakespeare professor slept with his graduate students, both male and female. I also knew that my introductory Sanskrit professor would not be getting tenure—and I knew it long before he did. I had sublet an apartment in New York for a summer while I was in graduate school from a couple who taught in the Department of English. They were vacationing in Tuscany. By the end of the summer, I knew that she was trying to have a baby (letter, desk drawer), that he was carrying almost two years' salary in credit-card debt (Excel spreadsheet, computer), and that *someone* needed a little discipline (whip, bottom of the closet, box marked TAXES, 1993–1995). In my little village in India, I knew who didn't have enough money to marry off his daughters, and I knew who was beating his wife. I squatted on my heels with the high-caste women and learned which men were impotent. I had always thought of myself as *curious*.

But I had lost a lot of my curiosity since my first day at CIA Headquarters. The knowledge that it was a felony to root out the wrong secrets had a chilling effect. I still followed my classmates' gossip with avid interest, but it never occurred to me to risk jail in order to find out the conclusion of the PINEAPPLE drama. Did the CIA sell crack in the ghetto? I didn't have a need to know, and ten years in a federal penitentiary marked the limits of my curiosity. How did we topple the Allende government? Beats me. I wasn't curious enough. I wondered if Stan had betrayed me, but I told myself I wasn't curious enough to find out. I remembered my mother searching through my father's wallet, looking for motel receipts. I didn't want to be like her.

But I also didn't want to be a fool.

That night, when Stan asked me how my day was, I began telling him about my interview with Janet. "I think she's gone nuts," I said. When I told him who the postcard was from and what it said, he stiffened.

"You didn't tell me you got a postcard from him."

"I didn't?"

"Does he write often?"

"Nope. First time I heard from him since he resigned."

"Do you still think about him?"

"Stan, for God's sake—isn't it bad enough that I have to explain my personal correspondence to Janet?"

"Have you been writing to *him*?"

"Christ. There wasn't even a return address. What's the *matter* with you?"

"Janet was on a fishing trip. Don't sweat it. Tell me about the rest of your day."

I decided not to tell him anything else about Janet's line of questioning. After all, I didn't want to contaminate the investigation.

If Stan had betrayed me—this was just an academic exercise—who would know? Janet and Nancy, to be sure. Janet looked lonely, and I pictured inviting her to a girls' night out, maybe at the Toledo Lounge in Adams Morgan, where we'd drink cosmopolitans and chatter. I imagined giving her tips on makeup and dating. *Janet,* I'd say, *just between us girls, should I be looking for a new boyfriend?*

I didn't think it would work.

Maybe my supervisor had access to my security dossier. What did I know about Bob? He liked me, didn't he? Perhaps Christ could help me through some difficult times. I tried to imagine how it would play out. Knocking gently on his door. *Bob, I really need your advice. This whole experience has left me feeling so empty inside.* I saw myself on my knees asking the Lord Jesus to save my ass, hustled off to the Agency's Christian prayer group, baptized in the Potomac. *And now that I've renounced Satan, Bob, there's one small thing I'd like you to do for Jesus. The Lord wants me to know what's in my security file.*

No, I knew in my heart that wouldn't work either. And I just wasn't curious enough.

. . .

Three days later, I found Stan at the cafeteria. I had told him that I wouldn't have time for lunch, but I had finished my morning cables early and decided to surprise him. On his tray was a Philly cheesesteak, accompanied by french fries, a tall Coke, and a slice of Boston cream pie. Whenever we had lunch together, he ate a green salad with fat-free vinaigrette.

"So this is what you do when I'm not around," I said. "I guess the dieting is getting a little old."

"Talk to me about it when you quit smoking, kiddo," he said.

"Stan, I just meant that you were looking great."

"I know *just* what you meant."

"Want to share my salad?" I asked. I was horrified at the thought of Stan eating that pie.

Stan looked at me like he was protecting his young. "I lost weight because I love you, but don't tell me what to eat," he said in a low, angry voice.

"I'm not, Stan." I said. "Cool down." I pretended to be offended, but a part of me liked the way he wouldn't let me push him around.

And another part of me wondered what kind of man has so much anger in his voice over a slice of Boston cream pie.

⟁

Brad, Iris's ex-boyfriend, was a security officer in the Central Eurasia Division. Stan now belonged to the Central Eurasia Division. Security officers might have access to security files. Brad had a weak spot—Iris—and I suspected I could exploit it. Iris had told me that Brad was making a nuisance of himself, calling her late at night, pleading for another chance.

I am not doing this, I told myself sternly. *No. That would be completely beneath me. I have my pride.*

I just wasn't curious enough.

. . . .

Stan asked me if I had heard anything from Janet or Nancy.

"How do you know about Nancy?"

"You told me—she's like a mom. Selena, stop this."

I couldn't remember what I had told him.

I got curious enough.

CHAPTER 9

~~~

D own on the Farm, recruitments had been telescoped. We'd go from first handshake to first substation wiring diagram in a matter of hours. The instructor would mumble, "Son's dying, pension wiped out in a pyramid scheme, they don't appreciate me at the office," we'd wink, he'd wink, we'd propose, he'd accept, and *voilà*. But in the field, they told us, it wasn't like that. In the field, patience was the key. Traitors must trust their handlers, and trust takes time. It's not as if we would have diplomas on the walls of our plush, professional offices testifying that we'd graduated cum laude from the Harvard Espionage School and were certified by the American Tradecraft Association. My diploma from the Farm was classified and stored in a secure facility. Nobody finds a handler by word of mouth. *Abdul, you must see my man about that dirty-bomb plot. He is a real artist with dirty bombs. I'd trust him with my life.* The Chinese were known to cultivate developmentals for more than a decade, although this Confucian forbearance was regarded among CIA officers as wholly unsporting. Stan was aiming for eight recruitments in his six years in the field. That was hugely ambitious. But I didn't really understand what my instructors had been telling us about patience until I spent two weeks listening to

Brad talk about his achy-breaky heart. *Man* were they ever right. There is nothing so dull as a man with a broken heart—except, perhaps, a woman with one.

∞

The door to Brad's tiny, windowless office was open. He was sitting at his desk, staring intently at his computer screen. He was a good-looking man, with thick sandy hair and blue eyes. His jaw was impossibly square; he had a broad, muscular carriage. He was the kind of guy who has to stoop to get through doors and complains bitterly about the size of the seats in economy class.

"Brad!" I said brightly, knocking on the open door.

He whipped around. I had never been in his office before, and he seemed surprised to see me. "Selena!" he said. "Long time no see. What brings you to my neck of the woods?"

I had prepared a plausible story. "Language cards," I said. "We're doing a review of embassy requirements and it looks like we haven't updated them in years. I need Kazakh, Uzbek, Ukrainian, Turkmen—"

"Don't those come from the sixth floor?"

I rolled my eyes. "Yeah, that's what they told me, too. But the woman up there told me that FBIS handles them now, and then the FBIS guy said he'd sent them to the regional security officers. You got 'em?" I sat down uninvited on one of the plastic chairs in front of his desk. A stack of files rested on the other chair.

"I don't *think* so . . ." He opened up the cabinet against the wall; papers fluttered out and fell to the floor.

"Take your time, Brad. How've you been lately?" I hadn't seen him since Iris broke up with him. I looked him in the eye. "Getting by?"

"Oh, you know. Hangin' in there . . . looking forward to Friday."

I needed a way to get time on target, as they said down on the Farm. I tried to remember what Iris had told me about his tastes. He liked jazz. I couldn't ask him to go to a jazz concert, though. Too much like a date. Did he collect stamps? Shoot birds? God, I hoped he didn't shoot birds. "Got anything interesting going for the weekend? Big plans?"

"Oh no, just hanging out. Chilling. Maybe play some soccer on Saturday morning, barbecue on Sunday at my cousin's place."

"Man, I haven't played soccer since I was a kid. Where do you play? You part of a team?"

"Just the interagency thing." I had seen the notices on the bulletin boards, but I hadn't paid much attention. The tournament was a team-building exercise for the Intelligence Community. The first game was CIA versus FBI. NSA and State and DoD were supposed to get in the act. Some GS-11 expert on policy coordination had probably dreamt the thing up to impress her promotion panel and then spent a year organizing it. *Oh God,* I thought. *Couldn't it have been birds?*

"That sounds like a hoot!" I said. "Do you think it's too late to sign up?"

∞

The soccer tournament had one redeeming virtue, I supposed. I couldn't imagine Stan would want to come. I brought it up with him on the drive home. We were listening, as usual, to his Russian tapes. "You know that interagency soccer thing?"

Stan paused the tape player.

"The thing with State and DoD? Yeah, why?"

"I was thinking I might go."

"To a soccer game? Against those striped-pants ninnies at State?"

"Fresh air. Exercise. Some people actually like that. When's the last time you played soccer?"

"Sixth grade. Haven't missed it since."

"You want to give it a try?"

"*Nyet.* I'd rather eat nails."

I pressed play on the stereo. I had thought that Stan was going to be more suspicious, and was vaguely disappointed that he wasn't.

∞

I arrived at the soccer field a few minutes early. It was a clear morning and the leaves were just starting to turn. A lot of parents had woken up and decided it was just too beautiful outdoors to watch cartoons. A lot of kids seemed unhappy about that decision. There were young mothers by the jungle gym, urging their kids to share the slide and for Pete's sake stop biting their sisters. Awkward fathers pushed strollers and carried diaper bags; they doled out bottles of apple juice. A pair of identical golden retrievers raced madly across the field to greet a beagle. An elderly Asian woman practiced a graceless but enthusiastic species of Tai Chi.

Brad was already there, stretching out and running in place on the spongy grass. The soccer pitch was dotted with big men in gray jerseys running synchronized wind sprints. The jerseys said FBI: WE KICK BALLS! and depicted an enormous G-man in a double-breasted suit towering over a terrified soccer ball. The ball sprouted little hands, with which it brandished a tommy gun. On the sign-up form, CIA employees had been instructed to wear blue T-shirts sans Agency insignia. I was wearing my light-blue COLUMBIA UNIVERSITY DEPARTMENT OF SANSKRIT T-shirt. I was feeling pretty sporty.

"Brad!" I called, and walked in his direction.

"You made it," Brad said with a smile. For a big man, he was surprisingly flexible, touching his toes and holding them, then leaning far back into the air to limber his spine.

"Wouldn't have missed it for the world."

Brad was about to say something, but before he could get the words out, a wiry, silver-haired man in knee-high socks ran by, slapped Brad on the butt, and shouted at us: "Time to huddle up, big guy. Let's huddle up!" He reminded me of a sheep dog rounding up strays. The wiry man loped off, and Brad and I followed him to a circle of blue jerseys that had formed on the edge of the field.

The soccer tournament was the kind of event that drew out the Agency lifers. I was the only representative, as far as I could tell, of the Clandestine Service. *These* were the kind of people who, when asked where they worked, *could* say, "the CIA." The man who had summoned us to the circle was the team captain. His introduced himself as Clive and said that he worked in facilities management. "I'm the fella who keeps you guys warm in the winter, cool in the summer." He chuckled at his joke, and we chuckled back.

Clive lined up a soccer ball in front of himself and kicked it across the circle to a tall woman wearing a T-shirt that read ARLINGTON VOLUNTEER FIRE DEPARTMENT. She stopped the ball with the side of her foot and said that she was a geographer; she kicked the ball to a stout man, who introduced himself as a bookbinder. The ball went around the circle: There was a psychiatrist who looked like a reptile, and two human resource consultants; there were a half-dozen men from packing and shipping—they had evidently come as a group—and a woman just shy of middle age who translated sign language. A cost estimator kicked the ball high in the air to a cost analyst, who stopped it with his head. When the ball arrived at my feet, I said that I worked on the Canada Task Force and passed it over to Brad.

Finally, the ball came back to Clive. He tucked the ball under his heel and stared at us intently. "Ready to kick some FBI butt?" he asked.

There was a low rumble of replies.

Clive repeated himself: "I said, are you reaaaady to kiiiiiick some FBI butt?"

We clapped hands and a man who had introduced himself as a press operator shouted, "Hooo-ah!"

Clive said, "That's the spirit," and assigned us positions. Everyone would get to play, he said—this was all about fun. He made himself a center and Brad a wing. I was put in the backfield.

I'd never been good at team sports. It wasn't that I was unathletic—in yoga, I had always prided myself on getting closer to God than anyone else in the class. I guess my problem with team sports goes all the way back to kindergarten, when I struck out in kick ball—but I'm not making any excuses.

The woman from the Arlington Fire Department showed me where to stand. My job, she explained, was to kick the ball thattaway—she gestured in the direction of the Feds' distant goal. I wasn't supposed to run upfield, she said; we had specialists for that. I was supposed to protect our goal. I imitated her crouch and practiced kicking an imaginary ball far down the pitch.

For the first few minutes of the game, the action was all on the other side of the field. Clive passed the ball to Brad, who bounced it off his meaty chest and passed it to the cost analyst. When Arlington clapped and said, "Woo-hoo," I clapped too, and added a throaty, "Way to go, guys!" Arlington back-pedaled when one of the Feds intercepted the ball and started to run toward her, so I retreated toward the goal as well, mimicking her defensive stance. The ball threatened to come in my direction once, but a speedy cartographer cut off the FBI pass and kicked the ball downfield.

After a little while, I began to get bored. There were butterflies in the grass, and birds chirping, and an agreeable bonhomie in the air. Someone on our team with a T-shirt that read LOU'S BAR & DELI shot at the opposing goal, and when the FBI goalie gracefully dove left to stop the shot, we all applauded. About twenty minutes had passed and neither side had scored a goal, but it was pleasant enough to stand in the sunshine.

I had just noticed that my T-shirt had a stain and was examining it very carefully when a chorus of voices started shouting my name. I looked up from my inspection to see three of the Feds pounding down the field in my direction. I assumed my defensive stance and tried to run after the ball, but the head Fed easily passed the ball to his confrere, leaving me standing all alone in a wide open field. I felt shame and sorrow.

I'll never know if the FBI would have scored; they never had the chance. The G-man who had passed me by, a burly fellow with a walrus mustache, was lining up his shot when the paws of God intervened: An enormous shaggy mutt, seeing the ball and wanting to play too, raced onto the field. The dog didn't snout the ball far, but it was just enough. The striker's shot sailed long over the goal.

"Goddammit!" someone from their team shouted.

"Attaboy, Pelé!" shouted someone from ours.

The confusion intensified when the dog's owner ran onto the field, trying to rein in his animal. He looked Mexican, maybe, and no older than twenty. I had noticed him earlier, treating himself to a little morning wake'n'bake on the other side of the field, and I can only imagine what kind of crazy bad trip he must have been having when he looked up and saw eleven enormous brutes in FBI jerseys thundering down on him. The poor kid stopped and turned a peculiar shade of pale. He dragged his dog off the field by the collar.

That's when it all went horribly wrong.

Clive picked up the ball and threw it to the referee. The dog had been an "act of God," said Clive, so the ball should be respotted in the center of the field. The captain of the FBI team disagreed: The dog was "an impediment on the field of play," he insisted, so the game should recommence exactly where it had been interrupted. The referee, some guy from the Secret Service, bought Clive's line, and the Feds were furious. "This is a game you play by the *rules!*" someone shouted. "In this country we live by the *rules.* You can pull that shit in *Zimbabwe* but not in the *goddamned United States!*" We maintained a stoical silence, refusing to reply to the G-men's taunts. Finally, the Feds were coaxed back, and play grudgingly resumed.

At halftime, Clive took me out of the game. I spent the second half lounging on the grass, watching the squirrels perform daring acrobatics in the trees. For a moment, I missed Stan. He would have gotten a kick out of them. At one point, I heard a shout: One of our guys, a graphic designer, had scored a goal. It was the only point of the game. When it was over, the Feds didn't offer us any of the beers from their coolers. We were grimly satisfied, and figured we'd put them in their place.

Great sport, I thought.

∞

After the game I asked Brad if he'd walk down to the Safeway with me to get a sandwich. His eager acceptance suggested that in the appointment book of life, all he'd penciled in for the afternoon—perhaps for the rest of his life—was "waiting for Iris's call." Maybe he'd scheduled some moping for the early evening, followed up by a brisk wallow in his own despair.

We talked soccer on the way to the deli section, where we ordered up a couple of tuna subs. I was surprised to find that he was almost as new to the game as I was.

"Back where I grew up, only the Mexican kids played soccer," he said.

I tried to pay for the sandwiches, but Brad wouldn't let me. He told me I could get the next one. We strolled back to the park and sat in the grass under a maple tree.

I asked him where he'd grown up.

"Oakland," he said.

Lilia had gone to Berkeley, and her then boyfriend had boxed at a place called King's Gym in Oakland. I went with them once. Some parts of Oakland were nice, but most of them were pretty rough.

I asked Brad about himself, and he told me his story in a long, halting monologue. I didn't have to say much to keep him talking. His mother was a post office clerk and his father had died of a brain aneurysm when he was a toddler. Growing up, he'd been bigger than the other boys, and quieter. In the seventh grade, he wrote a paper about the history of jazz that greatly excited his English teacher. She told his mother that he was gifted. Brad's mother decided her son deserved better than the drug-ridden local high schools. She arranged a complicated ruse to allow him to attend a better school, across the Bay. The school was for San Francisco residents, and the scheme required that all of Brad's official documents be sent to his grandmother's address in the city. "I got a lot out of it," he said. "I really came out of my shell." He was a reporter on the student newspaper and the lead in the school production of *Yojimbo*. He made respectable grades, and was accepted to UC Riverside. His brother hadn't gone to college and was still managing a convenience store. Brad wore an enormous class ring on his finger. When the CIA recruiter came to campus and explained the Agency's complicated benefits package, it had sounded like a good deal to him.

I steered the conversation gently toward Iris. "Iris and you are both such self-starters," I said. "I admire that."

Brad had told me about his father's death without notable drama. He said it as if he were telling me some other man's story. But at the mention of Iris's name, his voice grew thick and heavy: "I don't know . . . I don't know what happened there."

"What do you think happened?"

Brad turned the class ring around his finger. "I think she got scared. I think she wasn't ready for the kind of relationship we were having."

I've never heard someone with a broken heart say that he reckoned she just didn't love him. But then, I've never said that either.

"What do you think made her so scared?"

"The way I would always treat her right. Always treat her with respect. When I told her I would always try to be humble and compassionate, I think it scared her. Not everyone's *ready* to be treated right." This theory tumbled out of his mouth as if he'd explained it to himself many times already, in just those words. He didn't meet my eyes; he was staring out across the soccer field at the children playing on the slide.

"This hasn't been easy for her either," I said. "She's been going through so much lately."

He pulled a handful of grass from the earth and rolled it between his immense hands. "I just want her to know I'm there for her. That I'm not going anywhere."

It seemed cruel to me that such a sweet and gentle man could so wildly misunderstand a woman's heart.

⊙⊙

Stan smiled happily when I walked in the door after the game. He was in the kitchenette, taking a quiche from the oven. He had chilled a bottle of Sancerre, prepared a green salad, and set the table. I felt bad for having ruined my appetite with that sandwich. I took a quick shower, then, over lunch, recounted the story of the dog and the Feds and the poor Mexican schnook. He laughed. I told him about Captain Clive and the squirrels. "Did you feed them any nuts?" he asked, and looked disappointed when I said I hadn't. He told me that he kept nuts in his pocket when he went to the park. I ate as much quiche as I could.

We did the dishes together. When we finished, Stan grabbed the TetraFin and went over to the fish tank to give Milton and Sheldrake their lunch. "Oh no," he said suddenly. "Something's wrong with Milton."

That morning, Stan had told me that he was going to replace the gravel in the fish tank, explaining that fish waste and uneaten food, trapped in the gravel, tended over time to form poisonous nitrates. He had carefully changed the gravel while I was playing soccer. But now the goldfish was floating at the surface, its belly swollen. Stan put the little fish in a glass of Evian for an hour in the hope that it would revive. It didn't. "I think it's nitrate poisoning," he said. His expression was utterly forlorn. He gravely flushed the fish, which was rapidly turning black, down the toilet. "I should have taken him out sooner. When I changed the gravel, a poison bubble must have come up."

Sheldrake was swimming fretfully from corner to corner of the tank. "I was trying to make the tank safer," Stan said. "I was just trying to take care of them."

I tried to comfort him. "Stan, you were trying to do the right thing. You took good care of those fish—I know that. It's not your fault."

"Whose fault is it, then? He was alive two hours ago and swimming around. It's not like me to make mistakes like that."

∽

I came into the office Monday morning to find a cable that began: "C/O REGRETS TO INFORM HQS." That's *never* a good thing. C/O ROSENBLATT had scheduled a meeting with RAINBOW for Saturday evening in C/O ROSENBLATT's hotel room. RAINBOW arrived reeking of sweat. He accepted C/O ROSENBLATT's offer of a drink and began to curse. *"Son of a bitch! Son of a bitch!"*

C/O ROSENBLATT stayed calm. "Son, tell me what's wrong."

"I'm sitting at the fucking conference and the American son of a bitch . . . how the hell did he know our coho yield numbers north of the Fraser for the last two years? He sure as hell wasn't out there counting those fucking fish. *I was*. I told *you*. I thought you said this shit was *con-fucking-fidential*."

C/O ROSENBLATT went back to the basics he'd been taught at the Farm: Admit nothing, deny everything, make counter-accusations. "Son," he said. "I have no idea. Sounds like someone on your team has loose lips."

"It's not possible. It's just *not*. Only Lipscomb, you, and me knew the exact coho breeding numbers." Bill Lipscomb was the head of environmental studies for the Canadian Ministry of Fisheries. He was an ardent Canadian nationalist.

"Son, I can see how terrible you feel," said C/O ROSEN-BLATT. "You put a lot of work into those fish. Those folks might have taken a damn good guess—I mean, that's the way these things work in the business world, for sure, so it wouldn't surprise me—but I promise you, I never gave your reports to anyone who shouldn't have them. Neither would anyone I work with."

RAINBOW looked long and hard at C/O ROSENBLATT. *"Screw you,"* he spat, and walked out the door.

I went to my supervisor's office. "Well, what do we do now?" I asked.

He took a sip of his chamomile tea. He said, "I just *love* Mondays. Gonna be a big brouhaha with Agriculture over this." The negotiator's carelessness with the secrets we'd given him was incandescently stupid, but typical: Some of the Agency's senior hands sincerely believed that intelligence should never be shared with the customers, since they just couldn't handle it responsibly.

"There's not much we can do," he said. "ROSENBLATT handled it just right. He gave the guy a fig leaf if he wants to come back. Wasn't he about to go back to that little village he comes from? Let him have a good long think." The negotiations were scheduled to go into recess for a week; RAINBOW had planned to go back to Finn Slough to surprise his brothers by telling them that the *Mikko Hinhalla* would be safe.

"Sometimes people think it through and decide they don't want to know the truth. All we can do is sit tight and hope for the best. Send ROSENBLATT a nice cable. He's probably feeling a little down."

☙

Iris called me on Sunday night in tears. Things hadn't gone well with Max, the man who had phoned her while we were having tea. He had taken her to dinner the week before at Sequoia, a waterfront restaurant in Georgetown that was popular with journalists and junior congressional staffers. They sat on the terrace overlooking the Potomac. He made her laugh, and after dinner, as they walked together on the Mall, he told her delicious gossip about the senator he worked for. The evening was warm and sultry. They lay on the grass, staring at the lights twinkling from the Washington monument, and Iris allowed herself to be kissed. He invited her back to his apartment, and when she left the next morning, he promised he would call her soon.

He didn't, of course.

"Oh, honey," I said to her from time to time as she told me her story.

She snuffled and asked why she did this to herself. She missed Max, she said. She missed Brad.

"You poor thing," I said.

Would it be wrong, she asked, to just call Brad? She wanted to hear the voice of a man who loved her.

No, I said. I thought that would be *just* fine.

Monday afternoon, I stopped by Brad's office. I poked my head in the door.

"Brad! I brought you something."

He looked up from his desk.

I had stopped by Barnes & Noble the day before and picked up a copy of *Fleeing from Love: Why Women Sabotage Their Relationships with Mr. Right*. The cover depicted a heart cleaved in two by a thunderbolt. To make it look used, I'd battered it up a bit and written things like *Wow . . . powerful insight* in the margins.

"This really helped me," I said. "I think it'll help you understand Iris better."

Brad accepted the book and nodded solemnly at the title. "I'll look at this right away. I appreciate you thinking of me." He paused, and thumbed the pages. "She left me a message last night," he added reflectively.

I settled myself in one of the plastic chairs and arranged my features sympathetically.

"And?" I asked.

"And nothing. I was at my cousin's place, and I got back late. I didn't want to wake her up. I'll call her tonight."

I shook my head. "I can*not* believe she did that. I spoke to her yesterday. She was all sad about something silly, and she asked me if it was okay to call. I told her, '*No*. It is *not* okay. Men have feelings just like you do. You can't just call every time you need a boost. That's not *fair*. If you're not willing to be there for him when *he* needs you, why do *you* have the right to lean on him when you're low?' "

"I don't think Iris—"

"God knows I love that Iris, but sometimes she's so *blind*."

"I think she just—"

"Brad, you don't need to defend Iris. I love her too. But sometimes she's just spoiled. Don't call her back today. You'll see. Your phone will start ringing all hours of the day. And you know what? It'll do her good. She needs to see how *afraid* she is of someone who's good to her."

That week, Brad and I met for coffee every day. At three o'clock or so, he'd send me a message on the interoffice mail system, asking, "Wanna take ten?" I'd reply, "You bet!" We'd meet in the cafeteria, which by late afternoon was more or less empty but for the cleaning crews. Brad would carry our coffee to the table and settle into one of the chrome-and-plastic chairs. He swiftly understood that I was willing to listen to him talk about Iris, and was so grateful that he didn't ask why. I nodded thoughtfully while he spoke. At regular intervals I interjected comments along the lines of "That sounds really painful for you" (meaningful silence) or "I hope you're allowing yourself to cry over that" (meaningful silence). If I thought it appropriate, I would add something cryptic but sensitive, such as "Respect what your feelings are trying to say to you."

He told me about the first time he had laid eyes on Iris. "I know most men look at her and just notice how gorgeous she is. And, I mean, of course I noticed that, but that wasn't it. It was never just about her looks, it was that she was so natural, no airs, just laughing and—"

"Comfortable with herself?"

"Exactly."

Brad told me the story of their first date. He had taken her to the Pines of Italy, a family-style restaurant in Arlington with checkered tablecloths and red candles that melted sloppily over empty wine bottles. After dinner, the padrone came over to chat. He surveyed Iris and her legs, bunched his fingers to his lips, and kissed them explosively to indicate the wonder of the vision before him. Iris scanned the man's stained apron and his paunch, squeezed her own fingers to her own lips, and returned the gesture.

Brad shook his head. "That's when I *knew* I could love this woman."

Iris *had* been charmed by the Pines of Italy: She'd told me all about it—in the same cafeteria, in fact, over the same coffee. She liked the way Brad had opened the door of the car for her, waited until she tucked herself in, and then shut the door behind her. She liked the way he'd noticed that she was shivering and turned up the heat. She liked that he knew how the Agency worked. But she had made Brad take her back to the Pines of Italy three more times before she let him kiss her. It was a full two months before she stopped saying, "I want to wait, baby." The first time she woke up in his small condominium, she turned over and looked at him. His enormous body was sprawled across the bed like a felled redwood; he was slightly sweaty. She got up and brushed her teeth, then padded into the living room. She took in the sepia-toned Factory Outlet sofa and the matching recliner, the ash-veneer entertainment center. She opened the blinds and saw a parking lot. She wasn't sure what she felt, but it wasn't *thrilled*.

But Brad was nice—so unbelievably nice. No one had ever

been nicer to her. She had the feeling she could ask him to do outrageous favors for her—*Would you mind taking my cat to the vet for me? She coughed up a weird-looking hairball this morning, but I have a manicure appointment this afternoon so I don't have time*—and he would oblige, saying that he was always glad to help and that's what friends were for. Iris had been with men who weren't so nice; men who didn't call when they said they would; men who borrowed money from her and never paid it back, then tried to sleep with her sister. And you wouldn't know it from talking to him, she said, but Brad was a *monster* in bed.

Brad never asked why I found his relationship with Iris so fascinating. He told me that after they had been dating a few months, he woke up in the middle of the night to find Iris in the living room, settled in front of the computer, surfing the Internet, reading from a page of children's jokes—riddles and puns. Her innocence moved him, he said. He loved the way Iris would tire at the end of a long night and fall asleep in the car as they drove to his apartment, her hand resting in his. Once, Brad had picked her up from the bucket seat of his car, hoisted her easily in his arms, and carried her into bed without waking her.

I listened to these stories quietly, and when he was done, I nodded with infinite compassion, trying to hide my infinite boredom. I told him that he would feel empowered if he didn't call her and that he should grow a goatee.

"A goatee?" he said doubtfully, stroking his chin.

"I think it would suit you."

On Wednesday, Brad told me she had called him again the night before, leaving a long, rambling message. He hadn't called her back.

Brad was discovering how good it felt to make Iris see how *afraid* she was of someone who treated her right.

. . .

On Thursday night, Iris called me. She told me about a sale at Filene's Basement and a fight she'd had with her mom and a new secretary at the office who had lost a month's worth of expense-account receipts. She asked me about her wisdom teeth: She needed to have them out and did that hurt? I was finding it difficult to pay attention: Stan had challenged Peter Jennings to a rather noisy debate. I motioned for him to quiet down, but he ignored me. I asked Iris if maybe we could talk later.

"Honey, let me just ask you one thing—have you seen Brad around? He's dropped off the face of the earth. I'm kind of worried about him."

"Worry not," I said. "Saw him just today—he looked just fine."

"Really?"

"Yeah, he looked terrific. Don't think you need to worry for a second."

"Wow. That's a relief." Long pause. "Why, what's up with him?"

I let the line go silent for a moment, then said, "Will you be mad if I tell you what I really think?"

"Go on," she said reluctantly.

"Iris, I don't think you should even be asking those questions. I think you should just let the man get on with his life."

On Friday, I told Brad that there had been a time in my life when I had acted like Iris, afraid of a man who truly loved and respected me. I'd been a smart woman who made foolish choices. But I had done a lot of work on myself, like Iris was doing now, and I'd come to see that I deserved to be treated well. I told him how Stan and I liked to sing Elvis songs together as we drove back and forth from the Farm, and how he cooked for me, and how I *trusted* him.

But I added that things with Stan weren't perfect. I told Brad about Stan's anger and his jealousy. I said that sometimes Stan's temper frightened me. "Let's face it," I said. "Perfect relationships only exist in our fantasies. Stan and I have our challenges. But we're working through them."

He nodded sympathetically, told me that I should respect what my feelings were telling me, and went back to talking about Iris.

∽

Had I been asked to place a bet, I would have said that RAINBOW was more likely to poison the Fraser River with cyanide than speak to ROSENBLATT again. I guess I still had something to learn about folks.

On Monday morning, a cable from ROSENBLATT was waiting. After returning from Finn Slough, RAINBOW had called him on his phony business line. His voice shook. They met at a Toronto steakhouse, where C/O ROSENBLATT ordered shrimp cocktails and filet mignon for them both. RAINBOW, in his shabby parka, was underdressed. There were dark circles under his eyes. "You look a little tired," said C/O ROSENBLATT with fatherly concern.

RAINBOW was not in a talkative mood. He stayed quiet through the appetizers. "I'll keep working for you," he said finally. "But I swear to God, if that stuff leaks to the wrong people again, I'll stop." He said little else. The men arranged a time and place to swap his next report for his salary. C/O ROSENBLATT asked RAINBOW to prepare a dossier showing all of the Canadian Ministry of Fisheries' confidential estimates of salmon yields for the next seven years. RAINBOW left most of his steak untouched. "I'm doing this for my family," he said before he left. He wanted ROSENBLATT to know.

"Of course you are," said C/O ROSENBLATT. "That's why we all do this."

C/O ROSENBLATT asked the waiter if he could take the meal home in a doggy bag.

I closed the cable and imagined RAINBOW's trip back to the Fraser River. I saw him standing at the water's edge, his hands in his pockets, then reaching down to scoop up a stone, skipping the stone across the water. I imagined a lowering sky shading into the gray rapids, the flash of a jumping salmon's sapphire fins, the rattling call of a kingfisher. I imagined RAINBOW running his fingers pensively over the bow of the *Mikko Hinhalla,* then watching his sister-in-law separate the bills into piles: creditors who could be stalled and creditors who couldn't. I imagined his gork of a nephew with his arm in a brace, watching the other kids play. I imagined RAINBOW standing silently amid the cheatgrass and the blueweed at the banks of the Fraser River, contemplating the current and deciding that he had no choice.

I couldn't talk to Stan about the case. I wanted to know what he would think of it, but of course he didn't need to know. On the drive home that day, he asked what was on my mind. I said that I couldn't see why we needed to spy on Canada. "They're our friends," I said.

"We don't have friends."

"The *Canadians*? Come on."

"They're all enemies. Or potential enemies. They're not Americans. They're all pursuing their own interests, not ours. It would be great if we could all hold hands and sing 'Kumbaya,' but it just ain't like that."

"They're Canadians!"

"They're a bunch of self-righteous hockey players who wear stupid caps with tassels and kill baby seals. They coddle our draft dodgers and they fish in our water. Screw 'em."

"The Norwegians kill seals. And the Japanese. Not the Canadians," I said.

"Oh, for God's sake—it was a joke!"

"Espionage is a hostile act—it's something you do because you *absolutely have to*. You do it when you're confronting the Nazis, or the Soviet Union, or Iraq—not *Canada*."

"You do it when the *legally appointed* officials of your *democratically elected* government tell you to. The decisions are made in accordance with the law. They're made in the context of the Constitution and a system of checks and balances. Why do you think *you* should decide what's in the national interest? Who elected you? I have faith in our system. You live in the freest, most prosperous, most creative society in the world thanks to that system. If someone tells me we need to know what the Canadians are up to, why should I question it?"

"Because it's nuts! Why would we bother?"

"They may have reasons for needing to know that I don't have to understand. Isn't it rather arrogant to suggest that you, with your doctorate in Sanskrit, know better than the top officials of a government freely elected by the people of the United States?"

Maybe he was right. I didn't know anymore. The Canadians probably *were* capable of fucking us up.

Throughout that week, I choreographed the Mating Dance of Brad and Iris with the care of a zookeeper breeding pandas in captivity. I am quite certain that no one—but no one—had ever listened to Brad with the interest and rapt attention I displayed and that no one would again, unless he paid upward of $160 an hour. I gave him the best romantic advice a man has ever received from a woman, and damned if it wasn't working even better than I'd expected. He had stopped calling Iris, and Iris had started calling him. On Tuesday, Iris forwarded him a joke that was circulating on the Internet via e-mail; he didn't reply. That clearly chapped her hide: The next day she sent him an animated e-card, with a syrupy soundtrack, that told him how special he was to her and how special he would always be. When he told me about this—and told me that he still hadn't answered—I noted a distinct glint of sadistic pleasure in his eyes.

He asked me what I thought he should say to her if she called. He now permitted me simply to dictate his lines. I told him to get off the phone as quickly as humanly possible. I said that sooner or later she would show up on his doorstep, guaranteed. Then he could give her just a *little* crumb of hope. He could tell her that she looked nice. "Say that maybe you can go out again sometime for dinner again, but you don't want to make any big romantic promises. Tell her you feel a little sour on romance these days. Tell her you'll have to take it really, really slow. Get to know one another all over again. And do *not* tell her you love her, even if she says it first. You *can* say, 'You're very special to me, Iris, but I don't know what I feel anymore.' And then you *send her away* because you're about to go out. Got it?"

Brad nodded. The goatee was growing in quickly, and I thought it suited his new attitude. I suspected he did, too.

When Iris called and told me she had stopped by Brad's place to pick up her CDs and that he had seemed in a hurry to go somewhere else, I told her I thought she ought to move on and date other people. "You can't live in the past, Iris."

I told myself I was doing this for Iris's own good. If she returned to Brad, she would be returning to a man who loved her more than any woman could ever ask. The Maxes of this world, Iris clearly did not need. If I could help her to overcome her fear of being loved, was I not doing everyone a great favor?

After a while, case officers get good at this kind of logic. It's something of a job requirement.

On Thursday, I told Brad that I needed his advice desperately and that it was an absolutely confidential matter. He said he felt honored that I would choose to confide in him and would do his best to listen with compassion and respect.

I told him that his advice would be especially valuable to me because he understood how the Office of Security worked. I explained that I had sent a few indiscreet e-mails to my family "when I first got here and knew nothing about security" and that somehow the Special Investigations Branch had found out. "I don't know what this means," I said, "and I don't know what to expect, and I don't know why it's taking so long for them to answer my calls, and frankly, I'm worried."

He looked extremely concerned. "It sounds like you made an honest mistake and owned up to it," he said.

"Do you think they'll fire me?"

"I have to say I don't know much about what the Special Investigations Branch does. But I'm sure they'll figure out that you're a good person. You know, it bothers me. So many people here have *serious* problems. A guy in my division just left a whole 201 file in a taxi in Warsaw. We had to exfiltrate the asset because he screwed up so bad. As far as I know, they're not breathing down *his* neck. Why are they singling you out?"

"I don't know. I just don't know. I don't know why they singled Iris out, either."

"This goddamned place," he said, gesturing in a vague parabola. "There are just too many assholes here." It was the most aggressive thing I'd ever heard him say. It made me wonder exactly what his relationship with the CIA was like and whether it wasn't more complicated than I'd realized.

"Brad," I said. "Do you *like* working here?"

The minute I asked, I realized there was another mother lode of resentment left for me to mine. His brow knit together and he sat up a bit in his chair. "When I joined this place," he said, "I believed I would be judged by the content of my character, not the color of my skin."

I wondered where this could *possibly* be going. But I prepared myself to listen sympathetically and to take close mental notes. Brad explained that he'd now been passed over for promotion three times in favor of women of color—"don't get me wrong. I *love* women of color. I mean, you know that"—but truly, he said, he had been more qualified, more experienced and had put in his dues. It wasn't *fair*.

I agreed, I said. It was an outrage.

On Friday, I met Brad for coffee at our customary time. It was a pleasant afternoon. I suggested we take our cups outside to the courtyard so that I could smoke. We sat at a table near the Kryptos sculpture, a dense matrix of letters crisscrossed against a curving verdigris scroll, set in a stone-filled pond. No one knew what it meant and no one much cared anymore. Every so often some geek would post another crackpot theory about it on the Internet. A cryptologist from California had recently declared that he'd broken the code: *Between subtle shading and the absence of light lies the nuance of iqclusion.* No one knew what *iqclusion* meant. The Director of Central Intelligence, to whom the secret was historically passed by his predecessor, declined to confirm or deny the accuracy of the interpretation.

Brad wedged his legs under the table and yawned, stretching his neck from side to side and loosening up his jaw muscles for a *really* long discussion about whatever it was that Iris had recently said or not said and how she said it and what she meant to say and what she *really* meant.

We deconstructed Brad's latest phone conversation with Iris

for a few minutes. Our conversation revolved around the meaning of *miss,* as in "I've *missed* talking to you." This was the senti-
ment Iris offered Brad at (I imagined) about 7:15 the night prior,
since she'd hung up with me at 7:10 and I had suggested at 7:05
that it would be natural just to *miss* talking to Brad. Brad and I
discussed the plausible interpretations of her comment: Was that
an inclusive or an exclusive usage of the word? Was talking to
him the only thing she missed or the only thing she wasn't too
frightened to admit missing?

I told him that I had spoken to her too. She was very close, I
said, to insight. She was reflecting deeply on her problems with
intimacy and commitment. "I'm trying to help her acknowledge
her unhealthy patterns," I said. "I think it's really important that
as a friend, I speak the truth to her, instead of validating her excuses for not facing up to her fears." Brad couldn't have agreed
more. He put his left foot on his right knee. So did I. He
stretched out a kink in his neck. So did I.

The time had come, I decided, to get to the point.

Major fault line: Needs me to win back Iris.

*Ancillary fault lines: Resents the Agency because he's been passed over
for promotion. Resents them for taking Iris away.*

I burst into spectacular sobs.

"What is it?" he said with helpless, clumsy concern. "What's
the matter?"

I continued to weep. "I can't tell you," I gasped.

"You can. Please talk about it. You need to talk about it." He
reached over and touched my shoulder in a horribly awkward
but touching gesture of solidarity. He had the terrified look men
always get in the face of feminine tears.

I inhaled and tilted my eyes heavenward. In between sobs, I
forced out a question. "Brad?" I choked. "If you and Iris were to
get back together, would you be able to completely trust her?" I
took a tissue out of my handbag and began blowing my nose.

"I don't know," he said nervously. "I guess it would take time to rebuild the trust."

I took a few deep breaths, croaked out a few more damp sobs, and said, "Trust is *so* important." I spent a few moments on soft, subtle weeping. "Trust is really important. It's really hard to be in a relationship without trust." I blinked a few times, took a few more deep breaths, and then blew my nose again.

"You're having a problem with Stan, aren't you?"

I started to cry again, and nodded.

Brad squeezed my shoulder and looked at me earnestly. "You don't think he's cheating on you, do you?" I had no doubt he was prepared to break Stan's kneecaps with the butt of a hunting rifle if it were true.

"I think . . . I think it's worse . . . I think he may be the one who reported me to Security."

He exhaled.

So did I.

"Whoa," he said at last.

We let my confession settle in the air. I rubbed my eyes.

He sucked on the inside of his cheek thoughtfully. "I'm a security officer, but I would never report someone I loved for some minor infraction. That's just sick. Have you talked openly and honestly with Stan about your fears?"

"I have, but I don't know if I can trust him. It's driving me crazy. I want to trust him, but I just can't, and I don't know if it's because I shouldn't or if it's because I'm crazy." My eyes filled with tears again. It wasn't an act.

"Wow. I'm really sorry you're going through this."

"It's the *not knowing*. You know how you feel *not knowing* what Iris is thinking? Imagine magnifying that ten times. Imagine thinking that Iris had gone *out of her way* to stab you in the back."

His shoulders seemed to broaden; I could tell the thought enraged him.

"And I don't know why it is that around here they seem to pick on people like you and me and Iris. You know they wouldn't be investigating me if I were one of *them*."

Looking at him, looking at the anger on his face and feeling his protective hand on my shoulder, I could tell that it was going to happen. My body filled with an almost sexual tension.

"Selena, let me run something past you."

I nodded. *Yes. Oh God, yes. Don't stop.*

"They keep those investigations pretty tight, and I can't promise I could find out anything, but Stan *is* in my division—I might be able to ask a few questions and see what I could find out."

I remembered what they had told us down at the Farm: Treason should seem like *his* excellent idea.

"Would you want me to do that?" he asked.

I regarded him with wonder, like a Guatemalan peasant staring at an icon of the Madonna that had just commenced to weep. "Could you? I hadn't thought of that. Could you do that? I really just need to know the truth—you understand that, don't you?"

"Let me see what I can do."

God help me, I had recruited him.

—————⌀—————

CHAPTER 10

R AINBOW, unfortunately, was not alone in reasoning that
   if he and Lipscomb were the only ones with access to the
salmon-yield figures, one of them had loose lips. Lipscomb too
was capable of solving this equation. One week after his lunch
with C/O ROSENBLATT, RAINBOW was relieved of his job.
Placed on indefinite administrative leave and barred from attending further meetings, he had been told to begin looking for
new employment immediately. Lipscomb had told him how
very disappointed in him he was. "I don't know what happened
here," he said, "but I can't have you working for me if I can't
trust you."

    RAINBOW recounted this to C/O ROSENBLATT at their
scheduled meeting in the case officer's hotel room. He told the
story in the flat, robotic voice of a man in deep shock. He did not
cry or curse; he said only that he had no idea what he would do
now. RAINBOW was, I suppose, lucky. Had this been Iraq and
not Canada, electric shocks would have been applied to his geni-
tals. He would have been bound and hung by his feet; nails
would have been pounded into his hands; his tongue would
have been cut off while he was still alive. He would have been

immersed in a vat of acid, and if that didn't finish him off, his throat would have been slit like a sheep's—probably in front of his family, who would have received the same treatment. C/O ROSENBLATT did not, of course, try to cheer him up by pointing this out. He said only that he was deeply sorry to hear that RAINBOW had lost his job and was sure that he would land on his feet.

RAINBOW asked if he could keep consulting for Chicken of the Sea. "I still know more about salmon than anyone else in Canada," he said. "I could keep writing reports. It doesn't even have to be salmon—it could be sturgeon, trout, lobster . . . whatever."

C/O ROSENBLATT replied that he was terribly sorry, but the budget for consulting had just been cut. "I don't make these decisions," he said regretfully. "The guys in management do. Consulting's the first thing to go when they're tightening the belt. We've had to let a lot of good people go. It's a damned shame."

Without access, RAINBOW was of no use to us anymore.

RAINBOW seemed too beaten to be angry. He sank deeper into his armchair, as if he wished it would swallow him, and put his hand to his temple. An ambulance with a deafening siren passed by outside. C/O ROSENBLATT lifted his head instinctively in the direction of the noise, but RAINBOW didn't seem to notice. After a minute or so, RAINBOW looked up. His pale eyes flitted for a moment around the room; his face registered no interest in his surroundings. At last he rose and walked to the door. He carried himself as if his parka were lined with lead. He didn't say good-bye.

My supervisor hadn't seen the cable yet. When I told him about it, he shook his head. "What a shame," he said. "The irony is, Agriculture is going to be shouting at *us*, because they're not getting the numbers. They screw up, we carry the can. Tell ROSENBLATT to step up the development of SEAGULL—we need to get that guy on board soonest."

∞

The crisp, sunny autumn had become soggy. I wore a sweater that morning but was still cold when I hiked in from the parking lot. Virginia, the office's institutional memory, was warning me about the upcoming renovation of the parking lot. As she was telling me that I should plan to drive to work at least a half hour earlier, my phone twittered. I picked it up, assuming it would be yet another bozo who needed to know the name of the prime minister of Canada, but it was Brad. His tone was urgent.

He asked if I'd meet him in the cafeteria, but at that time of day, the cafeteria was packed, and I was worried about running into Stan. *That,* I thought, would be distinctly suboptimal tradecraft. Nan had once asked a logistics officer in the Turkrapistani Air Force to go bowling with her on a Thursday night. The instructor flunked her: That night was the county police bowl-off. "How was I supposed to know?" she asked petulantly. "That's *your* goddamned problem, Nan," the instructor told her. "You going to put *How was I supposed to know?* in a cable to Headquarters when your asset gets whacked because you paraded him in front of a goddamned police bowl-off?" I told Brad I needed to pick up a file in the basement, and asked him to meet me there, by the men's room near the yellow elevator. I couldn't think of a place in the building with less foot traffic.

I stood outside the men's lavatory, waiting. There was a dull ache in my stomach. I hadn't had breakfast. The muscles in my forehead and neck tightened. I heard the sound of a toilet flushing; a moment later a plump man with fat, mottled cheeks emerged from the men's room, shaking his hands dry. I heard heavy footsteps behind me and turned around: It was Brad. I walked in his direction and we met mid-corridor, near the closed door of an office marked only with a number.

"Hi," I said. I leaned against the wall and so did he. His jaw was twitching a bit, and he was shaking the pencil in his hand in a nervous, palsied rhythm.

Brad spoke: "All I could find out is that they sent a memorandum to the division to make sure he was paid overtime for coming in on a weekend."

"Who sent what?"

"The Special Investigations Branch. They sent a memorandum to our division."

It took a second to register. My heart began to gallop.

"When did they send it?"

"Stan was at the Special Investigations Branch a month before you graduated from the Farm. On a weekend. SIB wanted to make sure he got overtime."

It was a month before we'd graduated that Stan had gone back to Headquarters for that seminar on covert finance. It was then that he had come back accusing me of making a fool of him with Kirk.

They were paying him overtime to inform on me.

I looked at Brad and saw the pity in his eyes, and felt my own eyes cloud with tears. I could hear the hum of the fluorescent lights above me, and for a second I thought I would vomit. I realized I couldn't make it all the way down to the ladies' room. I would have to rush for the men's. Brad put out a hand to steady me, and the fear passed.

"Do you know what he said to them?" I asked.

Brad shook his head. He said he couldn't ask: He didn't have a need to know.

∞

Between receiving that news and returning to my office, *something* must have happened. After all, I went from the basement to my cubicle in Canada. I must have taken the yellow elevator—that would have been the most logical route. Perhaps I bid my fellow elevator travelers a good day; perhaps I stopped in the ladies' room to splash cold water on my face. I don't rightly know. My mind has considerably pushed the delete button on the memories of those minutes, presumably on the grounds that I would find them upsetting. I appreciate that.

Memory recommences in Technicolor and Dolby sound from the moment I returned to my office and sat on my padded swivel chair. The light on my phone was blinking; I entered my code to listen to the message: Stan had called to say his class would be over late that evening, and did I mind picking up his dry cleaning?

When he finished, the recorded operator told me to press three to repeat the message. I pressed three over and over and over, listening to Stan's familiar voice. The fucking hypocrite. *He wants me to pick up his fucking dry cleaning?* I thought about what Stan must have done and how he must have done it. The snooping—had he guessed my password, or did he crack it with some handy gizmo he'd borrowed from the office? I thought of him reading my mail, with that scandalized, guilty thrill that snoops feel. How did he justify that to himself? Did he tell himself he was just *curious*? He must have stored away in his mind the fact that I'd committed security violations, making mental note of my Achilles heel in the event he should ever need to exploit it. He deliberately marched to the Special Investigations Branch and turned me in. And he did it because he was a jealous, pathetic, vengeful fat fuck. Did he tell him-self he did it out of patriotism? Then he hid it from me, and lied about it—over and over and over. Not just in words but in deeds. I thought of every time he'd touched me since that weekend. I had been seduced under false pretenses. It seemed like rape.

Janet was right: I didn't owe Stan, that son of a bitch, *anything*.

⌒

Janet took notes this time, a lot of them. Her cast must have just come off; she still grimaced as she wrote.

"Let's review what you just told me," she said. "He told you that he wasn't like the other trainees and that he had special re-sponsibilities at Headquarters."

"Yes."

"He told you that he had designed operations known only to three other people: the DCI, the head of the Special Activities Branch, and the president of the European Central Bank."

"Yes."

"He told you that his involvement in this project occurred while the other trainees were in paramilitary training."

"Yes."

"And he told you that if either of you discussed this operation with anyone, you would both go to jail."

"Yes."

"But he said nothing at all about the nature of the operation."

"No."

"Are you absolutely certain of that?"

"Yes."

"Does he seem to have any unusual source of funds?"

"No."

"You did the right thing by coming here today, Selena."

∞

We had taken separate cars that day because Stan had a division meeting late in the afternoon. By the time he came home, I had already packed my belongings and put them in the car.

Stan walked in as I was carrying the last box out of the apartment. "What's going on?" he said. "What are you doing?"

I put down the box and stared at him, then shouted, *"How could you do that to me?"*

"Do *what*?" His eyes were panicky.

"Cut the crap, Stan. *I know.* You turned me in to Security. You read my mail and *you turned me in.*"

"Selena, calm down. Calm down. Don't do this to us. Whatever they told you, it's not true."

"You manipulative fat *son of a bitch.* How *could* you?"

Stan's face reddened. "Selena, don't talk to me in that tone of voice."

"Don't tell me what to do, you fat fucking sanctimonious prick!"

"Don't blame me because *you* sent those fucking e-mails! I'm not the one who spread my legs for the entire universe!"

I picked up my box and walked out the door.

∞

How many days elapsed between then and the next phone call from the Special Investigations Branch? Was it two? Three? I'm not sure. The next few days were foggy. I slept on Iris's couch, or tried to sleep. What obsessed me wasn't that he had turned me in—people do crazy, vengeful things in moments of jealousy. What I didn't understand was how *I hadn't known.* I had lived with this man in close quarters for months. We had talked about everything imaginable, sung songs together, shopped for groceries, taken bubble baths, broken bread, made love, woken up in each other's arms. I thought I knew him, but Iris was right: I didn't know folks. I should have been able to tell. I should have been able to tell from the moment he betrayed me, but I couldn't. He was that good.

This time, Nancy, not Janet, called me from the Special Investigations Branch and requested that I come in that afternoon.

She was right on time. She met me in the waiting room with a motherly smile and accompanied me to the interview room, holding the door open for me. "How are you, Selena?" she asked.

"I'm fine. Thank you."

"Let me explain what happens now. The Special Investigations Branch has concluded its investigation." She paused and took a deep, sighing breath; the corners of her mouth twitched. She opened the file before her and read from the page at the top: "The investigation team has established that Caesaria A. HESTER placed classified information on an unsecured computer and used this computer to access the Internet. Caesaria A. HESTER communicated with, and disclosed classified information to, members of households where foreign nationals reside. This has raised serious questions about her judgment and suitability for access to classified information."

"I'll say."

Nancy looked as if she didn't quite know how to reply to that, so she continued. "In and of itself, Selena, this is a serious matter. We had been prepared to recommend that you be placed on disciplinary probation for two years, and barred from consideration for overseas assignments or promotion during that time. However, another matter has come to our attention." I expected her to tell me that squealing on Stan—my patriotic gesture—had militated against such a stern punishment.

"Selena, we have received information that you have discussed the details of this classified investigation with at least three other people, one of whom is no longer an employee of this Agency."

And for the second time

—oh shit—

I found myself sitting in that interview room, completely unable to figure out how they knew.

I didn't have time to think it through. Nancy continued, "Selena, I'm sorry to have to tell you this, but in light of this information, the investigation team has no choice but to recommend that your security clearances be withdrawn."

"I see."

"The investigation team does not have executive authority. This decision must be formally adjudicated by an Employee Review Panel. You have the right to appeal any decision it makes to the Deputy Director for Operations. You may submit a statement on your own behalf to the panel. You have five days to do so. You must compose your response on a computer in a secure facility."

"Can I see the team's report?"

"No." I wasn't surprised.

I could fight it. I could respond. I had five days to respond.

I think she was expecting me to cry or plead or ask to be excused so I could collect myself in the ladies' room, but I didn't feel like doing any of that. I had done it all before; I was all out of tears. I smiled gently at her. I wanted to let her know that it was all right.

A calm came over me. I had been outwitted, I suppose, but somehow that seemed inessential. I considered what I had become—or what I had been all along, perhaps, but hadn't known about myself: I had betrayed my lover, I had betrayed my best friend, I had manipulated earnest Brad like a lab animal. For a moment I had a vision of Brad behind the bars of a cage, wait-

ing excitedly for me to bring him a banana. "Well *hello,* Bright
Eyes," I imagined myself saying, then turning to Bob, my supervisor. "It's amazing, isn't it? When you look into his eyes, he almost seems . . . *human*."

I remembered Ned, the man who drove us to Headquarters
on our very first day, and the way he'd looked at me with hollow
eyes, saying, *I wish I could start all over again.* I thought of RAIN-
BOW, haunted and destroyed, and the *Mikko Hinhalla*. I thought
of PINEAPPLE sadly waggling his head. I thought of malignant
Nathan telling Stan that I was sleeping with Kirk, and Jade, alone
in her bedroom, composing mad letters denouncing herself. I
imagined Stan turning me in; I remembered turning in Stan. I
thought of my mother wondering what had become of her
daughter, and of my sister, to whom I'd not spoken in months. I
thought of that night train to Marrakech. I no longer wanted to
ride it.

"I'd like to resign immediately," I said.

"That's the right decision, Selena."

"What will happen to Stan?"

"I'm not at liberty to discuss that," she said. "I'll go get the papers for you to sign."

She left me in the room with my thoughts. I suppose if this
were Russia she would have left me in the room with a revolver.
I wondered what I would do with myself now. I could go back to
studying Sanskrit, I guessed. I imagined various careers. Could I
run for Congress? Write a novel about what life was *really* like at
the CIA? If they ever watched the tape from the camera on the
wall, I wonder what they made of my expression.

She came back, and I signed the documents. They were much
like the ones I'd signed at the beginning. I was to protect forever
the secrets I knew, report prying inquiries, remain vigilant. The
resignation notice itself was the simplest form I had ever seen at
the Central Intelligence Agency. It said that I resigned from my

employment and relinquished the Agency from further obligations. I signed that one last, then handed her my badge, and it was done. For a moment, we both just sat there.

The discussion was over. I picked up my bag, put on my sweater, shook her hand with an odd composure, a serenity almost, and walked out of the Central Intelligence Agency forever.

EPILOGUE

He who thinks he knows, doesn't know. He who knows that he
doesn't know, knows. For in this context, to know is not
to know. And not to know is to know.

—*Kena Upaniñad*

N oise, dust, light, heat, motion, the smell of mold, bullocks
pulling carts, men pulling trishaws, cows wandering the
streets, Sikhs, Jains, Parsis, bodies everywhere, arms outstretched.
Every one of the bustling, humming, noisy billion people around
me, like me, convinced of the centrality of his own existence, the
inherent importance of his own life.

When I left the CIA, I had a little more than four thousand
dollars in my savings account. I left my car with Iris and asked
her to sell it for me and send me the proceeds. I took the train
from Washington to New York, where I saw my niece for the
first time. Then I flew to Amsterdam, and from Amsterdam to
Bombay.

I will never know the truth.

I'll never know who told Security that I had been sending
indiscreet e-mail. All the evidence pointed to Stan, but all
the evidence was circumstantial. Only Stan had the motivation and the opportunity. The timing of his visit to the authorities was too much to be a coincidence. I remembered the

expression on Janet's face when she said "You don't owe him any—"

Moreover, Stan had access to my computer. It made no sense to imagine that the NSA or the FBI were monitoring my e-mail. Why would they bother? I marshaled the evidence against Stan every morning, and all day long the jury deliberated.

The lawyer for the defense offered alternative explanations for the evidence. Stan had been involvd with something, something he couldn't tell me about. Janet had asked me questions about Stan. Perhaps Security was after *Stan,* not me. They were watching me only because I was with Stan. Perhaps Stan had been in the Security office that late spring weekend because *he* was under investigation, not me. That would also account for the evidence. The defense proposed wilder hypotheses. Could someone else from my class have gone to Security and said, "Take a close look at this one. I don't trust her"? Perhaps it was the same blistering cretin who believed I was an apologist for Jonathan Pollard? The defense insisted that reasonable doubt remained.

Every day I argued the case, only to conclude once more that Stan had snooped through my mail because he was jealous, because he was suspicious, because where women were concerned, he'd long ago learned to cut the deck before he played. In a moment of rage, he had gone to the Special Investigations Branch—while he was sharing my bed—to report what he had found.

But what if I had been wrong? What if he had done nothing but love me with all his heart, supporting me when I needed it most? Maybe I had treated him abominably, abandoning him without cause, accusing him of an egregious betrayal he had never committed, whistling up the hounds of the CIA's security apparatus to chase him like a fox.

Stan was a spy, and I knew he lied for a living, but so did I, and I trusted him. I thought he loved me. Perhaps I was wrong. I thought he would never harm me. Maybe I didn't know folks.

∞

I arrived in Mysore at early dawn. An impulse. I'd been there once before; Mysore University has an extensive Sanskrit manuscript collection. Mysore isn't big, but it is more than big enough to lose yourself in.

I had brought only a small backpack with me, with some toiletries and my wallet. Everything else, I had given to Iris or Goodwill.

I walked slowly from the train station to the market, feeling the heat.

It smelled of spices. Limes and apples were stacked in pyramids; outraged chickens clucked in their cages. Women in saris haggled with the squatting merchants, joining in the chorus of clucking: *pineapples, pineapples, two rupees.* I bought tiny bananas, like the fingers on my hand, from a man in a dhoti, then hot golden chickpeas scraped from an earthenware pot: *mangoes a thousand kinds mangoes a thousand kinds.* Children hawked garlands strung with jasmine by vats of powdered bindi dye—turquoise and fuchsia, ocher and crimson, teal, the colors bright as a sharp slap; the air wet and fragrant, heavy with sandalwood and incense, the smells intense and penetrating, as they are only in the tropics. The vendors sold small sacks of rice and potatoes, and spices, and huge bottles of coconut oil; they stared at me without apology and shouted, *come see come see best price.* Children followed me, hoping for sweets. Thin stray cats with rheumy eyes begged for scraps.

It was a universe far easier to understand than the one I'd left.

242 · Claire Berlinski

I would never know what Stan was talking about when he told me he was different from the other trainees. He boasted that he had designed operations so secret that only four people knew about them. Could those have been unauthorized operations? Illegal ones? Were the lawful appointees of our democratically elected government unaware what Stan was doing? Was *that* what the Special Investigations Branch really wanted to know?

Perhaps Janet and Nancy had set a trap for me, blackmailing me with my indiscreet e-mail so I would be forced to tell them what I knew about Stan. Had I walked right into it? My cooperation certainly hadn't worked in my favor in any way I could see.

I had no idea. I had no idea who Stan was. I knew he could lie and keep secrets so well that I would never have guessed, even had he been working for the Russians.

Perhaps Stan *was* working for the Russians. Perhaps that was why he had turned me in—to deflect attention from himself. I shook my head sharply when I thought this and told myself not to be insane. But then another voice inside my mind replied: That's not insane. If you work at McKinsey & Company, it is insane to suspect that your lover is a Russian spy. If you work for the CIA, it's not. Bank robbers rob banks because that's where the money is. Russian spies work at the CIA because that's where the secrets are.

A thin, filthy barefoot boy ran behind me, asking if I had seen the Mysore Palace and whether I knew Malibu Beach. I thought of the boxes of Cap'n Crunch I had pouched to poor PINE-

APPLE, and wondered what had become of him. The boy trailing me would have happily committed espionage for a box of Cap'n Crunch if the chance had been extended him. I bought him a few chapatis and an onion bajhee at a stall by the dusty red road. He shoveled them down his throat rapidly, using both hands.

I found a primitive but clean hotel—squat toilet, bucket bath, a mattress not visibly full of bedbugs, a merry proprietor with a Buddha's belly and a satyr's face.

In the mornings, I took my breakfast of yogurt and papaya and drank milky tea with cardamom at one of the cafés, reading the Indian newspapers, with their unrelenting tales of catastrophic accidents, burning brides, corruption, misery, and scandal: *Mysore, October 15. The mention of the word* donkey *led to a heated debate among the rival political leaders in the MUDA meeting, here this morning. The trouble started when MLC Mr. Y. Mahesh (JD) objected to MLA Mr. A. S. Guruswamy (Congress) who repeatedly asked the Commissioner Mr. Jayaram whether the tenders pertaining to consultant agency would be finalised within a month. Mr. Guruswamy strongly reacted saying that the JD MLC had challenged his common sense. Without a common sense, more than two-and-half lakh voters would not have elected him to the Assembly. MLC Mr. Mahesh added fuel to the fury when he said that "people vote even for donkeys in democracy." This led to a furor with MLA Mr. Shankaralingegowda and MLC Mr. Ramesh joining Mr. Guruswamy to demand an apology from Mr. Mahesh for calling elected representatives as donkeys. Mr. Mahesh argued that the MLAs, instead of demanding apology, should clarify whether the* "common sense" *was an unparliamentary word.*

Everyone in India, like me, the star of his own drama.

In the afternoons, I read novels and napped.

I passed day after day like this in the peculiar and uniquely Indian timelessness. I began doing yoga in the morning, at the lit-

244 · *Claire Berlinski*

tle school on Hospital Road. There was a famous yoga school in Mysore too, but I avoided it. It attracted all the Westerners who had for some reason dropped out of life, and I didn't want to hear them talk about the Eightfold Path, and I didn't want to answer questions about how I had joined their ranks.

∽

How did they know that I'd contaminated the investigation? They knew that I'd spoken to *three* people. One of them must have betrayed me. Or had I been under surveillance that whole time? God knows, I wasn't gifted at spotting surveillance, but there was no one but Iris, me, and the teapot in that room. Was the Mongolian waiter an informant?

Had Iris told Stan what I'd said? Had Iris told Brad? Had Iris told Janet and Nancy? But *why*? Why would Iris betray me, her best friend? Iris had a grudge the size of the Annapurna against the CIA—why would she inform on me? It wasn't possible that Iris was still *working* for them, was it? That she hadn't really been fired? I thought about it: Coca-Cola's headquarters were in *Atlanta,* not Washington. A year of training, then off to Europe—perhaps it was all an elaborate scheme to put Iris under deeper cover? I'd never really understood why they fired her. She was a good spy.

Could Stan have been the one who told them I had contaminated the investigation? He had the motivation, of course. After I left him, he could have gone back to Janet and Nancy and told them that I had spoken to him. Had he made a lucky guess in assuming I had spoken to Iris? Had he recruited Iris to his side? Had he recruited Brad? How did he *know* about Brad? He couldn't possibly have known. But Stan *always* knew about things—he knew all the gossip about the Agency's senior ranks, who was up, who was down. He had ways of finding things out. Had someone seen Brad and me together? Had Stan's paranoia been aroused when I told him I was off to play a game of soccer? I'd wondered why he didn't seem suspicious; it wasn't like him.

If he had figured out what I was doing—my God, he was good. He deserved to work there. If he still did. If I hadn't succeeded in destroying him.

∞

I thought about trying to restart my career in Oriental studies. I bought a notebook and took a few desultory notes about the gopuram of the Shweta Varahaswamy temple. I spent a few afternoons in the manuscript room of the Oriental Research Institute.

Sometimes I wandered to one of the luxury hotels in the center of the city and sunned myself by the pool, where questions of my entitlement to do so were never posed, because I was white. I met a South African backpacker by that pool, another impostor, young and vital and hard-bodied, muscles rippling over his perfectly flat abdomen. He was only nineteen. He was driving a motorcycle through India and had nothing interesting whatsoever to say and no anxieties about anything. He was serenely confident in his youth and beauty, untroubled by any incertitude about himself or anyone else, devoid of deviousness.

He took me to the Mysore wildlife sanctuary on his motorcycle. I rode with him through fields of sugarcane, my arms around his waist, hands on that hard young stomach as he flexed and eased around the turns. We arrived and it was beautiful and savage; great plumed egrets rose on the tips of their feet from the mist and ferns, spreading enormous ivory wings and beating them gently against the hot, perfumed jungle air. He told me that he had "never been with an older woman before," and I told him nothing at all.

At first I thought about Stan all day, every day, wondering what had really happened and where everything had gone. I turned it over endlessly in my mind, examining it from every angle. I would come back to the place I had started: Even if it hadn't *been* Stan, I knew it *could have* been: *Stan was capable of such a thing,* and surely that was the essential point. And then, my emotions reversing midcourse, I would be consumed with uncertainty and regret and shame for judging a man who had loved me so much with no evidence beyond a coincidence of dates and the expression on a bitter woman's face.

I missed him. I missed him for longer than I had ever thought I would. I missed watching him take careful pride in his fish tank. I missed him holding me in the morning as we lay sleepily under the covers for just five more minutes. Despite everything, in the end I loved him.

∞

I wondered if Brad had informed Janet and Nancy that I had contaminated the investigation. Could I have so misjudged him? *Was Brad a double all along?* The idea seemed ludicrous. I thought about his open, trusting face. I had approached *him,* not vice versa. But perhaps, as a security officer, he had been trained to recognize a pitch and he had seen right through me, gone right to Janet and Nancy, and cooperated with them. Brad knew that I had told Stan. He was close to Iris. It was his *job* to keep CIA employees on the straight and narrow.

CIA counterintelligence officers spend years on problems like this, sifting through the evidence, trying to figure out who was working for us and who was on the other side. To this day, the mystery of the Soviet defector Yurchenko has never been solved—was he a true defector or a double? Why did he evade his CIA handlers one afternoon and return to the Soviet Embassy? Had he meant to do that all along, or had he been so disillusioned with the CIA that he changed his mind? No one would ever know for sure. They say that espionage is a wilderness of mirrors, and they are absolutely right.

When I thought it over logically, Brad was the likeliest candidate.

Brad, wherever you are: Kudos.

∞

For months after I left, I had the dream every night.

I've been thrown out. Everyone else is still on the inside. They are flying away—flying away to Moscow, to Beirut, to Bangkok. They are wearing suits, and I realize that I am not wearing anything at all. They look at me with contempt and pity, and I try to cover myself with my hands. They whisper among themselves. I want to know what they're saying, but their voices are a babble. They are speaking a foreign language. I strain to understand, but it makes no sense at all.

I call Stan, but he laughs contemptuously and hangs up the phone. I want to call again, but I am at a pay phone in Mysore and it falls silent, spontaneously out of order. Then Mysore and McLean merge, and I am trying to drive from the Shweta Varahaswamy temple in through the front gates of Headquarters, but they've taken away my badge. When I try to pass, the guards pull out their guns. I explain that I used to have a badge, but they don't believe me. They yank my arms behind my back and march me away, and I feel terrible fear and shame.

In the dream, I run into Stan. He doesn't look like Stan, he looks like the president, but I know it's him. "Did you do this to me?" I ask.

"You'll never know." He sneers.

"It was you, wasn't it?"

"*Nyet*. You did it to yourself. I have important work to do. Leave me alone."

I try to hit him, but my arms are too weak and they won't move properly. My punches don't connect, my fists flail in the air. He glides away, laughing at me. I'm on the outside looking in. I'm all alone. I can't get back in. I start to cry with rage and frustration and humiliation.

I wake up damp with sweat, shivering—although I am in India and the night air is warm.

The hot season came, and then the monsoon. I sent my article about the gopuram to the *Journal of Oriental Studies;* they published it and sent me a small check.

I received a letter from Iris and a check with the proceeds from the sale of my car. She was doing just great, she said: She and Brad were engaged and couldn't be happier. She wrote that every now and again, she went out for drinks with Allison, who was still working at Headquarters. Allison told her the latest gossip: Nathan had formed a support group for Agency employees called Under Cover? Come Out of the Closet! Jade was apparently doing well in Central Africa, and had been promoted immediately. I imagined Jade running a small African republic as her personal dictatorship, a ring of skulls guarding her CIA station, where unspeakable rituals were performed to the sound of drumbeats around the bonfire at night.

At the end of the letter, Iris wrote:

> . . . I ran into Stan at the Pizza Factory the other day. He's gained back all the weight, and then some. He told me he'd resigned.

He's doing some kind of policymaking thing at the Department of Agriculture.

I read that passage over and over, then I put the letter away.

I would never know. I realized that now: No one would ever tell me the truth. The records were sealed in the bowels of the Central Intelligence Agency, the most secretive organization in the world, where they were guarded by passwords, combination locks, trip-wire safes, alarms, buzzers, armed guards, vehicle barriers, vicious dogs, and a twelve-foot-high razor-wire fence. Stan would never tell me the truth, and even if he did, how would I recognize it?

Ye shall know the truth, says the inscription on the Agency's marble wall, *and the truth shall set you free.* But I shall never know the truth.

⊂⊃

I wake up. I am in India and the dawn is warm. The perfume of chameli flowers stirs the air and mingles with the scent of jasmine from the tree on the temple grounds nearby. I hear the chanting of morning prayers. I am alone, no one is watching, and all of India is waiting for me. I turn on my side and then sit up; the loamy sweet air fills my lungs. I stretch, raising my hands so high that I can almost touch the lazy ceiling fan. The room is neat; the dhobiwalla has pressed my cotton clothing into crisp folds. In India, the money from the sale of my car will last a long time. I could take a train to Varanasi at noon. If I hurry, I could catch the morning train to Rajastan. But I don't need to hurry. There is a train every day. And I could also stay here. Paul was right.

I bring the bananas off the windowsill so the monkeys won't snatch them, and tidy the residue from the incense and the hashish, which I smoked the night before on the veranda, watching India pass before my eyes. The sun's rays splash over the peacock-green tiles of the temple and through the open window. I see Vishnu waiting for me outside in the serene garden. He is beckoning.

I shall never know the truth.

But I shall be free nonetheless.

ACKNOWLEDGMENTS

I want my brother to share the credit for this book, but he modestly demurs, waving his hand absently and saying that he prefers just to share the money. As he wishes. I insist upon saying at least this: He improved every line. He *wrote* many of them. He spent days and weeks with me revising every sentence, conceiving every character, plotting every scene. He forced me to excise at least a hundred thousand words of bad material to which I had become inordinately attached. "Please let me keep it, Mischa?" I would plead.

"No, Claire, it's not funny."

"It *is* funny! That line is *very* funny!"

"Do you see me laughing?"

"I guess not," I would say, crestfallen.

And he was always right.

The best ideas are his, the best jokes are his, and whether he admits it or not, the book is his as well.

Moving up the generational tree: I showed up on my father's doorstep in Paris on a bleak September afternoon, unemployed, depressed, unlucky in love, and absolutely penniless. I declared that I had no idea what to do with my life. "What would you like to do?" he asked kindly. I replied that *perhaps* I could write a novel. It was a scheme that would not inspire confidence in anyone but my father. "*Of course* you should," he said. He then put a roof over my head and food on my table for an entire year as I wrote. He was serenely confident that whatever I wrote would be worth reading, and he ignored everyone—and I do mean *everyone*—who told him to cut that shiftless daughter of his loose and let her get a real job. My brother and I have taken my poor father to the brink of ruin with our literary aspirations, and never once has he complained. Well, a few times, maybe. But with every right.

Then there is Jonathan Karp, my editor at Random House, who believed in this book so much that he bought it. His advice about everything was correct. I know I looked doubtful sometimes, Jon, but I say it now for all the world to see: You were right, I was wrong, and I'm woman enough to admit it. Above all, I am grateful to you for allowing me to return to my father and tell him his confidence was not misplaced and that Random House bought the damned thing.

Now to Kathy Robbins, my literary agent. I looked for the words to express my gratitude to you and came up only with this: *I love you; I love you so much. I would do anything for you.* Kathy is the world's finest literary agent, and the smartest and most beautiful, too, and if she asks for my firstborn child, I will give it to her—or 15 percent of it, anyway.

To my friends in the blogosphere who generously publicized this book on their websites: There are too many of you to thank individually here, but if you consult my website, www.berlinski.com, you will see that I have returned the links, with love.

And finally, a private message to someone who must remain nameless: There are no hard feelings, and don't worry: I didn't tell them anything.

My brother, Mischa, patiently suffered thousands of conversations like this, at all hours of the day and night. Often, when I was writing, I would call him long distance (*grazie mille,* Cristina, for allowing him to tie up your phone lines) or chat with him over the Internet, like this:

Claire says: Hello?
Mischa says: Hello!
Claire says: Oh good, you're there!
Mischa says: How are you?
Claire says: I need your help.
Mischa says: Why? What's up?
Claire says: My editor thought this line was clichéd: "The experiment indicated a strong relationship between smoking dope and getting high as a kite." What would you suggest instead?
Mischa says: What's his problem with that line?
Claire says: He said, "avoid the cliché," in the margins . . . I don't know why.
Mischa says: High as a kite?
Mischa says: Maybe that could be a little wittier.

Claire says: Like what? I've spent the whole day thinking about it.

Mischa says: Yeah, maybe he's right there.

Mischa says: Let's see . . .

Mischa says: Toasted.

Mischa says: Baked.

Mischa says: Stoned.

Mischa says: High.

Mischa says: Blitzed.

Claire says: None of those are better.

Mischa says: Which of those is funniest?

Claire says: "High as a kite" has a better rhythm.

Mischa says: Yes, but I see his point too.

Mischa says: The line could be even funnier, with a better simile.

Claire says: Yes. I've been racking my brains.

Mischa says: Have you had any contestants?

Claire says: No. Everything I think of is dumb.

Mischa says: Toasted like a waffle?

Mischa says: Baked like lasagne?

Mischa says: Nope.

Claire says: Nope.

Mischa says: Keep "high as a kite" for now.

Mischa says: Something better will come to you—if there is something better.

Mischa says: Our dad is always good on lines like that too.

Claire says: Yes, that's true.

Claire says: Maybe you could ask him.

Mischa says: I will.

Mischa says: P. J. O'Rourke would do an excellent job at finishing that sentence.

Claire says: Yes, Hunter S. Thompson might also be useful.

Mischa says: I'm starting to wonder, though, if two jokes in the same sentence is not overkill.

Mischa says: I mean, the WHOLE SENTENCE is a joke.

Mischa says: Do you really need a flashy simile?

Claire says: I thought it was fine the way it was.

Mischa says: It's very funny as is, and if the reader needs time

Mischa says: to puzzle out "freaky as a '74 Cadillac,"

Mischa says: then maybe it wouldn't be so funny,

Mischa says: you know?

Claire says: No, that's not even funny.

Claire says: It's trying too hard, you know?

Mischa says: Exactly.

Mischa says: I say, keep it.

Mischa says: That line made me laugh repeatedly.

Claire says: Yes, lots of people like it.

Mischa says: In fact, it's one of the very funniest lines in the book.

Claire says: OK. I'll keep it. Thank you!

Mischa says: Bye!

Claire says: Bye!

ABOUT THE AUTHOR

CLAIRE BERLINSKI was born in California in 1968. She grew up in San Francisco, New York, Paris, and the Pacific Northwest; as a teenager she studied philosophy at the University of Washington, then French literature at the Sorbonne in Paris. She moved to England in 1989, where she studied modern history and earned a doctorate in international relations at Balliol College of Oxford University. Her writings about politics, the CIA, and national security have appeared in numerous magazines and anthologies. She has also held a number of other jobs. She lives in Paris and Washington, D.C. She can be reached via the Internet at www.berlinski.com.